IMAGINARY

IMAGINARY

HELEN WALTERS

LIBRARY OF CONGRESS CONTROL NUMBER: 2018905416

ISBN: HARDCOVER   978-1-5434-0901-7

SOFTCOVER   978-1-5434-0903-1

EBOOK   978-1-5434-0902-4

Print information available on the last page.

Rev. date: 05/02/2018

To order additional copies of this book, contact:
Xlibris
1-800-455-039
www.Xlibris.com.au
Orders@Xlibris.com.au
769950

Chapter 1

He was patient. He had sat in this one spot for three days now. He sat and watched them, studying their habits, learning routines, and predicting their every move. It was almost time.

Tonight seemed colder than last night, and he fidgeted, trying to get warm without losing his line of sight. He watched as she moved from the kitchen to the living room and stirred the old man. The old man didn't look impressed and fussed and resisted her helping hands. She looked tired tonight, and the old man wasn't helping. She stepped back and put her hands on her hips and tilted her head back. He watched her close her eyes and take a deep breath, in and then out. She looked back at the old man and crouched beside him. She placed her hand on his arm and spoke to him. He couldn't hear what she had said, but whatever it was, it worked. The old man wriggled forward on the chair and pushed himself up and to his feet. She looked relieved and escorted him from the living room. She paused at the doorway and turned back to turn out the light. From here, he could see them walk up the passageway to the bedrooms.

A light was turned on in the distance, but he could no longer see them. Now he was ready. He was sure about this one. She was the one. He stood up straight and stretched his back, which had cramped from being in the one spot for so long. He reached down and found his bags; he put on the backpack and slung the larger bag over his shoulder. He walked among the shrubbery and then stealthily across the lawn. He stopped by the large tree at the side of the front yard and leaned against it. He looked around slowly and surveyed his surroundings. It appeared to be all clear; he was sure there was no one around.

He left the sanctuary of the tree and walked to the side of the house. He followed the path and stopped at the gate that led to the backyard. He knew this gate squeaked. He knew this because he had been watching them. He took a small bottle from his bag and squeezed a few drops on both gate hinges. Being ever so careful, he lifted the latch and slowly pushed the gate away from him – not a sound. He was pleased with himself.

He entered the rear yard and carefully closed the gate behind him. He looked around and took note of the yard. He didn't use a flashlight. No need – there was enough light from the full moon to light his way. Everything was where it had been last night. But last night, the gate was left open.

She really should be more careful about securing her property, especially with two small children in the house. It would be dangerous for them if they got out, he thought.

He followed the path around the edge of the house to the back door. He placed his hand on the door handle and turned it ever so slightly. He felt the latch release, and he was able to push the door open. The door made no sound. He stepped through the doorway and stopped. He listened for noise. There was only silence. He knew she did not set the alarm tonight.

Another careless mistake. He shook his head.

He turned and closed the door. He was quiet. He stood in the kitchen and looked around. It was dark, and he struggled to see. He wouldn't use a flashlight in here either. Her neighbour was nosey, and he wouldn't risk her seeing a light. He could see just enough from the moonlight coming in through the kitchen window to navigate around the furniture.

He located the laundry and looked up. He could see the manhole cover. It was right where he had expected it to be. It was above the washing machine. He placed his hands on the sides of the machine and pulled his body up until he could kneel on the top. With one foot on either side of the edge, he stood up tall and reached for the ceiling. His fingertips reached the cover. He pushed up a little and then slid the cover to the side. He needed to be higher to be able to grip the edge and pull himself up.

He stopped. He listened. A toilet flushed. He froze but controlled his breathing and stayed very still. A few seconds passed, and a door closed.

He relaxed a little and breathed out. He looked around for something to stand on that would give him a little more height. An empty washing basket was in the trough. He crouched and reached to the side. Effortlessly, he lifted the basket and placed it upside down between his feet. He stepped up with one foot and reached for the opening in the ceiling. He lifted the other leg up, and he now had the reach. He was athletic and flexible and strong but lacked height. He could now grip the opening enough to pull himself up and into the ceiling.

He stepped back down off the washing machine and placed his rucksack in the trough next to the washing machine. Again, he pulled himself up on the washing machine, and he lifted the rucksack from the trough and pushed it into the opening. Then with both hands gripping the edge and with the skill of a gymnast, he was able to pull his body weight up with just the use of his arms. His head and then torso went up into the roof. He bent his right leg and pulled it into the opening and placed his foot on the edge; now he easily pulled the rest of his body up. Balanced on the roof beams that ran next to the opening, he slid the cover back into place. He was in.

He was in complete darkness; there was no light coming in from anywhere. He reached into the side pocket of his bag and found a small miner's light. He placed it on his head and turned it on. He looked around. The roof cavity was completely empty. He smiled to himself. It was perfect. *No reason at all for anyone to enter this space.* He would stay on this side of the house for the rest of the night. He would wait until morning to move around.

He found a corner where the roof beams met and took out two industrial hooks. He twisted one of the hooks into the roof beam. The wood was hard, and it took much effort to get it all the way in. He stepped over to the next beam, making sure he stayed balanced on the joists. He could not step onto the plasterboard for risk of falling through. He screwed in the other hook and then removed

3

folded material from his bag. He made a hammock. It wasn't the most comfortable bed, but he must sleep now, and he could not sleep balancing on the thin wooden joists. He climbed into his makeshift bed and quickly went to sleep.

Chapter 2

His alarm woke him at 6:00 a.m. He stretched and carefully swung his legs over the edge of the hammock. It swung under his weight, and he must steady it before he manoeuvred himself from his makeshift bed. He crept along the joists to the other end of the house. His footsteps were silent as he stepped across from one wooden beam to another. He was now above her bedroom. He laid himself down and listened.

He heard her alarm ring, and he checked his watch to make sure he was in sync with her clock – ten past six, the same as the previous three mornings. He felt at ease knowing she was a creature of habit and he could easily predict her movements.

He concentrated hard and could hear her getting out of bed and walking across the room. She opened her bedroom door. Her footsteps were loud, and he heard her close the door to the bathroom. The water pipe near him clanked loudly, and it startled him. It was louder than he had anticipated, but now he knew that noise, and he would be ready for it next time.

He had with him a small tool bag. He reached in and took a small handheld drill from its pouch. From where he was, he could access all the electrical wires to the house, and he could tell where all the light fittings were. He slid forwards and leaned over the narrow joist in front of him and drilled a small hole next to the bracket securing her bedroom light to the ceiling. His drill was quiet and made only a small humming noise. The noise from the drill wouldn't be heard over the clanking of the water pipes while the shower was running. He placed the drill back into his bag and swapped it for a small black cable. He poked just the end of the cable through the hole, and he looked at the image on the screen of his phone. At the end of the black cable was a camera, and now he could see into her bedroom. He was satisfied with the result.

He stayed still for just a moment as the noise from the pipe stopped. She had turned off the shower. He was confident that she would remain in the bathroom for another eight to ten minutes. This was her routine.

He carefully got himself to his feet and made his way back towards the other end of the house. He positioned himself in the space he believed to be the kitchen and again carefully made a small hole next to the light fitting. He poked the camera through the hole and surveyed the area on his phone. He was correct with the location, and now he had eyes on her in her bedroom and the kitchen. He knew these two rooms to be the ones where she would spend most of her time when she was at home.

He checked his watch and knew she would be coming to the kitchen anytime now. He sat up and balanced on the corner where two joists crossed, and he watched the kitchen from his phone. She entered the kitchen.

He watched her every move. He was fascinated by her. Her walk was graceful. Her hair was flawless. He liked the way she hummed to herself when no one else was around. He sat and watched her. He didn't move, almost as if he was mesmerised by her.

She filled the kettle with water and put it on the stove. From the cupboard above her head, she removed two mugs and prepared them for coffee. The kettle whistled, and she moved back to the stove and removed it from the heat and finished making coffee. He enjoyed watching her.

She is perfect.

After preparing food for her family for breakfast, she left the kitchen, and now he could not see her. For a moment, he felt lost without having her in his view. He looked at the other end of the house as if he could see through the ceiling to where he thought she was.

He heard a door open and her voice. She was waking the children. He smiled to himself. She was where she was meant to be. *She is a good mother.*

He looked at his watch and knew he had less than five minutes to set up a camera in the lounge. He knew the lounge was the next room over from the kitchen, so he did not have to move far. He shuffled along and balanced over the light fitting. He drilled the hole and poked his camera into the ceiling of the lounge to have a look. Everything appeared to be where it should. He was satisfied with what he saw.

He stopped and looked up; he could hear thumping moving towards him. *It must be the children.* He took his camera back to the kitchen to watch.

Chapter 3

Al Jenner felt old. He was in his eighties and had to come to live with his daughter two years ago. His body was slowly succumbing to old age. He was born in this town and had never lived anywhere else; he never wanted to as he felt safe here. Al had seen the world dressed in his military garb and had immersed himself in many cultures on his army adventures. Not all ended with happy endings, and he had witnessed first-hand what humans could do to each other, so when he retired, he was happy to come home and see out his days here.

Besides his daughter Katrina, whom he resided with, he had three other children. John was the eldest and would be close to sixty. Michelle, fifty-five, was second, and there was Carrie, fifty-one. They were from his first marriage, which fell apart, and then he had Katrina. Al had spent all his good years serving his country and knew nothing else. He retired ten years ago, and the years were dragging by. He tried to get a hobby after the army, but nothing filled the void, and now he sat and waited for the end. Grateful for being part of his grandchildren's day-to-day life, he watched in awe as they grew right in front of his eyes. He missed seeing his own children grow from newborn babies to adults as he had spent much of his life away from the family home, protecting them from the enemy the government wanted eradicated.

Al heard the usual noises out in the hallway. His daughter was getting his grandchildren up and ready for school. He preferred to stay in bed while she did this until minutes before the bus came to collect them. He knew she meant well to have him move in with them, but he felt like he was always in her way. She never said anything to him, but he felt it deep inside. He hated knowing as he had aged and his health had deteriorated that he was becoming more dependent on her to take care of him. He lay in bed and stared at the ceiling. He breathed in deeply and let the self-pity take over.

There was a soft knock at his door, and he sighed. Each of the family had a different knock, so he knew who was there before a word was ever said. His daughter had the annoying motherly knock that involved the door opening at the same time. This bothered him to no end. He often thought about what the point of knocking was if you were just going to barge in without waiting for the invitation.

Her husband had a strong knock but was hesitant, and when he did come in, he looked at him with obligation. The old man knew that he was here because his daughter had got her own way and not because her husband wanted it. From the many overheard conversations, he knew her husband would have been happy for him to have been sent to an old folks' home and taken care of by others. He remembered one conversation clearly. Stephen sat at the kitchen table with his daughter and was holding both her hands, looking deep in her eyes like he was trying to hypnotise her. Her husband told her that nurses should be taking care of him and not her. She was too busy with her work and the children to be adding such a big responsibility to her life. Every time he recalled this conversation, he got mad. He was no one's responsibility.

And then there were his grandchildren. He adored these two little people. The elder was Nathan. He was ten and was full of energy. He spoke at a million miles an hour – and his knock was no different – and he loved to listen to when his grandfather told him stories of the war. He never gave him the graphic details – no need to give the boy nightmares – but he did tend to bend the truth a little to make him sound like a hero. The sad fact was he wasn't a hero. He did bad things in the war. It was about survival – or at least, that was what he had told himself at the time, and now at the age of eighty-five, he lived with the constant regret of his actions.

The youngest of his grandchildren was Paige. She had just turned seven and was her mother through and through. Her knock was soft and almost apologetic. She was always trying to take care of him.

At times, he wanted to yell at her to just leave him alone, but when he looked in her eyes, he only saw a gentle soul who had the purest of intentions, so he internalised his frustrations and let her be. She loved cuddles. She would climb into his lap and snuggle into his chest and sit for ages, and just when she was ready to nod off, his daughter Katrina would come and scoop her up and take her away. Dear little Paige would sleepily blink at him and blow him a kiss and whisper, 'I love you'. *How could anyone be cross at this perfect little human?*

This morning, the knock was soft and barely audible, so he knew it was his favourite little person. He tried to sit up and found himself struggling at such a basic task. The tiny knock was repeated. He cleared his throat and invited Paige in. She opened the door and poked her head through the small gap. She grinned at her grandfather. Her smile was filled with gaps where she had lost baby teeth, and he couldn't help but laugh a little. She emerged in full with her hands behind her back, strutting in a matter-of-fact way all the way over to the side of the bed.

'Now, Grandad,' she said with a lisp created by the missing teeth, 'Mumma said I should tell you that there are pancakes ready for breakfast, and you shouldn't fluff around getting up today because you *will* miss out.'

She stood at the bed with her eyebrows raised, waiting for a response. He pulled back the covers and twisted himself to get his legs out of bed. He leaned close to his little princess and kissed her on the forehead.

'For you, my little one, I will not fluff around and will be there in a minute or two. If it is OK with you, I would like to visit the bathroom before joining you for breakfast.'

With a satisfied look, Paige nodded and skipped out of the room, yelling back down the hallway to the kitchen to let her mother know that Grandad would be there soon; he just needed a wee first. He laughed and shook his head. He loved the innocence of children; they just said it as it was and didn't care if they were politically correct.

He heaved his tired old body fully out of the bed and picked his robe up from the chair that sat beside his bed. It was his birthday present from the children last year, and although it would never have been the one he would have picked out, he wore it every day in appreciation of their efforts to get him something. It was a velvet type of material in ruby red and had a bunny head sewn into it. He wondered if his daughter had even picked up on that, which amused him every morning when he sat at the table to eat his breakfast wearing the robe.

Slowly, he made his way to the toilet and then to the kitchen to join his family for breakfast. He sat at the head of the table and waited for a plate to be put in front of him. Even though he hated his increasing dependency on his daughter, he would never get tired of her cooking. He watched her at the stove flipping pancakes with no effort, and every pancake was perfect. She smiled at her father as she carried over his plate. She placed it in front of him and put her other arm around his shoulders and then gently kissed the side of his head.

'Enjoy, Dad,' she spoke softly in his ear.

He loved his daughter very much. She was in her mid-forties, and when she put a bit of effort into her appearance, she could make a room stop and stare. She reminded him of her mother. He was in his forties when she was conceived out of wedlock. He had an affair with her mother when his marriage started breaking down. He was not proud of what he did, the betrayal to his family, but if his beautiful Katrina was the consequence, he would never regret his choice. His wife left him when she found out about the affair, and his two older children had never forgiven him or spoken to him again. Katrina was different. She didn't agree or accept what he did to his wife, but he would always be her father, and that was enough for her.

Hungrily, he started on his breakfast and smiled at each of them when they looked his way. Her husband, Stephen, was away on business again. He liked it when he was away. It gave him a break from his own guilt about being here, which Stephen had a great way of bringing out.

As he was putting the last morsel of food into his mouth, he stopped with a jerk. He sat there, mouth wide open and fork half in. He just sat there like a statue. His family stopped talking and stared at him. Katrina leaned to the side and put her hand on his arm that was on the table.

'Dad?' She paused. 'Dad?' she said a little louder, but still, he just sat there, frozen in time. 'Dad?' she repeated with panic to her voice. 'What's wrong?'

He could hear her talking but couldn't seem to move. 'Shhh,' he said, moving the fork away from his mouth. 'Do you hear that?'

Silence filled the air. A minute passed, and not one word or movement was made.

'Dad, you're scaring me,' Katrina whispered, her eyes pleading with her father.

He finally moved and looked deep into her eyes. 'Do you ever feel like you're being watched?'

Chapter 4

He sat and watched them have breakfast. He mainly focused on her. She was a good mother. He watched her attend to her children. He was drawn to her. He zoomed in on her face on his screen and took stills of her smile. She didn't just smile with her lips; she smiled with her eyes. He could see the way she looked at her children. She adored them. She listened to each of them tell their stories, and she responded with the right words and nods of approval.

Her children adored her back. The little girl clung to her side like a shadow, and the boy became very animated when he told her about his dream and waited for her animated, surprised look back. When she responded correctly, the boy leapt from his chair and ran around the table, imitating a superhero. She giggled at him and then focused back on her shadow, who was doing her best to try and climb onto her and draw her mother's attention back to her. The old man just sat there, watching his family.

He manoeuvred his camera to focus on the old man. For a minute, he just watched him. The old man angered him. His breathing slowed and deepened the more he watched the old man. He could feel his blood getting hotter. He was becoming agitated, and he could feel his feet and legs becoming restless. He did not like this feeling. He did not like losing control and letting his emotions creep in.

He watched as the old man picked up the last morsel of food on his fork and stop. The old man was frozen, and now he became curious. He zoomed his camera back out so he could see all of them and could not see anything unusual. Slowly, they stopped what they were doing and focused on the old man. She was becoming worried and was talking to the old man. She appeared saddened, and her body now slumped as she leaned forward, trying to gain his attention. The old man didn't move. The old man didn't speak. Now he was holding his breath, waiting for something to happen. His mind wandered slightly. Was the old man having a heart attack or some kind of seizure? This couldn't be happening. The old man was ruining everything.

Finally, the old man moved. He lowered the fork away from his mouth and stared right into her eyes. He held his breath, listening hard to what he was about to say. And there it was. It was perfect. It was exactly what he wanted to hear. The old man was becoming paranoid and felt like he was being watched. His plan was working. He laughed to himself in his head.

She shifted the little girl from her lap and stood from her chair. He could hear her tell the children to go and finish getting ready for school. They ran from the room as instructed, and she went and stood by the old man. He zoomed in on her again and watched her expressions change as she was considering her words to the old man carefully. She placed her hand on the old man's shoulder and assured the old man that no one was watching them. The old man flicked her hand away and started muttering under his breath. It was loud enough for her to hear but not loud enough for him to make out what was said.

She breathed in deeply and stretched her neck from side to side. He focused on her face as closely as he could. He needed to see what her eyes were saying now. They were telling him she was worried about the old man. The old man pushed his chair back, making a loud scraping noise, and he left her alone in the kitchen. She sighed again and went about clearing the dishes from the table.

She carefully stacked the dishwasher and yelled up the hallway to the children that the bus was going to be here any minute. She opened the fridge and took out two lunchboxes and waited for her children to return to the kitchen to collect them. They rushed in and hugged her tight together and took possession of their lunchboxes and quickly left again. He heard the front door open and the old man bidding them farewell. After a loud bang, the door was closed again. The whole time the children were leaving, he watched her compose herself, and when the door closed, she left the sanctuary of the kitchen. He could hear her walk up the passage to her bedroom.

He got up from his perch over the kitchen and quietly crept along the roof and took his camera to the other end of the house. He crouched over the bedroom and poked the camera into its little hole and continued to watch her. She was partly dressed for work. She looked down at her blouse and noticed a mark. She rubbed at it and sighed in defeat.

She slowly unbuttoned her top. She was facing the middle of the room now, which gave him a clear view of her front instead of via the reflection in the mirror. One by one, the buttons were slipped through the button holes. He watched and took in every second. When the last button was free, she tipped her head back slightly and let the silky fabric fall from her shoulders. His heart raced, and every third beat was skipped. His blood was getting hot again – but this time not from anger. This was different. He liked this feeling. As the fabric fell from her body, she let it fall to the floor, and she walked right under him to the other side of the room.

She opened her closet and ran her fingers over the contents hanging in front of her. She tilted her head to the side. He was watching her from behind. He moved the camera angle down and followed the arch of her back. Her spine curved in at the small of her back and then out again at the top of her bottom. Her skirt sat on her hipbone under her petite waistline.

He watched her select a clean shirt from a hanger, and she turned to the middle of the room and slipped it on. This time, he focused on the front of her. She was wearing a cream bra with no distinct flirtiness to it. He could see her breasts being pushed up and to the middle, which gave her ample cleavage. If the shirt was buttoned up low enough, no one would be making eye contact with her all day.

He moved his eyes down her body under her bust and again noticed the clear definition of her ribs. From the front on, she had a slight hourglass figure as she had nice-shaped hips, which were the only things giving her any curves. She started buttoning up the clean shirt from the bottom up, which bothered him. This was not how it was meant to be done. *Shirts should always be buttoned from the top down.* He paid close attention when she got to her breasts. He let his breath go when she buttoned up high enough that minimal cleavage was exposed. Once dressed, she opened her bedroom door and started down the hallway.

He pulled his camera up and silently made his way to the lounge. Carefully, he poked his camera into the hole and waited. He heard noises from a part of the house he could not see and focused all his attention on trying to hear the conversation. He could not quite make out what she was saying when he heard a car door close next to the lounge window. Heavy footsteps followed and then a loud bang; it was someone knocking on the front door.

He turned his head back to the direction of the hallway and heard the clicking of ladies' heels on the tiles making their way to the front door. A friendly greeting was had, and she raised her voice to her father to hurry along; his driver was here to take him to the day centre. Muttering and a heavy shuffle came next, and the front door closed again. He sat up tall and turned towards the front of the house. Two car doors closed, and an engine started. A few seconds passed, and the noise of the engine was now off into the distance.

He looked back at his screen and saw just a flash of her as she walked past the lounge, and the door shut hard behind her. It only took a second before he could no longer hear the clicking of her heels down the footpath. She was gone, and he was alone. He was finally alone in her house. Now he could work.

He made his way across the wooden joists back to the manhole cover and removed it from its place. He sat on the edge of a joist and poked his legs through the space. He leaned forward and placed his hands on the side of the gap. With the grace of an Olympic gymnast, he lowered himself down, but with a loud thud, he landed on the washing machine. He made a mental note that he needed to come up with a solution as landing that hard and loud just would not do when it was time. He landed more quietly onto the floor and stretched. He hadn't realised just how much he had been hunched over. He looked around at his surroundings. Everything looked different in daylight, clearer. A positive feeling surged through his body. He knew everything would be perfect. His perfect night was not far away now.

His first task was simple but time-consuming. He needed to familiarise himself with everything inside the house. He had spent much time looking from the outside in, but it was different now that he was inside. He had longed to be inside her home for some time now since that first day he saw her at the coffee shop near his home.

Before he could start, he needed to eliminate the biggest obstacle: the house alarm. With an urgency to his stride, he made his way to the front entrance and keyed in the code. He had studied her the past few days, and from the right position outside, he could see her enter the code into the keypad.

With the alarm disconnected, he could start. He began in the common areas, looking in drawers and touching the furniture. As he walked around the house, he allowed his fingers to brush over the various surfaces. He walked slowly through each room; he was not in a hurry and needed to absorb the environment. Each room smelled different. He would stand in the middle of each room and close his eyes and let each of the smells come to him.

The lounge was neutral. There was a faint smell of nothing, nothing distinctive – shoes in one corner, dying flowers in another. The smell was boring. He moved from the lounge to the kitchen. Now here was different. The kitchen was key. The kitchen was where the family spent their time together, and soon, he would spend his time here with them too.

He stood as close to the middle of the room as possible and breathed in deeply through his nose. Facing the table, he could smell fruit, the sweet smell of ripening apples and pears. He turned towards the sink and could smell the musty damp coming from the dishwasher, which was slightly ajar. The smell of dirty wet dishes bothered him. Becoming agitated, he turned to face the bench. He cleared his mind from the dirty dishes and focused.

Towards the bench, he could smell something fake, a deodoriser of sorts – lavender. He could smell a fake lavender scent. He opened his eyes and let his sights and smells coordinate. He started his routine again. He faced the table and breathed in the smell of the fruit, but this time, he let his eyes take it in. As the ripening fruit omitted their inviting fragrance, he saw them and let his brain imagine their sweet flesh sitting in his mouth.

Next was the sink and the dank smell of dirty dishes. What he saw did not match what he had smelled. There were no dishes visible, yet he could smell them hidden in the dishwasher. Finally, the bench – his eyes scanned the area. Nothing was out of place. *She should be proud of her housekeeping.* He could see the pride she took in keeping a clean and tidy home. It reminded him of his childhood. His mother was a stay-at-home housewife, and there was never a thing out of place.

He spotted in the corner of the bench a glass jar with sticks sitting in a liquid. He walked over to the distinct smell of lavender. The fragrance was so strong, he felt a wave of nausea pass over him. That would need to go. He picked up the jar and stepped sideways to the sink and tipped most of the liquid out. He didn't want to make it obvious that something had changed, but he needed to get rid of that smell. He tore a piece of paper towel from the roll that was sitting on a stand next to the stove and wiped away any evidence that the jar had been tampered with. He carefully placed the jar back in the corner and turned his back to the bench and placed the paper towel in the bin, which was located inside the cupboard under the sink.

He allowed his eyes to scan the room again to ensure he hadn't missed anything. Satisfied with his knowledge of the room, he stepped through the door and into the hall that connected the kitchen to the lounge and the front door, approximately fifteen feet from where he was standing. One foot in front of the other, slowly and calculatingly, he paced to the front door. He turned on the spot and looked at the kitchen from a new angle. From here, he could see a few things he had missed from being inside the space. To the right, he saw the way the floor plan led a path from the front door, down the passage, through the kitchen, to the back door. He stood for a moment and just stared at the path. This was important. Knowing the exact detail of one exit to the other and where the path twisted and turned would be crucial to his plan.

To his left, he saw a small box that was on the floor just inside the doorway. With long strides, he stepped back into the kitchen and squatted in front of the box. He lifted the flap carefully, taking note of how it had been closed so he could ensure that it was placed back in the exact same way. The content was disappointing – books, old books that seemed to be forgotten and unloved. He closed the box and turned back to the passage.

He stepped forward and then pivoted to face the darkness – the hallway to the bedrooms. From what he had observed from the outside, to his right were two bedrooms. The first belonged to the old man, and the second was hers. He felt his pulse quicken slightly at the thought of putting his hand on the doorknob that led to her bedroom and turning it. His mind wandered to what he had seen earlier when she changed her blouse. He closed his eyes and remembered. He remembered the shape of her body as she slipped the dirty top off her shoulders. He remembered the shape of her breasts supported by a plain bra but pushed up enough to reveal ample cleavage. He remembered everything about her.

She is perfect.

He let his thoughts drift from his task at hand and indulged in the fantasy he was creating in his mind. No longer than exactly one minute later, he regained his focus and stared back into the darkness. To his left, he knew there were two other bedrooms belonging to the children and the bathroom and toilet. He was not 100 percent sure of the configuration of the floor plan, so he knew he would need to take his time and focus.

Chapter 5

Four steps into the darkness, he came upon the first door to his left. He stopped, turned, and waited. He looked back to his left to see the kitchen, and to his right, he could only see a corridor with closed doors. He turned back to face the first door, and he placed his hand on the knob and turned. It turned easily, and the door glided open.

He took only one step inside the room and looked around – pink. He saw a sea of pink. The covers on the bed were pink, the clothes strewn on the floor were pink, and the stuffed toys were pink. He didn't need to guess who this room belonged to. He looked at his feet to see a mess. There was no order in this room. It was chaotic and showed no respect for belongings. He pushed some clutter to the side with his foot and walked to the bed, which was under the window looking out to the rear yard.

He leaned over and touched the linen. It was soft and velvety. He sat on the bed and then lay to the side with his head on the pillow. The room smelled like bubble gum. It was sickly and sweet. The pillow smelled of fruity shampoo. The sickly smell became overwhelming, but he continued to lie on the bed. He looked around the room from the same angle as the small girl would if she were lying here. The bed was longways across the far wall, with her head at the kitchen end of the room. He moved his head slightly to look at the far corner. There was a toy box overflowing with stuff. He couldn't make out what the stuff was, but he knew most of it was never touched, just an accumulation of things given to the girl and, without thought, stuffed into a wooden box and left to collect dust.

The sickly sweet smell was starting to give him a headache. He rubbed his eyes and continued to lie on the bed. He moved his focus to the main area of the floor, to the collection of toys that had recently been played with. There was a Lego set half completed, a sticker book opened to a picture of a princess, pencils, and jewellery. It was the type you would find at a two-dollar shop, cheap and plastic and perfect for a child of her age.

In the corner between the wardrobe and the door was a laundry hamper. He sighed deep as he looked at the clothes hanging over the edge of the hamper and on the floor around it. How did someone fail such a simple task of putting the dirty clothes inside a square container? It confused and agitated him that this was allowed to happen. Why did she not teach her child the simplest of things?

He sat up and turned to put his feet back on the floor. Directly next to the bed was a side table with a lamp, a dirty glass, and a clock. He picked up the clock. It was an old-fashioned round clock that ticked and had hands and not a digital display. To no surprise, it was pink with a picture of a princess painted on the background. He checked the time on his watch and compared it to the pink clock. The girl's clock was three minutes ahead, so he turned the clock over and corrected the time. He placed it neatly back on the side table and rose to his feet.

He walked to the door and picked up the dirty clothes off the floor and placed them inside the basket. As he turned to close the door, he spotted something behind the basket. He bent down and slipped his hand behind the basket. His fingers gripped the cloth, and he gently pulled it out. He stood back up and held the cloth at eye level to see it. It was a small pink T-shirt with a picture of a kitten embossed on the front. It was creased badly, and he stretched the material, trying to pull it back to shape. The material was soft to touch, and he rubbed it on his face. He liked how it felt against his cheek, and he held still for a moment with his eyes closed. He opened his eyes again and folded the shirt into a small square and tucked it inside the top of his jeans. He needed to keep this close to him; this was special. He pulled the door closed and walked to the next door on his left.

Door number two – he stood up straight and focused. He placed his hand on the knob and turned. This one was harder than the first. He needed to give it a bit of effort, and it make a sharp clicking noise, and the tongue retracted into the door. He pushed the door, but it did not glide open like the girl's door. He had to push with a little force. Once it was open, he investigated what was stopping the door from opening easily. He crouched down and tugged at a figurine that had become wedged under the door. He held it in his hand and studied it. It was a little green army man holding a rifle, a common boy's toy, but it angered him. He gripped the toy hard and then threw it across the room.

The room was of similar size to the girl's. The window was in the same place, but the boy's bed was at the opposite corner on the far wall. He took two paces into the middle of the room and looked around. There appeared to be more order in this room. There was no clutter on the floor, and the bed had been made. There was no box spewing out toys but instead a desk. It was tucked in the corner at the foot of the bed. He felt far more comfortable in this room. It was neat and organised. He walked to the bed and sat in the middle on the edge. He did not lie down this time. He knew the boy did not lie on his bed and played; he would sit at the desk. He stood again and looked back down at the bed. There was a dip in the blanket where he had sat, so he turned and smoothed it out.

He walked over to the desk and pulled out the chair. It was not a cheap student chair on wheels. It was a heavy wooden chair that you would find behind the desk of an important person. The seated was padded but firm, and the detail in the woodwork was exquisite. Someone had spent a very long time hand-turning and carving this detail. He sat in the chair and leaned back. He liked how he felt in this chair, in this room. There was order and discipline. He started searching the desk for clues as to what made this small boy tick.

There was a shelf above the desk with a number of books on the military and two scrapbooks. He cast his eye over the titles of the books and raised an eyebrow. They seemed to be for a much older audience than the boy, who must have been only ten or eleven. They must have belonged to the old man at some stage. He reached up and pulled the two scrapbooks down. He opened the first and ran his fingers over the first page. It was a newspaper article. It was from the 1960s and gave details of the war that was going on at that time. There was a photograph of a military man in his thirties kissing his wife, who was holding a baby. He read the caption at the bottom and realised that the man in the photo was the old man. The newspaper photographer had taken it as army men and women were being rounded up and shipped off overseas to fight in a war that didn't belong to them.

He studied the look on the old man's face in the photo and saw something he didn't expect. It was not a look of sadness as he was leaving his wife and child but a look of shame. The old man didn't want to go but was being forced to. The photo captured that look, and it struck at something inside of him he wasn't expecting. It was as if he almost felt bad for him. He turned the page and then the next and quickly picked up the theme of the book. It was a shrine of sorts to the old man's army career. The final page was a photograph with the old man, perhaps in his sixties, being presented with a medal, and the story told of his bravery as he was retiring from the armed services.

He closed the book and put it back upon the shelf. This small boy idolised the old man and had turned him into a hero. The old man was no hero, and the boy needed to learn this.

The second book only had a few pictures and articles glued in of some famous sports stars. This book didn't seem to follow any particular pattern and seemed to be half hearted. Maybe this was the book he showed to people and kept his real hero to himself.

He put the second book away and turned in the chair to look at the rest of the room. The small boy also had a laundry hamper in the corner between the wardrobe and the door, but there were no dirty clothes hanging over the edge or slumped on the floor next to it. This boy took pride in his room and put everything correctly in its place. He felt a bond with the small boy.

He stood from the chair and pushed it back into place and walked to the other side of the room where he had thrown the soldier toy when he first entered. He leaned down and picked it up from the floor. He looked at it closely again, and instead of putting it back where he had found it, he put it in his pocket.

He left the room and closed the door behind him. It made the same loud clicking noise as when he had opened it. That could be a potential problem; he made a mental note to take care of that later.

He moved away from the small boy's door and walked farther up the hallway to where he was confronted with three doors. Systematically, he worked from left to right. Door number one was in a small alcove to his left. Two paces in, he was at the door. He opened the door to see a toilet. The room was a standard size for a toilet, with a small window in the centre of the back wall. It slid from right to left with an opening about a foot wide. He closed the door and turned to his right and stepped two paces back to stand in front of door number two.

He opened the door and pushed it away from him. It swung open easily to reveal the bathroom. It was rectangular in shape, with the door being in the right-hand front corner. A strong floral scent drifted out and into his nose. He immediately searched for the source. He saw another jar with sticks on the vanity. He sighed with displeasure. He did not understand her fascination with these jars and the fragrant oil. He regained focus and started surveying the room.

Directly in front of the door was the shower cubicle. It was surrounded by glass, no curtain. Next to the shower was the vanity unit, which had a large oval sink in the centre with a two-door cupboard underneath. Above the sink was a mirror. Curious, he stepped into the bathroom and wandered over to the mirror. He ran his fingers underneath and pulled slightly. It didn't budge. There was no hidden cupboard behind the mirror.

To his left was a bathtub under a large frosted window. The window had one opening panel, which looked like it would be two feet wide when opened. He leaned over the tub and released the window lock. The window slid open easily. From here, he could see most of the rear yard. He stood for a moment and looked out the window. He climbed into the bathtub and evaluated how easy it would be to get out through this window. *This could be a problem. The girl could open and climb out without issue. This would need to be fixed.* He stepped back out of the tub and checked for footprints – none. He exited the bathroom and closed the door behind him. *Now for the third door.*

He knew what was behind this door. This excited him. He breathed in deeply and took a moment to calm his heartbeat. He delicately placed his fingertips on the doorknob and ever so gently turned it. He felt the door move. He pushed the door and heard the bottom of the door brush the carpet. There was no resistance, and it opened fully. He felt his pulse race. His fingers started to tingle. His feet felt heavy. He stepped in and took a deep breath through his nose.

The scent drew him in. It was her perfume. It was soft and feminine. He could smell talc with an exotic floral undertone. It was subtle yet tantalised his senses. He needed to find the bottle. He needed to hold it and smell it. He needed to remember this aroma. He remained in control and consciously started to observe the room's layout. The room was square with a floor-to-ceiling window on the right-hand wall that gave a view to the front yard. The bed was off centre along the back wall. He stood and looked at the bed. There was no reason for it not to be centred. This bothered him. Above the bed was a ceiling fan. On each side of the bed was a table with a lamp, and one had an alarm clock.

To the right-hand corner nearest the door was a free-standing wardrobe, not very big. She didn't seem like the type who would have a lot of things. He would start here. He moved towards the wardrobe and stopped in front. He opened the two doors and saw a small collection of clothes neatly hung and appearing to be in order. From left to right, she hung short-sleeved tops, long-sleeved tops, skirts, pants, and then dresses. The wardrobe had two drawers at the bottom. He opened the top drawer to see her underwear. It was all neatly folded. He liked the way she had everything in order. It was a sign. The bottom drawer had pyjamas and tracksuit pants, again, all folded and neatly organised.

He stepped back from the wardrobe and now wondered where the husband kept his things. What had he missed? He walked in front of the window to the table. There was a small shelf in the centre that housed a single book. He picked it up and read the synopsis on the back cover – a crime thriller, not what he expected her to be reading; he picked her for a romantic. He walked around the bed to the other side table. There was also a book. He picked it up and turned it over – a motivational self-help book. This was definitely the husband's. With a sigh of contempt, he placed it back from where he had got it. He looked around the room again and was still curious as to where the husband kept his belongings.

He stood at the foot of the bed and tried to understand why they had it off centre. He stood and stared. Then he saw it. There was a distinct line in the wallpaper on the far-left wall. He walked over and looked up and down. He ran his finger over the gap and noticed a small indent about halfway down. He put his finger in the indent and pulled. A door glided open, revealing a hidden walk-in closet.

The closet was dark. He ran his hand up the inside of the wall and located a switch. He clicked the button, and a bright light illuminated the space. It was a generous-sized closet with shelving at the end and hanging space down one side. Again, all the clothes were neatly hung in order. This was her doing. He could see her eye for detail. She was meticulous with a hint of OCD. He smiled, turned off the light, and closed the door.

He turned and went to leave her room when he took note of a small vanity dresser tucked in the corner. From where he stood, he could see it was hers. He could see perfume bottles, a hairbrush, a jewellery box, and a photo frame. He went to the photograph and picked it up. It was of her, the husband, and the children. It was recent. He stared at the husband and instantly disliked him. He had a look in his eye that told lies. They told lies to her. The husband stood to the side of her and had his arm around her shoulder like he was holding a possession. He moved his focus briefly to the children. The girl sat on her mother's lap and looked happy, the way all children should look. The boy stood to the other side of his mother, who sat on a retaining wall, her legs dangling down, not quite touching the ground. The boy leaned into her side. He looked content, not happy but not sad either. He was a serious child.

Now he stared at her. Her eyes told the story. She was happy. She held the girl tight, and her head leaned on top of the girl's head. Her other arm was behind the boy; he figured her hand was on his back, pulling him close. Her body language confirmed she was devoted to her children and not so much the husband. He ran his finger over the glass where her face was. She deserved better than the husband. He was a liar.

He was startled back to reality by a car door slamming out the front of her window. He placed the photograph back in its position and swiftly made his way to the window. He exhaled in relief. It was a visitor for the neighbour. He left her bedroom and closed the door behind him. *One more room to go.*

We went back down the hallway to the last door. He didn't pause at this door. He opened the door with force and stepped heavily into the room. It was the same size as the children's bedrooms. The door was in the left corner of the room, a large window across the far wall. The bed perfectly centred against the right-hand wall. To the left of the bed was a single table with a clock, to the right a wardrobe and a desk. He immediately went to the desk – not much there: the morning newspaper, a few old books about nothing specific, and an old photograph in a new frame of a woman he presumed was the daughter's mother. He picked up the photograph and studied her face. It was definitely her mother. The woman in the picture was pretty and had the same soft look in her eyes as her daughter. He gently placed the photograph back.

He turned his attention to the wardrobe. He opened the two doors and stepped back to observe. There was minimal clothing neatly hung and two pairs of shoes at the bottom. On the shelf above the hangers were three boxes of different sizes. He reached up and lifted the first from its place and placed it on the bed. He removed the lid to see what was inside – old documents. He quickly flicked through the sheets of paper to see if anything caught his eye – nothing overly interesting here. He replaced the lid and put the box back on the shelf and slid the next box from its place.

This box was smaller than the first and appeared older. He opened the box – photographs and memorabilia. Now this box grabbed his attention. He kneeled in front of the bed, and one by one, he pulled the photographs out. There were some of another woman and children. He raised an eyebrow. *Another family?* Now he was intrigued. Further into the collection were photographs of when he was a boy with other children and who appeared to be his mother and father, typical photographs from that era.

It wasn't until he was almost through the collection that he came across photographs from the old man's time in the military. There were pictures of the old man and his unit. The old man looked so young and proud, and the men around him looked close. There were smiles all around. Then the photographs got darker, from a time long after that first group photo. The smiles had faded, and the faces looked worn. They were dirty and appeared exhausted. The innocence from that first day together had vanished. Now they looked like soldiers of war.

The next few photographs were similar. Some of the men were bandaged, one had crutches, and the old man looked like he had been dragged through hell. He had almost finished going through the pile when one last photograph was face down in the box, almost hidden in the corner. He put his finger under the picture and gently pulled it away from where it had got stuck in the corner of the box. There was writing on the back of the picture: *Sept 10th 1952.* He turned the picture over.

The photograph was of a village. Buildings were destroyed and still smouldering from fire. The old man was in the background, moving the body of a dead villager to a row of other bodies. He looked at the camera. His eyes were dark and sad; the rest of his face had no expression. On the other side of the picture, another soldier was on one knee with his head resting on his fist.

He stood up from the edge of the bed and put the photograph in his pocket. He picked up the box and flipped the lid closed and placed it tentatively on the shelf. For a brief moment, he considered returning the photograph. He didn't. He closed the wardrobe without looking in the third box.

He went back to the desk and picked up the photo frame. This time, he put it on the other side of the desk, and he took the newspaper. He went to the clock on the side table and added six minutes to the time. He wanted to see if these small movements would be noticed by the old man. He wanted to test his paranoia.

His first job was now complete. He had been into every room in the house. He knew the layout. He knew the different smells. He went back to the alarm panel and keyed in the code. The panel beeped at him with confirmation. He swiftly moved back to the laundry and pulled himself up into the roof.

There was one last job for the day, and then he could rest. He carefully drilled holes in the ceiling of the rooms he had not done the previous night. He pulled from his large bag multiple cables with tiny cameras at the ends and secured one in each hole. The cameras connected to his laptop wirelessly, and now his screen had seven small boxes, each box looking into a room.

28

He was tired and hungry. He stretched out in his hammock and allowed his body to relax. From his backpack, he pulled out food, small bars made from oats, nuts, and seeds. It filled him up for now. Tomorrow he would need to source more food, something fresh, something she would make.

It was only midday, but he needed to sleep. He needed to take advantage of the quiet while no one was home. He closed his eyes, and her image appeared. He liked this image and allowed his mind to shut down.

Chapter 6

The old man sighed and looked at his watch. He understood why his daughter shipped him off each day, but some days he just couldn't be bothered with the other old people. Today was one of those days. All they did was complain and moan about everything. If someone said the temperature was too hot, the carer would turn the thermostat down, and five minutes later, someone else would complain it was too cold. And the next person didn't like what the kitchen had made for lunch and so threw a tantrum that a three-year-old would be proud of. The old man did, however, have the utmost respect for the carers. They took all the bitching with a pinch of salt and smiled the whole day long.

The old man had a special connection with one young lass who, no matter how much he told her he didn't want to talk, always had a way of getting the conversation going. Today he just wanted to sit in the big comfy chair by the back window and watch the birds in the aviary that would come and sit on the window ledge and whistle at him. He felt at peace when he sat there, watching the birds do what birds did, but over she came anyway, all bright eyed and bushy tailed, chattering away like nobody's business. She walked past him and grabbed at a chair that was neatly tucked under a table and dragged it over to where he sat. She plonked herself down and put her hand on his arm and gave a gentle squeeze.

'So, Al, what's the gossip for today?' She let his arm go and shifted her body in the seat so she was almost facing him.

He tilted his head slightly so he could see her out of the corner of his eye and gave her the look. It was the same look he gave her every time, and it was the same look she ignored every time.

'Don't be like that. There has to be something you want to talk about.' She stood up from her seat and leaned over the arm of the big comfy chair and whispered, 'I'm going to go make us both a hot cup of tea, and when I get back, you are going to spill all your secrets, OK?'

It was a rhetorical question; he knew that. He liked the way she would give him a few minutes to ready himself for the onslaught of questions she would have for him. He needed to think of a topic that wouldn't probe too deep but satisfy her need to know stuff about him.

He sat back in the chair and watched two birds out the window fight over a small twig. He closed his eyes for a moment and enjoyed the last few moments of being alone. Out of his left ear, he could her the clinking of Carla carrying two cups in one hand, which meant she also was bringing back a plate with biscuits or maybe even cake. He sat up and opened his eyes, and a smile almost appeared when he saw chocolate cake on the plate. She was good; she knew what bribery to bring to get him to talk.

Carla carefully placed the cups on the table next to the big comfy chair and handed the old man one of the plates of cake. He thanked her and greedily ate two big bites of cake. His taste buds exploded, and he could feel his mouth fill with saliva in anticipation of the next bite. He heard Carla giggle, and he turned his whole head to look at her.

'Oh, Al, you make me laugh. I've never seen someone eat cake like you. I love watching how much you enjoy it. Did you know I make the chocolate cake you enjoy so much?'

The old man stopped mid-chew and shook his head; he really had no idea this was her creation. He couldn't help but smile at her now. She had got to him. She was patient and understanding, and empathy just oozed from her. The way she talked with him was genuine. She didn't mock or belittle him, and when he spoke on a matter that was sensitive, she remained quiet but attentive. She really cared about all the folk that came here. She was the reason he didn't fight with his daughter on the days he had to come.

Licking the last bit of icing from his top lip, he made eye contact with Carla in a way that told her he was ready to talk. She leaned over and took the plate and fork from him and delicately placed them on top of her plate on the table.

'So, young man, what do you have to say for yourself?'

'Did I ever tell you the story about the time I found my grandson sitting in the kitchen on the floor with both his hands pulling apart his sister's birthday cake?'

Carla let out a hearty laugh. 'No, you haven't told me this one.' She sat back in the chair and waited for story time to commence.

'It was Paige's second birthday. Nathan would have been five, and he had been a right little shit all day. He was jealous that his baby sister was getting all the attention. He had popped all the balloons out in the yard after his mother had spent an hour blowing them up. I'd never seen her this cross before at either of the children. She adores them and is so patient and forgiving – but not this day. She put Nathan in a time out and went and found more balloons. Meanwhile, her good-for-nothing husband was out picking up the birthday cake. He had been gone far too long. It doesn't take an hour and a half to go to the bakery ten minutes away. So my daughter was frustrated with her husband, and now little Nathan was playing up. After his time out, she asked him to come and help her carry out the paper plates, plastic cups, and the like. Well, you should have heard her yell at him when she saw him throw them on the ground and start stomping on them.

'I was in the lounge with baby Paige, watching her play in her portable cot, so I got up to investigate. I took Nathan by the hand and brought him into the lounge to give Katrina a break. I sat on the lounge with him and read him books to keep him amused. Every now and then, I would see him glare at baby Paige and then snuggle deeper under my arm.

'Eventually, their dad came back with a big white box from the bakery. Nathan was ever so excited to see his dad. He ran after him to the kitchen and, within a minute, came back with his bottom lip quivering. When I asked him what was wrong, he climbed back on the couch and said he wasn't allowed cake yet. He wasn't even allowed to look at it.

'So about another hour passed, and the house was ready for the party, and guests slowly started to arrive. Nathan became distracted when some kids around his age turned up, and he had friends to play with. I moved outside and found a comfy spot in the background to watch the festivities.

'Food was had, games were played, and presents were opened, and I heard Katrina say it was almost time for the cake. I watched her look around, and then she locked on to me. She walked over and asked if I had seen Nathan. I said I hadn't but offered to go inside to have a look. I got up and wandered into the kitchen. I couldn't see him, but I could hear something coming from behind the table. I walked around the table, and there he was, on the floor with the big white bakery box and both his hands in the cake. He looked up at me with a grin so big, you couldn't help but laugh. He had pink frosting covering his face and cake up to his elbows.

'Well, I let out the biggest laugh, which caused Katrina to come inside. She was holding Paige on her hip, and the look on her face was priceless. I'm not sure if she was going to cry, yell, or laugh. After a few seconds of silence, Paige started wiggling, trying to get down off her mother's hip. Kat was still stunned and put her down. And then Paige, like a rocket, ran over to her brother, squatted down, and plunged both her hands in the cake too. She picked up a scoop and shovelled it into her mouth and starting giggling like only a two-year-old girl can.

'Well, Kat lost it and started laughing so hard, she couldn't breathe. Her husband had come in, wondering where everyone was at, and saw the ruckus. He had the camera in his hand and started taking photos of the mess. In the end, they had to go out to the party and tell them there was no cake unless they wanted to eat it off the floor. Well, this got the other kids excited with deafening squeals, and the kitchen was filled with kids eating cake from the floor. This would have to be the funniest end to a party I have ever seen.'

The old man finished his story and focused his eyes back on Carla. She sat there with a smile so big and laughing. He couldn't help but start laughing too.

'What a great story, Al. I wish I had been there to see that. Now I'm going to clear these plates and then come and get you ready to go home. Your driver will be ready to take you shortly. Is there anything else I can get you before you go?' Carla stood up and picked up the stack of dishes from the table and paused, waiting for a response.

'No, thank you.' He turned back to the window and started watching the birds again.

Chapter 7

His alarm was set for 3:00 p.m. She would be home with the children at half past three, and he wanted to be awake and ready to watch them. He tipped himself out of the hammock and turned on his laptop.

Shit! It only had half its battery life remaining. He felt himself become agitated. He needed to have full power to ensure he got through the night, and there were no outlets in his space. He has approximately thirty minutes to rectify his problem.

He crawled to the manhole and slid the cover away. He poked his head down and listened for noise. Silence. He stuck his legs out first and lowered himself. *Thud.* He really needed to land quieter; he would work on this. He slid off the top of the washing machine and took off his backpack. He removed the laptop and connected the charging cable. He plugged it into the spare outlet near the washing machine. Now he must wait.

He looked through the doorway into the kitchen. He could smell the fruit on the table. He was hesitant. He knew the alarm was on and there was a sensor in the far corner of the kitchen. The sensor didn't reach him in the laundry room. Hunger was getting to him; he felt pain in his stomach. He checked his watch. He still had twenty-five minutes until they were due to arrive back home.

He took a deep breath and swiftly moved to the front door and entered the security code. The light on the panel went out. Quickly thinking what he could do while the laptop was charging, he moved effortlessly down the hall to the toilet. He relieved himself and flushed. He went to the bathroom and washed his hands. He opened the cupboard under the sink and looked at the contents – nothing interesting: aspirin, perfume, cotton buds, and spare toothbrushes.

He hurried back to the kitchen, stopped at the table, and looked at the fruit. His stomach rumbled again, and he picked up two pieces of fruit. He put them in his backpack and pulled out his drink bottle. He went over to the sink and filled it to the rim from the cold-water tap. He wiped drops from the bottle on the dish towel when he got a strong smell of the fragrant lavender oil. He disliked this smell and walked over to the jar and picked it up. He remembered the bin under the sink and dropped the jar in. He checked his watch again – ten minutes until she would be home. Back to his laptop, he checked the progress – 90 percent charged. He would give it two more minutes. He would not risk any longer than that. He would not be caught.

He heard a car pull into the driveway.

'She is early,' he grumbled to himself.

He tugged at the laptop cable and pulled it from the outlet and from the laptop and rolled it back up. He slipped it into the backpack together with the laptop. He zipped the backpack shut and put it on. He placed the washing basket back on top of the machine and climbed back up.

He heard the key in the front door. He looked in panic in that direction. He hadn't reset the alarm. Now he felt tense as there was not time to fix that. He hurriedly climbed back into the roof and knocked the basket off the top of the machine. It hit the ground with a plastic thud.

He held his breath and listened – nothing. He slid the cover closed and sighed deeply. He made his way back to his camp and sat gently back into the hammock. *That was too close. That can't happen again.*

He unpacked the laptop once again and set it up. He now saw every room in the house. He looked for his beauty and watched her in the kitchen. He reached into his backpack and grabbed the piece of fruit he had taken from the kitchen. He bit into the pear and savoured the sweet juice that filled his mouth. He sucked where he had bitten and drained the juice from the flesh. He stopped for a moment and let the juice sit on his tongue. The sweet juice set his taste buds into a frenzy, and he felt the energy returning to his body. He hungrily finished the pear and wrapped the core in tissue and placed it back inside his backpack. Now he was ready for the rest of the family to come home.

Chapter 8

It was four o'clock, and the old man's driver pulled up to the house. They exchanged pleasantries, and the old man got out of the car and shuffled to the front door. He opened the door and was greeted by the wonderful sounds of giggling. He could hear Katrina in the kitchen talking with the children. He closed the door behind him and made his way to the kitchen.

'Grandad!' Paige squealed with delight when she saw the old man come through the door.

His heart filled with joy, and his face beamed as he hugged his granddaughter. He looked over at Nathan, who was much quieter than his sister, and he looked up from his homework and smiled at his grandfather.

'Hey, Grandad.' His voice was soft but friendly. 'How was your day?'

'Just fine, thank you, Nathan. How was school?' The old man pulled out the chair at the end of the table and waited for Paige to scramble to his lap.

'School was good. Got a B plus on my math test. Teacher said it was the highest in the class.'

'That's wonderful news. Well done!' The old man turned his attention to his daughter. 'How was work, Kat?'

His daughter looked up from her coffee and grinned. 'Great. Thanks, Dad. Was asked to extend my hours again today. Told them I would need to discuss with the family before I decide. Don't think

I will though, not while the kids are still so young. I like being able to pick them up from school and not have to use a baby sitter.'

'They won't be little forever, Kat. Just make sure that you don't miss the opportunity.' He smiled at his daughter. It didn't matter what opinion he had. She was going to do what she wanted no matter what anyone else said, so he knew it wasn't worth saying anymore.

The old man hugged his granddaughter, who was still snuggled into him. 'Paige, dear, I need to get up.' He helped her slide off his lap, and he gripped the table for support while he stood. 'I'm going to go and read the paper until tea time if that's OK.'

He didn't wait for a response and made his way down the hall to his room. He needed some quiet until it was time to eat, and now was the time when the kids needed to do their homework.

He opened his bedroom door and stopped. Something didn't feel right. He looked back down the hall and hesitated.

They only got home a few minutes before me, he thought to himself, *and they never go in my room.*

He shook his head and entered the room. He sat on the end of the bed and slid off his shoes. With a heavy sigh, he got up and went over to the desk to retrieve his paper. It was gone. Puzzled, he stepped back and looked around his room, wondering if he had put it somewhere different. He knew he hadn't, so it had to be here on the desk. He put it there every morning before he left for the day centre as every night before the evening meal, he sat at the desk and read it.

His feet ached, so he sat heavily on the desk chair. He went to call out for his daughter when something caught his attention: his photograph. *Why is it over there?* He could feel heat rising in his cheeks. First, his paper was missing, and now his photograph was in the wrong spot. Out of the chair, as quickly as his old body could manage, he stormed out of his room and back to the kitchen.

'Have you been in my room, Kat?' His tone accused her; it was a statement rather than a question.

'Not tonight, Dad. Why?' She stopped what she was doing at the sink and faced him, curious as to the meaning of the question.

'My paper is missing, and my photograph was in the wrong spot.' He stared hard at her as if he was trying to intimidate a confession out of her.

'Sorry, Dad, it wasn't me, and the kids haven't left the kitchen since we got home. Are you sure you didn't take it with you this morning?' Kat turned back to the bench and continued preparing dinner.

'I never take the paper with me!' he snapped at her harshly. 'Someone has taken it and has been touching my things.' He turned his attention to the children and glared at them. 'Which one of you has been in my room?'

Nathan looked up from his homework and stared blankly at his grandfather. 'Not me, Grandad. I know I'm not allowed in your room.'

The old man caught the eye of Paige. Frightened, she got up from her chair and clung to the back of her mother. The force caused Kat to drop the potato she was peeling onto the floor. She spun around and bent over to retrieve the runaway potato. She looked at the fear on her daughter's face and shot a dirty look at her father.

'No one has been in your room, Dad! No one has taken your paper, and no one has touched your stuff.' She pulled Paige close to her and held her as if she was protecting her from a threat. 'Dinner will be at six. Why don't you go in the lounge and watch the early news?'

She turned her back to the old man and handed the potato to Paige and whispered an instruction. Distracted from the moment earlier, Paige went about washing the potato.

The old man was frustrated. He left the kitchen and went back to his room. He sat on the end of his bed and looked at the clock. He would not leave his room until six. He would stay here and sulk.

Someone has been in here. I'm not making this up. She looks at me like I'm stupid. I know the paper was here this morning.

He let his thoughts and emotions consume him for a few minutes. He lay down and waited for six o'clock. His body acted his age, but he knew his mind was still all there. He was certain of that.

The old man lay and stared at the clock. He watched every minute pass. He had lain here for over an hour, and he was still angry. Finally, the numbers on the clock changed to read six o'clock. He willed his tired old body to sit up and turn so his legs hung over the bed. He pushed himself forward and stood up. Pain seared through his feet and into his legs. He let out a small moan of discomfort, followed by a deep breath in.

One foot forward was all he needed to do to get his body moving. One step and then another, and he was off, shuffling his way down the hallway to the kitchen. He pulled his chair out and sat with a huff to let his daughter know he was there. She looked up from the stove and smiled at the old man. His mood softened, and he let his anger go.

'Smells good, Kat.'

His daughter turned back around and looked up at the clock above the door. 'Won't be long, Dad. It's almost six, and we will eat.' She moved away from the stove to the doorway and yelled to the children to wash up and come to the table.

Puzzled by her last comment to him, the old man turned in his seat to look at the clock – five minutes to six. He felt his frustration rising and turned back to face Kat. 'Is that clock slow? I came out of my bedroom at six o'clock.'

Kat stopped what she was doing and pulled at her sleeve to reveal her watch. She looked up at the clock and back at her watch. 'No, the clock is right. Maybe you have accidently changed the time on the clock in your room. I can fix it after tea if you like.'

Now at a boiling point, the old man thumped the table with his fist. 'I have not changed the time on my clock, I did not move my photograph, and I did not lose the newspaper!' His voice was raised and angry.

The children stopped in the doorway. Kat looked at Paige, who looked like she was about to cry, and Nathan looked frightened.

'Lower your voice, Dad, you're scaring the kids.' Her tone was serious. 'No one has touched your things, and you are the only person who goes in your room. I will fix your clock after tea and look for the paper. Please, for now, just calm down so we can enjoy dinner.'

Kat placed a plate in front of the old man and then went over to the children, who were still standing in the doorway. She pulled them both close and kissed the tops of their heads. She took Paige by her little hand and led her to the table and helped her into a chair and pushed her in. Nathan sat next to his grandfather but said nothing.

Kat returned to the table with food for the children and for herself. She sat opposite her father and studied his face. She could see he was frustrated. She always knew there would come a time when he would start to slow down mentally. Tonight he looked old. He looked tired and worn. She slumped in her chair and started to eat.

I don't know if I am ready for this. Maybe Stephen is right and we should look at nursing home options. Her heart broke a little at the thought of her father being put in a home. Mortality was kicking in, and she knew he wouldn't be around forever.

There was only silence as the four of them sat at the table and ate. Nathan finished first and excused himself before clearing his plate. Paige finished but didn't look up from her plate and waited for her mother to finish. The old man was pushing his food around on the plate and hardly ate anything. He looked up at his daughter with sadness in his eyes. He didn't mean to get angry and yell, and he certainly didn't mean to scare his favourite little girl.

'Paige, I'm sorry I yelled before. I didn't mean to scare you.' He looked at his granddaughter, who was still staring at her plate. 'Will you forgive me?' His voice was soft and gentle. He reached out and put his hand over her small hand that was on the table.

Paige looked up, still pouting. She nodded at the old man and then pushed herself backwards and almost ran from the room. A few seconds later, he heard her bedroom door close.

'Kat, I really didn't mean to scare them. I am sorry for that. It's just frustrating.'

He looked Kat in the eye. She looked back, and a tear escaped and ran down her cheek.

'Aw, don't cry, honey. I promise I won't yell anymore.'

Kat leaned over the table and squeezed his hand. 'I know, Dad.' Still leaning over, she pulled his plate towards her. 'I will put this in the fridge in case you get hungry later, OK?'

She stood from the table and carried plates to the sink. He sat at the table and watched her as she put plastic wrap over his uneaten meal and put it into the fridge. She picked up one of the kids' plates and went to the bin to scrape the few small pieces of food into the bin. She placed the plate on the bench and then turned towards the old man. She had a hand on her hip, and her brow was furrowed. He looked at her in a way that questioned why she stood like that.

'Did you throw out my reed diffuser?'

'Your what?'

'My reed diffuser. The jar that sat on the bench here that had lavender oil in it and little sticks that sat in the oil.'

'No. Why would I throw it out? It stank, but I didn't put it the bin.'

'Huh' was her response, and she reached into the bin and pulled out the jar. She didn't say anything else, but he knew from her look she didn't believe him.

He got up from the table and walked to the lounge and sat in his chair. The remote was still on the arm of the chair from where he had left it the night before. He pointed it at the TV and pushed the red button. Voices started talking to him, and he crossed his arms over his chest and stared off into the distance.

Chapter 9

He sat high up in his perch and listened to everything. From his laptop, he watched the drama unfold, and he was very pleased with the outcome. He nestled himself in his hammock and balanced the laptop on the joists at an angle where he could see it all while relaxing in his makeshift bed. To his other side, his backpack was just within his reach. He stretched his fingers and pulled it ever so slowly towards him. When it was close enough for him to grab with a firm grip, he lifted it and placed it on his stomach.

He unzipped the main pocket and rummaged around. He found the other piece of fruit he had taken from the bowl on the table and placed it at his side. He was still hungry, and this would do for him for now.

As he went to do the bag up, he paused as something caught his eye. He reached back in and delicately pulled out some fabric. It was the top he had taken from the little girl's room. He placed it on his chest and continued closing his bag and placed the bag gently on the ground next to him.

He picked up the shirt and held it at arm's length so he could see it more clearly. The light was fading outside and made the space he was in almost pitch black already. He had the glow of the laptop screen providing him with light for now, but it didn't provide him the brightness he needed to take in all the details of the shirt. He reached to the side again and retrieved his bag. His miner's light was in the small front pocket and was easy for him to find. Again, taking caution, he gently placed the bag down.

He slipped the light on his head and felt for the tiny button. Now he could see. He held the shirt at arm's length again, and this time, it was illuminated by the torch. It wasn't very big, but it was very pink, and embossed into the front of the fabric was a cat. He ran his fingers over the glittery detail and tried to imagine the girl wearing the shirt, her bright eyes and toothless grin and that annoying high-pitched squeal only a small girl was physically capable of making.

He brought the shirt to his face and smelled the fabric. He remembered her room smelled like bubble gum, the sickly sweet smell that made him feel ill. He breathed in deeply for a second time and held his breath. He allowed the scent to linger in his nostrils before releasing the air from his lungs. The fragrance on the shirt was nothing like the little girl's room. It had the faintest aroma of laundry detergent, and that was all. He was a little disappointed but lay still, rubbing the material on his cheek.

Lost in a daydream, he hadn't noticed movement on his screen. It was the noise of the little girl that startled him. With a jolt, he opened his eyes and turned to focus on the images on the screen.

The old man was still in the lounge, staring at the television. The boy was in the bathroom, brushing his teeth, and the little girl was nowhere to be seen. He scrunched the shirt in his hand and looked at the other boxes. Her mother was in the kitchen and looking at the doorway, looking perplexed. A second later, the little girl appeared in the kitchen, looking like she was about to cry. He stared at the two girls and concentrated so he could hear the conversation.

In between sobs, it was established the boy had splashed water at her in the bathroom and then put her toothbrush out of reach. He rolled his eyes and sighed. He couldn't understand why she was crying over this. *It's just a toothbrush.*

Her mother pulled her close for a moment in comfort and then stood up from the chair. She took the little girl by the hand and led her into the hallway.

In an instant, he had lost sight of the both of them, and now he realised his error. He had not put a camera in the hallway, and he had no spares. He tried to sit up, which proved difficult in the hammock as it began to sway with his movement. Agitated, he heaved himself up and was now in an upright position. As he steadied the hammock from swinging, the apple rolled out from under him and rolled off the edge. With a thud, it landed on the plasterboard.

His blood went cold, and his skin tingled. His heart began pounding so loudly, he could hear the blood surging through his veins in his ears. Nausea took over. A stupid mistake – he was not concentrating.

He looked back at his screen and saw the mother and both the children in the bathroom oblivious to what had just happened. She was doing her best to sort out the squabbling between the two little people.

He moved his eyes to the lounge and the old man, and there, on the screen, was the old man, staring at the roof. It appeared as if he was looking right at the camera. So here they were, staring at each other, hearts pounding, and no one moved a muscle.

Chapter 10

Katrina walked into the lounge and startled her father, who appeared to be staring off into space. 'What are you thinking about, Dad?' she asked as she sat in the lounge chair next to her father.

'There is something moving around in the roof.' The old man looked at his daughter with concerned eyes.

'What makes you say that?'

'I just heard a thud coming from the roof. And earlier. I got a feeling that we were being watched.'

Katrina rolled her eyes slightly at her father. 'There's nothing moving around the roof, Dad. If there was, I would have heard it, and there is no one watching us.'

The old man frowned at his daughter. 'You think I am making all this up, don't you? I suppose you think I am losing my mind.' The accusation in his voice was unsettling.

'Dad . . .' She paused for a moment, carefully selecting her words. 'I don't think you are losing your mind or making this up, but over the past couple of days, you don't seem to be yourself. I'm worried about you.'

The old man shifted himself in the chair and picked up the remote and started flicking through the channels, ignoring his daughter. Katrina sat there in silence next to her father and waited for him to say something. From the kitchen, Kat heard her phone ring, and she stood up from the chair.

She turned to her father. 'I will be back in a few minutes. Would you like a cuppa?'

The old man grunted and nodded. Katrina walked out of the lounge and into the kitchen and snatched up her phone, which was buzzing on the table.

'Hey,' she said softly. 'How's the trip going?'

She pulled out a chair from the table and sat facing the doorway. For a few minutes, she sat and listened to her husband fill her in on the past couple of days at the conference he was attending. She replied with the applicable 'that's great' or 'sounds interesting' periodically. She missed her husband when he was away. She missed being able to have an adult conversation after work.

Several minutes into the phone call, she got up from the table and went to the bench, filled the kettle, and put it on the stove. She tucked the phone between her ear and shoulder and proceeded to get two cups from the cupboard and prepared them with sugar and a tea bag and waited for the water to boil. She leaned back against the bench and waited for her husband to eventually ask her how she was going. And finally, he asked her.

'The kids are great. I was hoping you would have rung a little earlier so you could have spoken with them. They miss you. I miss you. Are you still going to be home Friday night?' Fighting back anger, she retorted to the response. 'What do you mean you won't be back until Sunday afternoon? What is so important that you need to stay another two days?'

There was silence again. She dropped her head in disappointment and rubbed at her temple. 'A fishing charter? Oh, how lovely for you.' She wasn't often sarcastic to her husband, but he had a habit of staying for the weekend after conferences and leaving her to do all the running around after the kids with their weekend commitments. More often than not, both the kids had different activities at the same time at different locations, and somehow she had to be in two places at once.

'Well, I hope you enjoy yourself while I'm here raising your children on my own.' She started pacing around the kitchen. 'No, you're not sorry. If you were sorry, you would say no to the charter and come home and be with your family.'

She opened the fridge and snatched at the milk, slammed the fridge door, and put the milk carton on the bench.

'Actually, I will be like this because you do this to me all the time.' She had now raised her voice. She could feel her face burning. 'Oh, and not that you care, but it seems like Dad is now starting to lose his mind. He is convinced that there is something in the roof and someone is watching him. Of course, I haven't heard anything or got that feeling, so now I have to deal with his paranoia. But hey, at least I can count on you for support. Oh wait, no, I can't – 'cause you're too busy *fishing*!'

Katrina ended the phone call abruptly and threw the phone onto the table. She leaned on the back of the chair, hanging her head, and took a few deep breaths to try to calm down.

The phone rang again. *Fuck off!* She sniggered to herself and flicked the phone to silent.

When she regained her composure, she went about making the cups of tea and grabbed a packet of biscuits from the top shelf, where she kept a few treats for herself that the kids couldn't see.

Armed with hot tea and biscuits, she went back to her father in the lounge and placed the cups on the table. She got herself comfy and tore open the packet and offered the sweet treats to the old man. He smiled at his daughter, and his eyes were filled with empathy. She knew he had heard the yelling. His old fat fingers fumbled with the biscuits, and he ended up with two landing on his lap. They looked at each other and laughed. With the mood lightened, they sat and watched the TV together, and once again, all appeared peaceful in the house.

Chapter 11

He lay in his hammock, very pleased with himself. The old man was starting to act crazy, and his daughter was starting to think he was losing his mind. His plan was working. He was getting excited at how well it was going.

He continued watching his laptop screen. He continued watching her. *She is perfect.* She sat in the chair near the old man, watching the TV. From where he was, he could hear her laugh. He watched his screen and saw her smile. She smiled with her eyes, and it lit up her face. He wanted more than ever to touch her, smell her, and see that smile up close.

The day was finished, and he watched her as she turned off the TV. She helped her father up from his chair and walked him down the hall, turning off the hall light as she passed the switch. Tonight she came back and set the alarm and then disappeared back into the hallway. She was in his blind spot again. He became agitated. He sat up and swung his legs over the hammock and leaned in closer to the screen, wishing for her to appear somewhere again. He held his breath and listened for any noise. *There.* He heard her gentle 'good night' to her father by the old man's bedroom door.

He moved his focus to another square on his screen. The old man appeared on the screen. Closing the door behind him, he shuffled past the bed, and he sat down at his desk and started reading a book.

His eyes darted to the square containing a black image of her room. He held his breath in anticipation – nothing. He stared harder at the screen, willing her to appear – nothing. His eyes darted to all squares, looking, searching for her – still nothing. He exhaled and focused on his hearing, listening for her movement in the house.

A noise at the far end of the roof eased his tension. A toilet flushed, and a door closed. Back to his screen, he saw her in the bathroom. His heart rate slowed again, and he breathed in deeply. He watched her. She washed her hands and leaned into the mirror, looking closely at her face. She tilted her head to the side and ran her hand down her throat, stretching the skin. Disappointed, she stood up straight. She picked up her toothbrush and put on a generous amount of toothpaste. She watched herself in the mirror as she brushed. She spat and turned on the tap and scooped water with her hand into her mouth. She rinsed and spat again. She washed her toothbrush and picked up the small towel hanging next to the sink and dried the toothbrush and wiped her face. Precisely, she folded the towel and rehung it on the hook. Without looking back, she left the bathroom and back into his blind spot.

He didn't have to wait long until she had reappeared on his screen. This time, she was in her bedroom. His heart beat faster. She walked over to the bed and stood at the end. She rolled her neck around and rubbed one shoulder. As her head tilted back, she closed her eyes. She was directly under the camera. In an instant, his body temperature peaked, and his heart skipped a beat.

She finished stretching her neck and looked over at her laundry hamper. She stepped closer and started unbuttoning her blouse. The satin slipped effortlessly from her shoulders, and with two fingers, she lifted it away from her body and let it fall into the basket. She reached behind her back and unzipped her skirt, and with a finger tucked into each side, she worked it away from her hips and let it fall to the ground. Now in just her underwear, she bent down and retrieved the skirt. With little thought, she tossed it into the hamper.

He sat there as still as a statue. He barely breathed. He just watched her every movement. *She is breathtaking.*

Now she reached with one hand behind her back and expertly unfastened her bra. She slid one strap down her arm and then the other. She hung it over the edge of the hamper. He only saw her back but tensed in anticipation, waiting for her to turn around. He finally blinked. She removed her underwear and dropped it into the hamper.

She turned around and walked towards the door. He started to fidget. He put his hand over his mouth. She turned off the light.

He could no longer see her. He breathed in once more and lay back in the hammock. He closed his eyes and let the image of her naked body fill his head. He felt dizzy. He did not like the way she took over his thoughts, controlling his mind, distracting him from what he needed to do. He couldn't do anything just now but wait. He must wait until he was sure everyone was asleep.

He opened his eyes and tried to dismiss her image from his brain. He must focus again. He reached into his pocket and pulled out the small soldier figure he had taken from the boy's room. He stared at it. He remembered what he must do now. He was again focused. He looked at the screen and saw no movement, but it was still too soon. He was patient, and he waited. He would wait until the time was just right.

It didn't take long for the house to be still, with all occupants sound asleep. He shut down his laptop, put on his backpack, and crept to the manhole cover. He lowered himself to the washing machine and, this time, landed silently. He slid off the machine to the floor and effortlessly made his way to the front door. He keyed in the security code and smiled when the active light went out. He waited and listened. Silence filled the house.

He went back to the kitchen and removed his backpack. He opened the fridge and found a container filled with the leftovers from that night's dinner. He placed the container in his bag and took out a drink bottle to refill with water. He picked up a jug from the top shelf and filled his bottle, being ever so careful not to spill any water. He put the jug back and replaced the cap on his bottle and placed it back in his bag.

The moon was bright tonight, and light streamed into the kitchen, making his job much easier. He looked around and saw the jar he had placed in the bin earlier back on the bench. Smiling to himself, he walked over and gently picked up the jar and lowered it to the bottom of the bin, taking his time not to make any noise. Next to the jar, he saw the biscuit packet she had left out. He moved his backpack over to the bench and, with soft fingers, put the packet in his bag.

He leaned back against the bench and looked around. *That's enough for now*, he thought. He wouldn't do too much at once – small things over the next few days and nights, just enough to get her to question the old man's sanity.

He put the backpack back on and swiftly moved from the kitchen to the front door, re-entered the code to the alarm, and quickly went back to the laundry room and disappeared up into the darkness.

He hopped across the beams and back to the safety of his camp. He eased himself back into his hammock and opened his backpack. Feeling his stomach rumble, he removed the container he had helped himself to from the fridge and took off the lid. He closed his eyes and smelled the contents. It'd been almost a week since he had eaten a proper home-cooked meal. He had no cutlery and so used his fingers to shovel the food into his mouth. Greedily, he scooped the food from the container and devoured the contents in just a few minutes. With the container empty, he sucked the remnants off his fingers and lay back, feeling very satisfied.

Tiredness started taking over, and so he replaced the lid and put the container back in his bag. He took out the drink bottle and thirstily gulped half of the water. A loud burp escaped, and he chuckled a little. *Better out than in.*

He placed his bag down next to his bed and folded his arms across his stomach. Slowly, his body relaxed, and he felt a heaviness in his legs. One last sigh, and he drifted off to sleep.

Chapter 12

He was awoken by his alarm at 5:45 a.m. Sleepily, he opened his eyes and looked around him. He was surrounded by darkness. He pulled his phone from his pocket and unlocked the screen. He scrunched his eyes from the brightness and slowly started to focus. He leaned across and woke up his laptop. Slowly, each camera was activated, and he observed each room. The house was quiet, and all the inhabitants were sound asleep. He swung his legs over the side of the hammock and stretched his back and took another scan of the rooms on his screen – no movement from anyone. He sent his laptop back to sleep.

He picked up his backpack and moved across the roof to his exit. Quietly, he descended to the laundry room and landed silently on top of the washing machine. He stretched up and replaced the cover.

He stopped and listened. Silence filled his ears. He slid off the washing machine and made a quick dash to the back door – unlocked again. He smiled to himself as her carelessness amused him. He left the house and breathed in the fresh morning air. His lungs felt cold, and a shiver ran up his spine. The weather was turning, and he could smell rain in the air.

He walked quickly along the back of the house and down the side to the gate. Hesitantly, he lifted the latch and slowly pulled the gate towards him. The gate moved noiselessly, and he left the backyard. He closed the gate behind him and turned to face the street. He looked around. The sun hadn't risen yet, and the neighbourhood was quiet. There was a small amount of light coming from the street light. He walked past the lounge window and the front door and stood in front of the old man's room.

Shielded by a row of rose bushes, he could not be seen from the street. He tapped on the window, softly at first, and when he could not hear any movement from inside, he tapped a little harder. He sensed the old man stirring from his slumber, so he tapped again. He heard a groan. The old man was awake.

He reached behind his back and broke a small branch from one of the rose bushes. A sharp pain seared through his finger. He jerked his hand back and saw blood starting to drip from the side of his little finger. He puts the side of his hand to his mouth and sucked the blood from the wound. The taste was metallic and gave him an instant sense of nausea. He held his hand at eye level and saw a small splinter protruding from his finger. He carefully pinched it between two of his fingers and pulled it free. He sucked at the wound one more time and watched to see if the bleeding had stopped.

'Fucking roses,' he angrily muttered under his breath.

He held the stick he had just torn from the rose bush tightly in his hand and, with the splintered end, dragged it across the window, letting it make a scratching noise.

He heard another groan come from inside, and this time, he heard the old man thud out of bed. He scratched the window again and then quickly leaned with his back against the bricks, out of sight. He looked to his side and saw the curtains move in the middle of the window. He couldn't make out the old man, but he could hear him grumble loudly. The curtains closed, followed by the thumping of the old man heavily walking back to bed.

He waited a minute to let the old man settle back in bed, and he scratched the glass with the stick, this time faster and louder. The thud of the old man getting out of bed was louder, and he quickly took shelter back against the wall of the house. He turned his head slightly towards the old man's window and saw the curtains move ferociously. He laughed internally. This time, he could make out the silhouette of the old man leaning against the glass. He sucked in his torso and flattened himself up against the house as much as he could. He didn't move a muscle. He held his breath. The old man stood in the window for what seemed like an eternity. He saw the curtains close again, and he exhaled.

This time, he waited several minutes just to let the old man think the noise had gone. He moved back in front of the window. He stood dead centre, and this time, he knocked on the glass. This time, he did not move away. This time, he wanted the old man to see him.

With a furious grumble and an anger to his stride, the old man whipped back the curtains and saw him standing there. The old man jumped back in fright and lost his balance and toppled to the floor. The old man cried out in pain and looked back at the window. He stepped closer to the window and stared back at the old man and smiled. The old man yelled out. He heard her hurrying from her bedroom. He waved at the old man and left the window.

He walked quickly to the footpath and walked with an urgency in his step up the street to the corner. He rounded the corner and kept walking until he reached the main road. He knew not far from here was a group of shops; one shop served breakfast from six.

He checked his watch. *Ten minutes until they open.*

He slowed his pace as he knew no one was following him. It took him only seven minutes at a slow pace to reach the shops. He saw a middle-aged man inside the shop getting the restaurant ready for the day. He waited near a phone booth close to the street. He watched the shop and waited for the front door to be unlocked and the Open sign to be switched on.

At three minutes past six, he walked up to the front door and pushed it open. A bell above the door announced his arrival, and the man whom he had been watching through the window came out from the kitchen and greeted him with a big friendly 'good morning' and a smile. The man introduced himself as Harry and ushered him over to a booth. He placed a menu in front of him and walked away.

He studied the menu and was ready for Harry when he returned to take his order. He was famished and ordered a large hot breakfast of bacon, eggs, hash browns, toast, and mushrooms. Harry took his order and filled up his mug with steaming hot coffee. He leaned over the mug and let the aroma of the coffee fill his nostrils. He sat back and stared out into the empty restaurant, his mind filled with thoughts of what was happening at the house. His mind replayed the moment the old man opened the curtain and saw him. He sniggered when he recalled the look of fright on the old man's face and watched him crash to the ground, hearing his muffled cry for help.

Lost in his daydream and pleased with how the day had gone so far, he was brought back to the now when Harry returned to his side with a plate piled high with food. The plate was placed in front of him, and he nodded his thanks to Harry. Without much grace, he ate his food and finished the mug of coffee. He sat up tall and stretched his back.

He looked around and caught the eye of Harry, who was slumped over the counter, reading the newspaper. Harry stood and turned away from him. He watched Harry and saw him pick up the coffee pot and turned back to face him. Harry lifted the pot with a raised eyebrow, and he nodded in favour of a refill.

He didn't take his eyes off Harry. He liked to watch people. People fascinated him. He liked to imagine their faces when bad things happened. Sometimes he made bad things happen just to see their faces. He wondered what Harry would do if something bad were to happen right at this moment. Would he drop the pot filled with hot coffee? Would he rush to someone's aid? Or would he freeze and do nothing?

Harry, oblivious to his thoughts, refilled his mug and then picked up the empty plate and asked if he wants anything else. He looked up at Harry and smiled. He shook his head and then turned away. Harry took the plate to the kitchen and then returned to the counter and continued reading the newspaper.

He sat in the restaurant until four minutes till eight o'clock. He slid out from the booth and took his wallet from his back pocket. He removed twenty dollars and left it on the table. He acknowledged Harry as he left the restaurant.

He crossed the carpark to the phone booth. He took coins from his pocket and picked up the handset. He dialled a number and listened to the ringing – three rings, four rings, and then . . .

'Hello?'

Chapter 13

Startled, Katrina sat up in bed. She looked at the clock sitting on the table next to her pillow – 5:45 a.m. She sleepily got out of bed and found her dressing gown. She sighed as she opened the door and stepped into the hallway. When she heard her father cry out again, her pace quickened, and she burst into his room.

She panicked as she saw her father lying on the floor, struggling to get up, clearly distressed. She fell to her knees beside him and put her hands under his shoulders, using her body weight to push the old man into a sitting position.

'Stay there, Dad.'

She stood and walked back to the doorway and turned on the light. The brightness from the globe sharply illuminated the room, and they both squinted while waiting for their eyes to adjust. Katrina came back to her father's side and helped the old man to his feet. She guided him to the edge of the bed and steadied him as he sat backwards onto the bed.

'What happened?' Her voice was soft and filled with concern. She sat next to him and held his hand, which was still shaking.

'There was something knocking on my window, and when I opened the curtain, he was standing there.'

His words were stuttered and shaky. Katrina looked at her father's face; his eyes were frightened, and his body slumped next to hers.

'Who was standing there, Dad?' She tried not to come across as condescending, but she was getting frustrated with his behaviours over the past couple of days. A sadness filled her chest as she started to accept his age was finally catching up with him.

'It was him. I told you the other night we were being watched.'

'Did you recognise him? Is it someone you know?'

'No. I don't know his face. He laughed at me when I fell. He just stood there and laughed.'

Katrina squeezed her father's hand and got to her feet. She walked over to the window and looked out. From over her neighbour's house, the sun was starting to make an appearance, and shadows were starting to form. She looked at the roses and couldn't see anything out of place.

Surely, if someone had been standing there, I would see evidence, wouldn't I? Katrina stood by the window for some time, questioning her father's story.

'Mum?' A small voice came from the doorway.

Katrina turned to see Nathan standing there.

'What's going on?'

His eyes were locked on his mother, and she knew she couldn't brush this off; he was smarter than that.

'Grandad took a tumble when getting out of bed, honey, but don't worry. He is going to be all right.'

Nathan switched his focus from his mother to the old man, who was still sitting slumped on the edge of the bed. 'Grandad? You OK? Want me to get you a glass of water or something?' Nathan stayed in the doorway and waited for the old man to respond. His look of concern for his grandfather was heartbreaking.

'Yes, please, Nathan. That would be nice.' He looked up at the small boy and smiled as best he could. He knew not to tell him about the intruder knocking on his window; he didn't want his grandson to be scared in his own home.

Nathan left the two adults and went to the kitchen.

Katrina came back to her father and crouched in front of him. 'Thank you for not telling him about the stranger in the window. I don't need him having nightmares about this. You know how vivid his imagination is.'

'I know, Kat.' The old man pushed himself to his feet and took a second to control his balance. His hip hurt from the fall, and he was feeling nauseous. He walked around to the other side of the bed and sat heavily. He pulled his feet up and slid them under the covers.

Katrina finished tucking him back into bed. 'How are you feeling now, Dad?'

'Thirsty.'

He smiled and looked past his daughter as Nathan returned with a glass of water. Katrina stepped back and let Nathan pass and place the glass on the side table

'Thank you.'

'That's OK, Grandad. Want anything else?'

'No, I'm fine. Thanks, son. I will rest here until breakfast is ready if that's OK with everyone.'

'Of course, Dad. I will come and get you at seven thirty. Rest now.'

The old man looked wearily at his two caregivers and then closed his eyes.

Katrina put her hand on Nathan's shoulder and ushered him from the room. She quietly closed the door and kissed her son on the top of his head. 'Go back to bed for a while, honey. It's too early to be up.'

Nathan yawned and walked up the hall to his room. He stopped by his door and looked back at his mother. 'Is Grandad really OK?'

'Yes, honey.' She tried to smile and reassure her son. 'Grandad is getting old is all. It happens to everyone eventually.'

Nathan dropped his head and disappeared into his room.

Katrina went to the other end of the house to the kitchen and put on the kettle. There was no way she could go back to sleep now. She gazed up at the clock on the wall – six o'clock. *I'm up now, I guess*, she thought and went about making a cup of tea.

She hated being here without her husband for support right now. Even though she knew Stephen wanted her to put her father in a nursing home, he would always hug her tight and tell her she was doing an amazing job looking after him on top of everything else she did. She needed that hug right now. She needed to hear those words. She stared into her cup, searching for the answers.

Broken from her daydream by the irritating noise of her alarm ringing madly from her bedroom, she walked almost at a jog down the hall and into her room. She smacked the alarm as if it were a bug and frowned as it fell from its place to the floor. In a swipe of frustration, she snatched it back up and put it back where it belonged.

She rubbed her eyes and shook her head. *The day can only get better.*

Showered and dressed, Katrina went about with her daily routine. She opened the kids' bedroom doors and roused them from sleep. She took her place in the kitchen and made lunches for school, followed by breakfast. A little after seven, she stomped up and down the hall, barking orders at the children, and at seven thirty, she smiles with victory as once again, she had them both sitting at the table, dressed in school uniforms, and Paige had even brushed her hair.

'Nathan, honey, can you please go and tell Grandad it's time for breakfast?'

'Sure.'

Nathan got up from his chair and flicked Paige on the ear as he walked past, and she squealed as he vanished from the room.

'Mumma! He hurt me again. He always hurts me.'

Katrina looked up from what she was doing to see Paige's pout as she rubbed her ear.

'Sweetie, he's your brother, and it's his job to be annoying. Did he really hurt you, or are you exaggerating?'

'Mumma!' the small girl hissed. 'You always take his side.'

Amused by the sulking, Katrina put a plate of bacon and toast in front of her daughter. 'I saved you all the crunchy pieces.'

Paige looked up and soon lost her pout. 'None for Nathan?' she asked slyly.

Katrina leaned on the table and kissed Paige on the nose. 'None for Nathan.'

Smugly, Paige smiled at Katrina and picked up the crispiest piece of bacon she saw and crunched it loudly just as Nathan sat back at the table.

'Hey, where's mine?' he responded in protest and looked disappointed when he scanned his plate for the fought-over crispy pieces of bacon.

'Sorry, kiddo. Next time, don't antagonise your sister as you walk past.'

'Whatever.'

'OK, what's going on?' said a voice from the hall, followed by a slow-moving old man. He took his place at the table and thanked Katrina as she handed him a plate.

'Mum's playing favourites again,' retorted Nathan, still searching his plate.

'I highly doubt that, Nathan.'

'She is!' he responded sharply. 'Just because I gave Paige a little flick as I walked past, Mum gives her all the good bacon.'

The old man looked at his little princess and was greeted by a cheeky grin. He couldn't help but smile at her.

'It's true, Grandad. Mum loves me the best.'

Nathan looked up, hurt, and Paige stuck her tongue out at him.

'Mum?' He looked for comfort from his mother.

Katrina sat at the table and tilted her head at Nathan. 'You know that isn't true, honey. I love you both the same.' She turned to her daughter. 'Paige, that wasn't nice.'

Paige stood up from the table and grabbed the last piece of bacon from her plate. 'He started it.' She threw the meat at her brother – 'Here you go!' – and made a quick dash down the hall.

Nathan jumped up and gave chase. 'You're so dead!'

A door was slammed, followed by a second door. Katrina and her father looked at each other and laughed.

She dropped her head into her hands and rubbed her eyes. 'Well, this has been a great start to the day. Thank god the bus will be here soon and they can be the school's problem for a few hours.'

She cleared the plates and checked the time again – a few minutes before eight. She yelled down the hall, and within a minute, both her children left the sanctuary of their rooms and collected their school bags from her. She hugged and kissed them both and watched them leave the house. From the front door, she could see up the road to the corner where the bus collected them, and right on time, they left her care for the day.

She closed the front door and headed towards the bathroom to finish getting herself ready when she heard the phone ring. On the second ring, she changed direction back to the kitchen. On the third ring, she reached for the handset. On the fourth ring, she picked it up.

'Hello?'

There was a pause.

'Oh really? I have to work today, but I will be home again around four. Will there be a technician in the area then?'

The old man looked at his daughter and gestured to ask what was wrong. She shook her head at him and concentrated on what the caller was telling her.

'Fantastic. See you then.' She replaced the receiver and looked at her dad. 'Seems the alarm isn't working properly. They say that it is intermittently turning itself on and off at their end. They are sending someone out this afternoon to fix it.'

The old man nodded at his daughter. 'Good. After what happened this morning, we definitely want to be sure the alarm is working.'

Katrina walked past her father and looked out the lounge window. 'Your ride is here, Dad.' She continued to the front door and opened it for the driver. 'Morning, Dan. Dad is coming now.' She kissed her father on the cheek as he shuffled past her. 'See you tonight, Dad. Have a great day. Oh, Dan, can you please get the girls to keep an eye on him? He had a fall this morning, and I just want to make sure there are no injuries. He seems OK, but they would know better.'

'Sure thing, Kat. Come on, Al, let's get you into the car.'

Katrina closed the door behind the two men and sighed. She decided to make another cup of tea and have just ten minutes to herself before leaving for work. She was exhausted already, and the day had only just begun.

Chapter 14

He hung up the phone and was pleased with himself. He would arrive at the house at 4:00 p.m. as arranged, less than eight hours until he would be with her again.

He left the phone booth and started to walk. He must return home and collect some more things. The walk home took him thirty minutes. He opened his front door and was greeted by a comforting silence. He entered his home and looked around. He relaxed when he was sure nothing was out of place. No one had been here. He was alone.

He had been in the same clothes for days now and felt dirty. He showered and changed into fresh clothes. Now he could work.

He went into his garage and opened his van. He removed two toolboxes and placed them on the bench. He opened them both and removed the contents. He placed them down in precise order. Every item had its place, and every item had its use. He went back to the van and removed a folder. He opened it and removed a folded piece of paper. He unfolded it and laid it next to the rows of tools and studied it. It was the plans to her house with the details of the security system. He must study the plans before he returned. He could not make any mistakes.

He was interrupted by his phone ringing. He grumbled as he answered it. A chirpy young girl apologised for interrupting his leave, but they were stuck and needed someone to attend an urgent job. He agreed and hung up abruptly. This was not how his day had been planned. There was a beep on his phone, and the details of the job were displayed. A smile escaped the side of his mouth, and suddenly, he felt control returning.

He repacked his toolboxes and carefully folded the paper, making sure he used the same creases. He loaded up his van and returned to the house and to his bedroom. He opened his wardrobe and removed a shirt from a hanger. He slid it on and buttoned it up and then tucked it neatly into his trousers. He looked in the mirror; looking back at him in uniform was an electrician. On his left breast pocket was his name badge – Simon. Simon the electrician was ready to work.

It took twelve minutes to drive to the urgent job. He parked out the front and walked empty-handed into the front door. He was greeted by an older lady dressed in a crisp white blouse and black slacks.

'Hello. How can I help you?' She smiled at Simon.

'Hello. I'm Simon, and I got a call that you have a fuse that keeps shorting out.'

With relief written all over her face, the lady moved out from behind the counter. 'Thank you for getting here so quickly, Simon.' She extended her hand. 'I'm Susan. We've had issues all morning with one fuse that keeps turning off the main lights in the common room, and the oldies are causing quite a bit of trouble for the carers.'

Simon shook Susan's hand and followed her past the counter, down a corridor, and through a door that led to a large room. The room contained shelving down one side and a large table in the middle. There was a sink and a fridge under a window.

'This is our staff break room, so please feel free to make yourself a cuppa whenever you like. The circuit board is just over there.' Susan pointed to a large metallic box on the wall.

Simon nodded. 'Thanks, Susan. I will take a look and then go and get my tools out of my van. Do you have any issues if I need to wander through other parts of the building to check out what's going on with your wiring?'

'Not at all, Simon. Just be warned. When you go into the main area where our clients spend their day, they will all be experts and tell you how to do your job.' Susan chuckled and walked away.

Simon opened the metallic cupboard and started inspecting the circuit board. It was an old building and so shouldn't be too complicated. He went out to his van and retrieved his tools. About fifteen minutes into the job, he figured out the problem. He found a young girl wandering the corridor and got her to point him in the direction of the common room as labelled on the faulty fuse. He opened the door and stepped into another world.

It looked like an oversized lounge with couches and large chairs scattered all around. There were two televisions on opposite sides of the room, surrounded by elderly folk. There was a kitchen at the back with a large opening and serving counter. He could see two women with their hair bundled into nets in the kitchen preparing food. At the back of the room were large windows overlooking a garden. One window looked into an aviary. There were two high-backed lounge chairs in front of that window. In all, he counted sixteen elderly and four carers besides the two kitchen staff.

He must have looked lost when a tiny old lady stood in front of him.

'Can I help you, dear?' She had a tiny croaking voice and could hardly be heard.

Simon looked down at her and shook his head. 'I'm fine, thank you. Just trying to locate the problem with the lights.'

She smiled a toothless smile at him and, with the help of a stick, very slowly wandered away. The conversation caught the attention of the only male carer, who nodded at Simon and then made his way over. He shook Simon's hand and looked up at the lights.

'They've been playing up all day, and the natives are getting restless being in the dark. It's not too bad when the sun is out, but when the clouds come over, it's almost impossible to see in here. They tell me that light over there' – he pointed towards the window overlooking the aviary – 'has been making a crackling noise, so when the fuse went out the last time, we left it off and called you.'

'Thanks for that. If it's just a faulty light socket, it shouldn't take more than half an hour to replace and test all the other lights just to be safe. Just to let you know, I am going to have to cut power to the building before I replace it. Sorry.'

The carer smiled at Simon. 'OK. Give us five minutes to let the staff know so we can prepare for the chaos. Hopefully, the girls in the kitchen can bring out food. That should distract them for a little bit anyway.'

Simon chuckled. 'Good luck. I will be as quick as I can for you.'

The carer gave a friendly pat on Simon's shoulder and walked towards the other carers to prepare them. Simon left the room and went back to the reception area to update Susan and get the OK to shut down the power.

Within minutes, he could hear the moans and groans as the power went out. He picked up his toolbox and made his way back to the common room. Most of the oldies had been moved out into the garden, and the carers were seating them for an early lunch.

The groundskeeper entered the room and noisily dragged a ladder behind him. 'Thought you could use this. Bit easier than you having to unload yours.'

Simon took the ladder and thanked the groundskeeper. He set the ladder up behind the two chairs looking out at the aviary. He could see the balding head of an old man sitting in the chair. Simon wondered if this was him. He took his foot off the first step and went to walk around and confront the old man. He stepped back when a young girl walked in.

'Al, there you are. Come on, we are going to spend some time outside while the lights are getting fixed.'

'I don't want to' was the gruff, rude response.

Simon smiled. It was him. He looked at the girl and walked around the other side of the chair. He smiled at the old man. The old man stared back, and slowly, the realisation hit him. The man from this morning was standing in front of him. The old man gasped for air. Words escaped him. Before Simon could say anything, the male carer returned to help the young girl move the old man outside. He grabbed the old man's hand and elbow and heaved him to his feet.

'Come on, Al, we need to leave the electrician in peace so he can get the lights working again.'

The old man struggled and tried to resist being moved. 'It's him,' he croaked

'Who?'

'Him! It's him!' The old man kept repeating himself as he was led away to join the others outside.

Simon laughed out loud. *Yes, old man, it's me.*

In thirty minutes, as promised, Simon had replaced the faulty light socket and tested the others. Satisfied that the job was completed perfectly, he went and stood by the window, looking out into the garden at the old folk. He saw the old man sitting at the table, just staring back at the window. He sniggered as he walked away, knowing that he would be seeing him again very soon.

He collected his toolbox and returned the ladder to the groundskeeper. He spoke for a moment with Susan at the front counter and then left the building. He drove home and reversed the van back into the garage, closing the roller door to shut out the world. Back at his bench, he once again unpacked and sorted his tools and unfolded the plan of her house. He was in a good mood. The day so far had gone better than planned.

Chapter 15

Katrina arrived home with about ten minutes to herself before the children would get home from school at three thirty. She kicked off her heels and pushed them to one side with her foot. The cold from the tiles instantly relieved some of the ache in her feet. She opens up the fridge and grabbed the jug of cold water. She leaned against the bench and poured a glass and stood there listening to the quiet, knowing it was all about to change any minute.

On cue, her blissful silence was interrupted and turned into squeals and chatter as the children arrived home. She was instantly attacked by Paige, who just had to be picked up and hugged. Katrina knew she was getting too old to be picked up, but she loved the attention, and little Paige would soon enough grow up and require less and less cuddles. Nathan walked over to his mother and hugged her free side. He tossed his school bag on the floor next to the table and left the room.

Katrina peeled Paige from her side and sat her on the table. She tenderly kissed her forehead and stepped back. 'How was school, sweetheart?'

'Good.'

'What did you learn today?'

'Nothing.'

'OK, who did you play with at lunch?'

'No one.'

The one-word answers were tedious, and they had the same conversation every day.

'So you are telling me that you learned nothing and played with no one today. So what did you do all day then?'

'I don't remember.'

Katrina huffed and walked to where she had kicked off her shoes. She bent over and picked them up. 'I'm going to get changed, and then I will come and make you a snack, OK?'

She didn't wait for a response and left the kitchen. In her room, she removed her blouse and skirt and replaced them with her favourite comfy pants and a T-shirt.

She heard a squeal from the kitchen and the front door closing. Dad was home. Katrina walked back through the kitchen to the front door and was surprised to see Dan waiting for her.

'Hey, Dan, what's up?' She furrowed her brow as the only time Dan came in at the end of the day was to tell her when something had gone wrong.

'Hi, Katrina. Don't mean to bring bad news, but your Dad got a bit upset earlier today. The staff calmed him down, but he was muttering something most of the afternoon, they tell me.'

'Oh? What happened? Did they tell you anything else?'

'Just that he got upset when the electrician came to fix a light. He kept yelling that the electrician was following him and that he has been watching him. At least that's the story they could piece together.'

Katrina let out a loud sigh and stretched her neck. 'Dad was convinced this morning that someone was outside his window, watching him. I found him on the floor after he fell. He's been acting strange for the past few days. Anyway, thanks for filling me in and getting him home.'

'No worries, and I will see you tomorrow. Enjoy your evening.'

Katrina closed the door behind Dan and leaned back against it. She was saddened by what she had just been told.

'*Mum!*' Nathan yelled from the kitchen. 'Where are you?'

'Coming, honey!' she yelled back.

She pushed herself back off the door and went to the kitchen to start preparing something to eat. She got about halfway when there was a knock at the door. She quickly poked her head into the kitchen and saw the two children sitting with her father at the table.

'I will be back in just a minute. The alarm guy has just turned up.'

Back at the front door, she swung it open a little too quick and lost grip of the handle, and the door banged into the wall.

'Shit, sorry about that. Hi.' She smiled at the man on the other side of the screen door.

'I'm from your security company.'

Before he could say anything else, Katrina opened the screen door and invited him in. 'Hi, come in. I'm Katrina.'

She extended her hand, and he ever so gently took it in his. She looked at the name badge embossed onto his shirt. His eye followed hers, and he released her hand and pointed to his name.

'I'm Bradley. Nice to meet you.' He smiled at her and held her eye for a second too long. He quickly looked away.

Katrina stepped back, still smiling at him, and pointed to the alarm panel on the wall just near the door. 'It's all yours. I will be in the kitchen if you need anything.'

Careful not to make eye contact again, he turned towards the alarm panel. 'Thanks.'

Katrina returned to the kitchen to sort out the kids. Paige was sitting on Grandad, and Nathan was investigating the contents of the fridge.

'Would you shut the fridge door, please, Nathan? You are letting all the cold air out.'

Nathan backed up and swung the fridge door closed. 'But I'm hungry,' he whined at his mother, who heard the same story every day.

'I know, and if you give me a minute, I will get you something to eat, the same as I do every afternoon.'

She sidled up to her son and put her arm around his shoulder. He looked up at her and smiled.

'Can you please start your homework while I get some food?'

Nathan huffed and dragged a chair away from the table. He heaved his heavy school bag onto the table and removed some books.

'Paige, honey, it's time to do reading with Grandad in the lounge, OK? Can you please go and get your reader from your bag and go and wait in the lounge?'

'OK, Mum.'

The little girl scrambled off her grandfather's lap and left the kitchen. Using the table for support, the old man got up and followed her to the lounge.

With the house again quiet, Katrina set about making a snack for the kids. She cut up some cheese and put it on top of some crackers and filled up three plates. She placed a plate near Nathan, who was fully engrossed in his history book and didn't notice. She picked up the other two plates and headed for the lounge.

Quietly, she stood by the doorway, watching her daughter and her father snuggled together on the couch as Paige read to him. The old man listened to every word and patiently stopped and corrected when necessary. Katrina didn't have the same level of patience when it came to listening to Paige read and so was very grateful that her father enjoyed this time with his granddaughter. Eventually, they noticed her standing there and beckoned her to come in. She handed them each a plate, and they wasted no time devouring the food.

Happy and content with the state of play with each of her charges, she turned her attention to the tradesman by the front door. 'Hey. How's it going? Is there a problem with the alarm? I was concerned when I received the call this morning that it was playing up.'

Bradley paused and turned to face her. He put down his screwdriver and wiped his hands on his pants. 'Looks like there is a wire inside the panel here that is causing the problem. I'm going to go ahead and fix that, and then if it is OK with you, I would like to check all the sensors around the house just to be certain they are all doing what they are meant to. Can you explain to me what settings you use? I will make sure it is all perfect for you.'

Katrina beamed at the man standing in front of her. He had a sweet aura about him and spoke to her without talking down on her like she was an idiot, unlike the mechanic last week who kept referring to her as 'darling' and said that maybe next time, her husband should come with her so he could explain all the technical stuff to him. That infuriated her no end, so to be spoken to by a tradesman with respect won her over instantly.

'I only use the two settings—the full alarm, including internal sensors when we are not home, and the night setting when I go to bed, which should just be the door and window sensors.'

Bradley smiled at her and nodded. 'Good. Sounds like you are doing everything right. When you have a moment, could I please trouble you to show me where your internal sensors are? I will give them the onceover when I have finished with this panel.'

Still smiling, Katrina turned and pointed to the one sensor in the corner in the passage where the lounge and kitchen met. 'That's the only one. I figured when it was installed, if anyone were to break in, they would come through either the front door or back door and this sensor would catch them as they moved through the house. It's only a small house, so I didn't think it worth putting any down the other end. But all the windows and doors have sensors anyway, so hopefully, they would get set off first before the internal one is even needed.'

Impressed at her logic, Bradley nodded. 'You're right. If your window and door sensors are working properly, the motion sensor there shouldn't even be needed. So what I will do for you is check every window and door before I go just to make sure you and your family are safe.'

Katrina sighed with relief. 'Thank you. After this morning, that will put everyone's mind at ease.'

Bradley tilted his head and gave her a questioning look. 'Is everything OK?'

Katrina looked behind her and lowered her voice. 'My dad, bless him, is getting on, and he is convinced that someone was knocking on his window this morning, and then his carers said he got spooked by an electrician at the respite centre today, so if I can assure him that our house is safe, hopefully, he will settle down again. So I really appreciate you taking the time to check everything.'

'Don't worry, Mrs . . .'

'Just call me Kat.'

'Don't worry, Kat. I will take good care of you.'

He bent over and retrieved his screwdriver and went back to work. Feeling a sense of calm, Katrina went back to the kitchen to help Nathan with his homework.

Chapter 16

The drive from his house to hers was eight minutes. To gain her trust, he must be there at least ten minutes early. *Women seem to be easier to control when you are early.* He would leave at twenty minutes to four.

He checked his watch – two o'clock. He packed his toolboxes and loaded them into the van. He moved into the house and removed his laptop from his backpack and plugged it in. He could not risk it running low again. When it was fully charged, he knew he should get eight hours of vision, more than enough to watch over the house for the evening.

He had spare time to fill in. He went to his bedroom and opened his closet. He reached up high and retrieved a box. He took the box to the kitchen and set it down on the table. He sat in front of the box and removed the lid.

One by one, he removed the contents and placed them neatly in a row on the table. Once the box was empty, he placed it on the floor. He pulled his chair in closer to the table and picked up the item on the left and held it to his face. The fabric was silky against his face. He held it to his nose and breathed in. Disappointed, he removed the fabric from his face. The fragrance had gone. He played with the fabric between his fingers and closed his eyes. The scent may have gone, but he still had his memories.

I see her sitting on a bench at the park, wearing a pale blue silk blouse. She is leaning back with her elbows resting on the back of the bench, watching as the people pass by, her soft brown curls gently moving in the breeze. I recall it being sunny, and she was wearing an oversized pair of sunglasses. She is a picture of perfection. I must have her.

She checks her watch and gets up. I follow her back to her work and wait outside for her to finish. She always finishes on time. I know this because I have been watching her. She comes out with another lady. The other lady will not do; she is not perfect.

She waves goodbye to the lady and walks to the bus. I wait with her. I get on the same bus as her. I sit behind her. All I can smell is her perfume. I want to touch her. I must touch her. Her fragrance is making me hot. I must have her.

I get off the bus at the same stop. I hang back and then follow her. She walks quickly, but I keep up. She arrives home and opens the front door. I stay over the road and watch her.

I see another silhouette in her house through the lounge window – a male figure. I remember this made me mad. How dare she be with another man. I must have her. The man leaves. I enter.

I find her in the kitchen. She is surprised to see me. She yells at me. I get mad. I grab her. Her perfume is too much. I must have her. I pull her to the floor. She fights me, but she is weak. I pull her arms above her head and hold on tight with one hand. She starts to beg. This turns me on more. I like her begging. I must have her. I take a cable tie from my pocket with my free hand, and bind her hands together.

Now she is sobbing. I don't like this. It makes me sad, so I grab at a cloth from the kitchen bench and cover her mouth. She shakes it off. Now I am really mad. She is not doing as I want her to do. I slap her face hard to make her stop crying. I hate crying.

She starts to beg again. Now this makes me happy. I must have her. I look at her blouse. It is pretty, and I don't want it to get dirty, so I unbutton it and let it fall open, and I see her bra. Black and lacy – I like this very much. I need to see more.

She starts fighting again. I hit her face again to make her stop. She does not stop. She makes me very angry. I hit her face hard two more times. Now she is still. Her eyes are closed. I must have her.

I take out my knife. I must see how she bleeds. I take my knife and gently run the tip from her throat down to where her ribs divide. I *find where it becomes soft. I push on my knife. It cuts her skin easily. A small flow of blood escapes the wound. It is bright red. This makes me happy. I leave my knife in her. I run my finger up under the flow of blood and put the drops on my tongue.*

She tastes so sweet. I feel my body getting hot. I feel a sense of excitement surging through me. I must have all of her. I pull my knife out of her. The excitement is too much to contain, and I push my blade into her body over and over and over, each time quicker than the last until I feel my body explode and the excitement fades.

She lies there, so still. Her eyes are still closed, her lips parted. I remove the tie from her hands and place her arms back down to her side. Blood is ruining her pretty blouse. I take my knife and cut a segment to take with me. She was perfect.

He looked down at the piece of faded blue fabric and smiled. She was his first, and he liked how he felt that very first time. He wanted that feeling again.

He moved to the second item and picked it up – the top of a tiny bikini. He closed his eyes again. He needed to remember.

It is a scorching hot day, and she has not left the house in days. I am irritated, having to wait so long and not seeing her. I wish I could see in the house. I need to see her. She is perfect.

A small white car pulls in the driveway, and a young girl gets out and goes to the front door. She is dressed in a bikini top with a flowy skirt. She looks around while waiting for the door to open. I haven't seen her before, but she too is perfect. The door opens, and I see her. I must have her. I must have them both.

I cross the road and walk down the side of the house. I can hear laughing and water splashing. I feel happy. I wait at the corner and peek into the yard. I watch them for an hour, splashing and laughing. I feel excited. I must have them both.

They get out of the pool and lie on towels on the grass. They are lying on their stomachs and don't see me come close. I already have cable ties at the ready. As I get closer, it appears they are both sleeping. They are both perfect. I must have them both.

Before she realises what has happened, I have her hands bound behind her back. Her friend stirs from her slumber and does not have time to react before I have her restrained too. I have them both sitting up with their hands behind their backs. They are younger than my first. I think they are still at school.

I pull her to her feet and put my knife to her throat. Her friend starts to cry but follows my instructions perfectly. Her obedience makes me happy. I walk them inside, where we can have privacy from the outside world. They sit on the chairs that I move from the dining table. I tape their legs to the chair so they cannot run away. I must have them both.

She must watch so she too can feel the excitement I do. I want to share this moment with her. I move her friend so they are facing each other. I stand behind her friend and smile at her. She pleads with me, her voice like an angel. I feel hot and more excited. I untie her friend's bikini top and put it in my bag. I need something to remind me of this moment. I must have her now.

I take her friend's chin in my hand and pull it up. I have my knife in my other hand, and I hold the blade to her throat. I can feel her pulse racing on my fingertips. This makes me more excited. I look over to her and make sure she is ready to share this moment with me. She begs me some more. Her face is perfect.

I move my blade to an angle and push it into her throat a little bit. I don't take my eyes off her. She is crying. Her friend is crying. I don't like crying. I yell at her to stop crying. She stops and starts begging. That feels better. I quickly move my blade across her throat. I feel her head go heavy in my hand. I carefully release my grip on her. I smile at her watching me. I come to the side of her friend and drop to my knees.

I see a flow of red running from her neck down her chest and painting her small breasts red. My excitement is peaking. I kiss her friend's neck and lick her wound. She tastes wonderful. Her friend was perfect. I look over at her. I must have her.

I stand up and step over to her. I ask her if she enjoyed that. She shakes her head and screams. I don't like this attitude and smack her face. How dare she scream. Such a horrible noise. My excitement recedes. She looks up at me and begs me to untie her. I ask if she is going to be good. She smiles and nods. I really must have her. She is perfect.

I remove the tape from her legs and make her sit on the floor next to the table. I cut the tie from her hands and then make her lie on her *back. I pull her arms above her head and tape her hands and wrists to the table leg. She lies on the floor, looking at me. She is perfect.*

I walk over to her friend and cut the tie from her hands and the tape from her legs. I gently lift her body and lie it next to her so she can be next to her friend again. I stand over the two of them. I have taken the friend's top to remind me of this moment, so I feel it is only fair that I have hers too. I stand over her and lean down and remove her top. I go put it in my bag so I don't forget to take it later.

I look at her from a distance. She is wiggling and begging me again. My excitement returns. I must have her. I go back and sit on her to stop her wiggling. I look at her ample breasts, much bigger than her friend's. I put my hands on them and spend a moment appreciating them. I lean down and kiss one. My excitement peaks again. This is the feeling I want. I pick up my knife, and while kissing her breast, I push it into her side. I feel her body tense under me, and I cannot contain my excitement anymore.

I sit up and pull my knife from her. I hold it up and watch the glistening red liquid drop on to her. She is shaking. I am shaking also from excitement. She is feeling this too. My excitement is now out of control, and I take my knife in both hands and plunge it into her stomach, over and over, faster and faster until I explode.

The feeling is fading. I have blood on my fingers. I must taste her. The sweetness tingles on my tongue. She was perfect.

I untie her hands and lay her right next to her friend. Best friends forever.

He looked at the table and picked up the other bikini top and held them both to his face. They were the perfect double act. He put the two items back in his box and looked at the table. *Two more items.*

He looked at his watch – half past three. He didn't have time to remember the others just now. He would come back to them another time.

As if he were handling something fragile, he placed each item one by one back in the box and covered them with the lid. He picked up the box and returned it to its space in the cupboard and collected his things, ready to go. He closed and locked his door and opened the garage. He sat in the driver's seat and took a moment. He was ready.

She is perfect.

Chapter 17

He pulled up outside of her house at twelve minutes to four. He stepped out of his van and went around to the side door. He slid it open and removed his toolbox and backpack. He retrieved a work order he had made up from his bag and placed it onto a clipboard. He put on a cap and tucked in his shirt. It was a different shirt to what he had worn that morning. Simon the electrician was his day job. This was different. This was personal.

He carried his belongings and placed them down on the stoop and rang the doorbell. Patiently, he waited and heard her walking towards the door. She flung it open and greeted him with a smile. She was breathtaking. *She is perfect.*

She pushed open the screen door and introduced herself. 'Hi, I'm Kat. Thank you so much for coming so quickly.'

He returned the pleasantries. 'Hi, Kat, I'm Bradley.'

'Come on in. The alarm is just here.'

She showed him the alarm panel. He sniggered to himself. He already knew.

She left him to his work and walked away to the kitchen. He opened his toolbox and removed a screwdriver. He carefully removed the cover, exposing the wiring. It was an old system and easy to manipulate. He kept his back to the kitchen so his face could not be seen.

He heard tiny footsteps coming towards him. He stopped working and looked down over his shoulder to see the little girl looking up at him. She had her hands behind her back and was twisting from side to side, smiling.

'Hello.'

'Hi.'

He didn't want to be rude to the children. They could be easily offended, and he didn't not want the child running back to her mother and putting her off the side.

'What's your name?'

'Bradley. What's yours?' He smiled a little at her but tried to look busy enough so she would go away.

'Paige. What are you doing?'

'Fixing the alarm so that you are safe.' He didn't look at her.

He could hear heavy shuffling footsteps coming. The old man was behind him. He continued working and did not look at him.

'Paige, sweetheart, let's leave the man to do his work, and you come and read to me like your mother asked, OK?'

The little girl spun and skipped away towards the old man, who had collapsed onto the couch. Bradley sighed in relief. He did not want the old man to recognise him just yet. It was too soon for that.

Ten minutes passed, and he had manipulated the security system so it appeared to work but the signal went nowhere. He was putting it all back together when Kat came over to him. She asked a few questions, and he assured her that he would take care of her. She smiled at him, and he knew he had her trust.

She left him again, and he finished putting the panel back together. He wanted to test her boundaries, so he sought her out, head down, careful not to let the old make see his face. He could hear her in the kitchen. He stepped into the doorway and smiled at the boy sitting at the table next to his mother.

She looked up at him and then stood. 'Hey, all OK?'

'Yes, ma'am. I was wondering if I could check the window sensors now just to make sure nothing else is wrong. The control panel is all OK now.'

'Sure thing. Follow me, and I will show you.'

She glided past him, and he caught a hint of her perfume. He felt his body temperature rise, and he quickly followed. She took him into the children's rooms first. He inspected the sensors and assured her they were fine.

Next, they went into her bedroom. She entered first and stood by the bed. He followed and stepped past her deliberately, a little too close. The scent of her perfume was stronger, and he found it hard to concentrate. He just wanted to touch her. He wanted to taste her. He had to have her.

He looked at the sensor on the window, and he could see her reflection in the window. She didn't take her eyes off him. The excitement built, and as he turned to face her, she left the room. He paused, let the tingling subside, and then followed.

The last room to check was the old man's. She opened the door, and as she was about to go in, the small boy yelled for her help. She apologised and said she would return.

He quickly entered the room and removed the empty dish he had taken the day before from his backpack and placed it on the old man's desk. He pushed it to the back, out of view, unless you came all the way in. He moved quickly and went to the window and pretended to check the sensor when she came in.

'All good in here, ma'am.'

'Fantastic. Thank you.'

They both left the old man's room, and like a puppy, he followed one step behind her back to the front door. He had her sign the fake work order, and he tidied up his tools.

'Here's my number if you have any issues, OK? No need to go via the office. I'm only around the corner, so anytime, just ring me, and I will come straight over.'

As he picked up his toolbox, Paige came running over and hugged her mother's side.

'See you next time, young lady.' He nodded at the little girl, who smiled back.

He looked up to see the old man had come over. 'Sir.'

He raised an eyebrow at the old man and opened the front door. As he turned to close the door behind him, he saw the realisation on the old man's face. He winked at him and shut the door quickly.

A few long strides later, he was at his van. He hadn't locked it to enable a hasty departure. After a slight look over his shoulder at the house, he drove away, feeling very pleased with himself.

Chapter 18

'It's him! It's him!' the old man screeched over and over, getting more and more upset.

Katrina quickly sent the children to their rooms so she could deal with the meltdown that her father was having. 'It's who, Dad?'

'It's the man who was outside my window, and it was the electrician at the centre. It's him! I know it is!'

The old man grasped at the doorway, his legs unable to hold him up any longer. Katrina rushed to grab his arm and helped him to the closet chair. His breathing became laboured, and sweat started to bead on his face. In fear that her father was having a heart attack, Katrina called for an ambulance.

Within minutes, help arrived. Two paramedics entered the house and immediately took over the care of the old man. Katrina watched as they calmed him down and monitored his vitals. Her children were at her side, holding her hands tight, not saying a word.

The older of the paramedics stood and came over to the three of them and indicated that they should speak in private. Katrina, still clinging to her children's hands, left her father and led the stranger to the kitchen. Without talking, she opened the fridge and took out a treat for the children and gave them a look they knew that they should go outside to play.

'Kat, can you tell me how long your father has been acting differently?'

Katrina crossed her arms and fought back the tears. 'It's only been like this for about a week, maybe. He's started acting paranoid and getting mad, and now he thinks every man he meets is someone watching him. I don't know what to do.'

'His heart rate is now back to normal, and he seems to have calmed down. I would like to take him to the hospital just to have a check done on his heart. I can have the doctors look into the sudden change in his personality if you like.'

'Thank you. Do I need to come with you?'

'Not just yet, but if you can have the neighbours watch the kids soon, I'm sure the doctors will want to talk to you.'

'OK.' Katrina rubbed her eyes and walked the paramedic back to the lounge, where his colleague was preparing the old man to be taken to the hospital.

'Katrina, where are they taking me?' Her father started to resist the help of the paramedics. 'Katrina?' he demanded

'They need to take you to the hospital to check to make sure your heart is OK. Dad, please don't fight them like this.'

'I'm not going anywhere, and you can't make me!' He aggressively pushed at the hand of the younger paramedic. 'There is nothing wrong with me! Now leave me alone!'

'Come on, sir, we are only trying to help you.' The older man, trying to intervene, took the old man by the elbow and started to guide him to the front door.

Sharply, the old man pulled his arm away and glared at everyone. He raised his voice. 'I said I am not going!' He pushed past his daughter and set off for the safety of his room.

Katrina stared at the floor and let tears escape. She fumbled in her pocket, looking for a tissue, when the older paramedic put his hand on her shoulder.

'I'm going to refer your case to one of the senior geriatric doctors when we get back to the hospital and see what he can suggest, but as your father is refusing help and we cannot see any immediate danger to his health, we can't force him to come with us.'

Katrina was exhausted. She tried to smile at the two men who came to help, but she just couldn't. They collected their belongings and left the house, leaving her to deal with her father.

Lacking any motivation to think about dinner, Katrina went out to the backyard and suggested pizza to the kids. With squeals of excitement, the kids rushed back inside and snatched the menu off the fridge door. While the kids studied their options, Katrina went to check on her father. She stood in front of his door and took a deep breath and then knocked gently.

'Dad?' She waited for a response. 'Dad, can I come in?'

'You are going to anyway, so why bother asking?'

Katrina opened the door slowly and saw her father sitting on his bed, shoulders slumped, facing the window. She went and sat next to him and held his hand.

'I just want to help you. You know that, right?' She looked at the window, trying to see his reflection.

'You think I am going crazy.' He took his hand away from hers. 'I know what I saw, and I know that the man who was here fixing the alarm is the same man who was at the centre earlier today, who is the same man who was outside of my window this morning, and I don't really care anymore if you believe me. I know what I saw.'

Katrina stood up and walked away from her father. 'OK, Dad.' She didn't want to argue anymore. 'I'm ordering pizza for tea. What type would you like?'

He turned slightly towards her. 'I don't want pizza. I would like what we had last night if that's OK. That is, if no one ate the leftovers already.'

'Of course, you can. I will let you know when it is ready.'

Katrina closed the door behind her and joined her children in the kitchen, who were ready with their request. She watched Nathan place the order online and had Paige set the table ready for the delivery. With smiles and happiness filling the kitchen once again, Katrina relaxed and poured herself a glass of wine. She rarely drank, but the need at this moment was too strong.

She sat at the table and listened to the children chatter between themselves and let the soothing feeling take over as she savoured each sip of wine. She leaned back in the chair and closed her eyes for a moment, her head starting to tingle from the alcohol, and she liked how she felt. She allowed her mind to go blank for a few minutes before coming back to reality.

'How long until the pizza is here, Nathan?' She touched his shoulder as she went to the fridge to organise food for her father.

'The timer says six more minutes.'

'Great, 'cause I'm starving.' Katrina opened the fridge and leaned in, looking for the container with the leftovers. She moved a few things around and then shut the fridge door. 'Hey, guys, did either of you eat the leftovers from last night?' Her eyebrow was raised in question.

Both kids stopped and looked at her, shaking their heads.

'Huh. OK, then I wonder where they went. Let me just go ask Grandad.'

She went back to her father's room and knocked on the door. Before she could say anything, he opened it.

'I thought dinner would be ready, so I was already on my way to you.'

'Actually, Dad' – she hesitated – 'I can't find the container with the leftovers in it. Did you have it already?' She really didn't want to ask as she knew he would get cranky all over again.

'No,' he said back. 'Not me. I'm going to the bathroom, and then I will come to the table.' He walked off, not bothered by the question. 'Can you be a dear and grab my glasses for me? I will do some reading with little Paige after we eat.'

Katrina entered his room and scanned the bedside tables for his glasses. She couldn't see them and so walked in farther to check his desk.

'Oh, for Christ's sake.'

She saw the empty container and felt herself suddenly get angry. Snatching the container, she stomped out of his room and slammed it on the sink. Her father appeared a second later.

'What's the matter?' He took his place at the table and waited for Katrina to reply.

She paused before answering. 'I found the empty container in your room, Dad. I just asked you if you already ate the leftovers, and you lied right to me.'

The doorbell rang. The children ran to the front door, eager to take possession of the pizza. Katrina followed them with money to pay the driver. Like a stampeding herd, the kids ran back to the kitchen, pizza in hand, and hurriedly sat at the table.

Katrina was right behind them. She placed a slice of pizza on a plate and put it in front her father. 'If you don't want this, I will make you a sandwich.'

He said nothing and stared at his plate.

The children finished eating and were excused from the table. The old man still sat in silence. Katrina cleared the plates and went about tidying the kitchen.

'I'm not hungry anymore.' The old man slowly rose from the table, leaving his uneaten food behind.

Katrina heard him walking up the hall to his bedroom and then the bedroom door close. She was on the verge of tears. Feeling a mix of anger and sadness, she poured a glass of wine and sat at the table, staring into the glass. She was lonely and missed her husband. She needed to hear his voice.

For a few silent minutes, she sat at the table and sipped at her glass of wine. She looked up at the clock and sighed. It was time for her nightly challenge of getting the kids to bed. Determined to get this done quickly, she threw back the last mouthful of wine and stood up with renewed energy. She placed the empty glass on the sink and headed towards the kid's bedrooms.

Without knocking, she opened Paige's door and smiled. Her little girl was sitting on the floor with her stuffed toys surrounding her, and she was reading them a story.

'Honey, can you please quickly finish the story and put your PJs on? Thank you.'

She didn't wait for the response, and she closed the door again. The next room was Nathan's. She stood outside, knocked, and waited for the OK before she opened the door.

'Half-hour warning until bedtime, OK?'

'Yes, Mum.'

Nathan got up from his desk, where he had been studiously reading, and walked over to his mother and hugged her waist. Surprised by the unprompted affection, she held him tight. It was like he knew that was exactly what she needed. She stepped back, and Nathan walked past her to the bathroom.

So far, so good, she thought, and now she was becoming suspicious at how well this was going.

She went back to Paige, and when she opened the door, Paige was in her pyjamas and putting her toys back on the shelf. Now Katrina was getting very suspicious.

'Wow, Paige. You are already changed. That was quick. Come on, I will come with you while you brush your teeth.'

'It's OK, Mumma. I can do it by myself.'

'OK, then I will come and tuck you in when you are done.'

Katrina stepped back from the door and watched her daughter skip up to the bathroom, where Nathan was already brushing his teeth.

Here we go, she thought to herself. *Let's see how this ends.*

But to her amazement, Nathan helped Paige with the toothpaste, and they stood there together with no shoving or fighting. Shaking her head, Katrina walked back to the kitchen. *What is going on here tonight? The kids are getting along far too well.*

Her thoughts were interrupted when the phone started ringing.

'Hello?' she said to the unknown number.

'Hello, Mrs Elliot. I'm following up to see how your experience was with our technician who came to see you today.'

'Oh, hi. He was great. He was on time and polite and finished reasonably quick.'

'That's great to hear. We will keep an eye on the system for you, and if we see anything unusual, we will contact you again.'

'OK, great, thank you.'

'Have a lovely night, Mrs Elliot.'

'You too.'

She ended the call and went back to getting the kids ready for bed, feeling better about the day. With Paige all tucked in and Nathan having a few more minutes of reading time, Katrina thought she'd better check in on her father, who had disappeared into his room after tea and hadn't made an appearance since.

She knocked on the door and waited – no answer. She knocked again a little louder in case he didn't hear her the first time – still no answer. She opened the door slowly and peered into the dark room. She could make out his body under the covers and heard his congested breathing. She carefully closed the door again and went back to the kitchen. She couldn't remember the last time she was without company for the evening.

She poured another glass of wine, picked up her phone, and sat on her own in the kitchen. She dialled her husband's number – no answer. She left a message and ended the call. She always wondered what he did at night-time when he travelled for work. Disappointed, she wandered to the lounge and lay on the couch. Kat turned on the TV, flicked through the guide, and settled on a rerun of a police drama. Getting comfy with one of the fluffy cushions, she soon drifted off to sleep, curled up on the couch. Little did she know she was being watched.

Chapter 19

Silently, he crept back into the house, wary not to wake his sleeping beauty. He slithered up into the roof and glided to his bed. He turned on his laptop and focused only on her.

He watched her sleep, his eyes glued to the screen. His breathing slowed, and he started to feel numb. As she moved on the couch, a strand of hair fell across her face. He ran his finger over the screen as if he could move it away from her eyes. *She is perfect.* He breathed in deeply through his nose and was sure he could still smell her perfume, as if the smell had been burned into his brain. He wanted her so badly now, and he felt his pulse quicken the more he thought about her.

She stirred again, and this time, she awoke. She sat up tall and stretched her arms high above her head. He watched and copied her movement. As he stretched his arms, he banged his knuckles on the roof. A sharp pain rushed through his hand, and he bit his lip, trying not to swear. Irritated, he resumed his attention back to her.

She had moved quickly to the kitchen and rinsed her wine glass and left it upturned on the sink. She opened the fridge and removed a small piece of food and kicked the fridge door closed. She walked over to the table and shoved the food in her mouth as she grabbed her phone, which was half hidden under one of the kids' books. He turned his head to the side to watch her face as she ate the morsel of food, and he could tell from her expression it was sweet and juicy. As she savoured the sweet delicacy, he felt his heart speed up. She had this look on her face that he needed to see up close. He had to find out what she ate.

She gracefully walked up the hallway to her bedroom, turning off the kitchen light behind her. He hated this small gap in time where he lost sight of her, for what was in reality a few seconds felt like minutes to him. On his screen, he saw her again. She was alone in her bedroom and had closed the door. He wanted to go to her now. He had to have her now. He was becoming agitated as she was so close to him, yet as he reached out, he could not touch her.

She unbuttoned her blouse and let it delicately slide off her shoulders. She dropped it into the hamper, and then she reached behind her back and unbuttoned her skirt. She pulled at the zip a little, and then when it behaved, she let the skirt fall to the floor. She stepped out of the crumpled skirt and bent over to pick it up. She was facing away from the camera, and as she bent over, he struggled to contain himself.

She is perfect, and I must have her.

His skin was clammy, and he was having trouble focusing. His urge was strong, and he could feel his pulse in his fingertips. His mouth was open as he tried to suck in oxygen. He watched her with everything he had, and she did not disappoint.

She walked to the side table and turned on the small lamp next to her bed and then turned off the main light. The room was now dimly lit, and the shadows danced on the curves of her body. She moved back to the bed and pulled back the covers. She removed her bra and knickers and let them drop on the floor; she lay naked on the sheet. She picked up her phone, and the look gave away her husband had not sent her anything. She placed the phone down, rolled onto her side, and slid open her the drawer on the bedside table.

He watched intently, unsure of what she was looking for. She removed something small and held it just in front of her face. She twisted the end in her hand and smiled. She slid herself down off the pillow and placed it between her legs.

Stunned, he sat straight up. His perfect beauty had another side to her, a side he did not expect. He did not blink. He did not take his eyes off her. He held his breath. He was feeling something inside he did not expect. Like a shot, he left his bed and carefully scurried to the other end of the house. He lay balanced on the beam above her room and listened. He needed to hear her pleasuring herself. He needed to hear what she sounded like as she reached her climax.

He held his breath and closed his eyes. She was faint to start with, and he had trouble making her out, but within a minute, he could hear her moan. She got a little louder, and her moan became more intense. With his eyes closed, he could picture her naked body lying on the bed with her hand between her legs, and he pictured the way she was moving in time with the sounds he could hear.

He started rocking his body in time with her moans, picturing himself lying there with her. As she moaned faster, he rocked a little faster, and when she let out a throaty moan that lasted for several seconds, he felt himself lose control and almost his balance. With a strange sense of pleasure, he got back to his feet, and with a euphoric dizziness, he made his way back to the hammock.

He fell into his bed heavily and heard a creak come from the beam above that was holding up one end. He rolled his eyes back into his head and let an overwhelming tiredness take him away. He tilted his head slightly so he could see the computer screen, and as he blinked heavily, he could see the house was in darkness. His beauty was resting, as were the rest of the occupants.

He felt safe here. He felt like this could be his forever home.

Chapter 20

Katrina lay in bed, staring at the ceiling. Her alarm hadn't yet buzzed, but she was already wide awake, thinking about where her life was at right now. She felt a lump in the pit of her stomach, so she rolled onto her side and tried to forget. After several restless minutes, Kat gave in and decided to get up. She sat on the edge of the bed, her head hung, staring at the ground. She rose to her feet and felt a surge of nausea rush from her stomach to the back of her throat. She wasn't going to work today; she needed a day on her own at home.

Dressed in track pants and a jumper, Kat turned off her alarm and headed for the kitchen. It was only Thursday, but it felt like the week was never-ending. As silent as a mouse, she set about preparing the children's school lunches and packed their bags.

Knowing that she would be spending the day alone, she felt the nausea subside and the knot in her stomach fade away. For a brief moment, she thought she was supposed to feel guilty about taking the day off from work, but she didn't. She felt relieved. With her mood improved, Kat set the table for breakfast and gently woke the children.

Paige and Nathan were quieter than normal this morning, and Kat knew they were feeling the effects of her father's sudden personality change. In just a few days, he had gone from a soft and gentle soul who did nothing but adore his family to angry and paranoid, losing his temper at the children and hallucinating about a man stalking him. It saddened her no end as she thought about putting him in full-time care at the nursing home. He seemed to like his days there and said the staff treated him well, so maybe it was time. She knew for sure her husband would agree, so there was no point bringing it up with him when he rang.

She sniggered out loud. 'He would actually need to ring for us to have a conversation.'

'Who needs to ring, Mumma?'

Startled, Kat looked up. She had been lost in her thoughts and forgot that her children were at the table. Quickly thinking of an answer, Kat stuttered, 'Just someone from work, honey.'

Thinking nothing further of it, Paige resumed eating, but Nathan stared at his mother. She smiled back and sipped at her coffee.

'Mum,' Nathan hesitantly spoke, 'when is Dad coming home?'

Katrina sighed long and hard and looked deep into Nathan's eyes. She knew he understood her statement, and she couldn't lie to him. She was convinced her son was an old soul who understood things far beyond his age. She knew her son was aware of how much time his father spent away from the family and that when he was here, his mind was somewhere else.

'He tells me he will be home Sunday afternoon, sweetheart.'

'So he is going to miss my football final.' It was more a statement than a question, and she could hear the disappointment in his voice.

'I'm sorry, Nathan, but it does seem that way. But don't you worry. Paige, your grandfather, and I will be there cheering you on all the way. And then after, it will be your choice where we go to lunch.'

She grinned at her son and hoped she had done enough to get him back to being excited for his final. Nathan finished his breakfast and stood by his mother. She placed an arm around his waist and pulled him close and tight. She felt his weight shift as he leaned in closer to his mother. It broke her heart to see how much her husband's absence was crushing Nathan's spirit.

Nathan pulled away from his mother's embrace and left the kitchen. She heard his bedroom door shut softly.

'Now, Miss, how about I help you get ready for school?' Katrina turned her attention to her daughter, who seemed to have more breakfast on her face than what had been consumed.

With a dramatic sigh, Paige got up from her chair and headed for her bedroom.

Katrina called after her. 'Bathroom first, please! You need to wash your face before putting on clean clothes,' and a louder, more dramatic sigh echoed back. Kat smiled and cleared the dishes from the table.

It had just gone seven thirty, and both children were ready for school. There was just over half an hour until the school bus was due, and her father's driver would be here. She knocked on her father's door and waited for a response. She could hear movement on the other side of the door, and then without warning, it swung open. He father was dressed and standing there, holding onto the door handle. He looked old today, and his lips were tightly pressed together while he almost glared at Kat.

'Morning, Dad,' Kat said, trying to be as cheerful as she could. 'Are you hungry? I have some raisin bread ready for toasting and a cup of tea, perhaps.'

'No, thank you,' he responded gruffly. 'I'm not hungry. When will my car be here?'

'In about thirty minutes.'

'Good.' He started to step back and then started, even harsher at Kat. 'I'm going to ask to stay overnight at the centre. I don't like it here anymore.' He turned his back, not waiting for a response, and shuffled back to his bed, where he had packed a bag.

Kat felt a heat inside surge through every inch of her body. Her head went dizzy, and her throat thudded and went dry. She was speechless, and without warning, her legs lost the strength to hold her up. She grabbed at the wall and managed to steady herself. She was in no way prepared for what just happened.

Back in the kitchen, Kat used the table to hold some of her weight as she slowly sat in the chair. The heat in her body faded but was quickly replaced with sorrow. She was dumbfounded and stunned and confused. She knew he was getting old and his mind was starting to go, but for him to just come out with a statement like that without any warning crushed Kat deeply, and she didn't know what to do.

Kat needed her husband. She needed him to put his arms around her and just hold her. But he wasn't here. She hadn't spoken to him in two days. For the first time in her life, she felt so completely alone with no one around for support. She sat with her head in her hands for a few minutes, letting the sorrow and loneliness consume her. When the tears started trickling down her cheek, she knew she needed to regain her composure. Her children were still here, and she would not let them see her like this. She rinsed her face with cold water at the kitchen sink and patted her eyes with her jumper. There were ten minutes left before they needed to leave for the school bus.

Katrina found her phone and rang the nursing home. She hoped that someone would be there already to talk to her. Her spirits lifted when, after only four rings, she heard a voice talking to her. Katrina spent the next ten minutes talking to the senior nurse and had agreed it would be best for Kat and her father if he spent the night there. After Kat ended the conversation, she let the relief flood her tired brain.

She called for the children and sent them off to the school bus. She stood in the doorway and watched them run to the corner only a few houses away where the bus would stop. And she heard, as reliable as always, the squeak of brakes as the bus came into sight, and the children were whisked away. At the same time her children disappeared from sight, a car pulled into the driveway, and a friendly young man exited the vehicle.

'Morning, Kat,' he greeted her with a smile so bright. 'Big Al ready to go?'

'Sure is. I'll go tell him you're here.'

Kat turned to go back into the house when she was startled by her father standing barely a step behind her. 'Dad, you frightened me. I didn't hear you sneak up on me.'

'I didn't sneak,' he snapped. 'Can you fetch my bag from my room?'

'Dad,' Kat said softly, 'I know it's been tough the past couple of days, and I am sorry for that. I hope a couple of days away from here will help you.'

She kissed her father's cheek as she stepped past. She heard him grumble something as he stepped out of the door, but she couldn't make out what it was.

She entered the old man's room and picked up the bag that was sitting, waiting for her on the end of his bed, and then added a few snacks from the kitchen as she came back through the house. She hoped that a small sugary gesture would win her back some brownie points.

She placed the bag on the back seat of the car and went to the passenger door, where her father was already buckled in. She held his hand and tried to make eye contact.

'I love you, Dad. Don't ever forget that.'

She kissed his cheek again, and this time, he looked up at her. His glare had softened, and he attempted a smile.

'I love you too, Kat.'

Katrina closed the car door and stepped back as the car reversed away from the house. She stayed there and waved as her father disappeared from sight.

Slowly, she walked back to the house and closed the door behind her. She was alone at last. She listened to the silence and smiled. It was a rare opportunity to have the house completely to herself and she didn't need to think about another person's needs all day. First thing she would do was ring in sick from work, and then she planned to take a very long hot shower. And after her shower, she had absolutely no plans, and that was what excited her the most.

Chapter 21

He sat there, a bundle of excitement. Everything was working out perfectly, and he hadn't had to intervene to get things moving. It almost seemed too easy.

He watched her on his screen as she paced the kitchen on the phone, talking to her employer. He watched her smile brightly as the conversation ended, knowing she had got away with her little white lie. He watched her as she glided effortlessly out of the kitchen without a care in the world, her fingers brushing the wall and door frame as she moved. He held his breath as she momentarily disappeared from sight, as she walked down the hall to the bathroom, and then exhaled in relief as she came into view again. And he fixated on her as she undressed to take a shower.

He sat up tall and puffed out his chest. Today was the day. Today was the day he would have her. *She is perfect. She will be mine.* He felt a burst of excitement in the pit of his stomach thinking about it. But he had work to do first.

He grabbed his backpack and waited at the manhole for the noisy water pipes to wake up, telling him she was in the shower. He braced himself like a runner waiting for the starting pistol. And there it was, the metallic rattle of the pipes banging as the water rushed through them. He slid the cover to one side and lowered himself down into the laundry room. This time, he didn't bother replacing the cover; he needed every second to prepare for what was about to be a perfect day.

Quietly, he moved around the kitchen to the back door and turned the lock. He passed the window and made sure it was fully closed and latched. With every step he took, he listened for a change in noise from the bathroom.

From the kitchen to the front door and from the front door to the lounge, he checked every lock to ensure they were secured. He stood at the entrance to the hallway. He listened. He could still hear running water. He grinned. He made it to the first door and opened it. The pungent smell of sickly sweet little girl hit him in the face, and his stomach churned. He stepped inside and closed the door behind him. He took a deep breath through his mouth and tried to ignore it.

He watched his feet as he stepped through the room, making sure he did not step on any of the obstacles that littered the floor. He leaned over the bed to the window and checked it was closed. Scanning the room, he found a container filled with small plastic beads. He took a few and pressed them into the window track. He knew the girl was small, and this should make it almost impossible for her to open the window quickly.

He crept back to the door and put his ear to the crack. He couldn't hear anything, so he opened it just the tiniest amount and listened again. The water had been turned off, but he did not know if she was still in the bathroom. He opened the door farther and took one step into the hall. He went to take another step when the bathroom door opened suddenly.

His heart jumped up to his throat, and he could hear his pulse in his ears. Swiftly, he stepped back into the girl's room and pushed the door almost closed without letting it click shut. He gripped the doorknob tight. He took in the air slowly and deeply. He grinned and laughed a little in his head. He loved the excitement. He was having fun.

He needed to move to the next room, but he couldn't predict how long she would be in her bedroom. He leaned up against the door frame of the little girl's room with the door open just the smallest amount. He didn't wait for long when he heard her footsteps coming. She was walking slowly, and she stopped outside the girl's door. He could smell her perfume. He closed his eyes and let his senses absorb her fragrance. He could hear her breathing, and he was sure he could feel her breath on his cheek. She was barely two inches away, and he wanted to reach out and touch her.

He opened his eyes and moved the door open just a fraction, and he could see her. She was right in front of him, and he felt his body heat up. He was getting light-headed, and he put his fingers slightly though the crack in the door. He could almost feel her. He looked at her face; she was lost in thought. Just another millimetre more, and he would feel her skin on his fingertips. He could feel the heat of her skin. He moved his hand forward again, and his finger brushed the fine hair on her arm.

Startled from her daydream, she scratched the spot where his fingers touched and walked away from the door.

He retracted his hand back into the room and ran his fingers over his lips. He was very pleased with himself.

The sound of the kettle starting to boil and the scraping of a chair on the tiles gave him the opportunity to exit the little girl's room and creep into the boy's. He knew he could not be seen from the kitchen, and he could hear her moving around the kitchen, so he took the opportunity to move up the hall and into the next room.

Once inside, he wasted no time jamming the window track with a ruler he had picked up from the boy's desk. If either of the children were to be an issue this afternoon, he would pick it to be the boy. The boy had a calm demeanour and was smart; he would need to take control of him early. The girl would be drawn to her mother, and he would use that to his advantage over both of them.

Back at the door, ready to move, he listened for her. He did not need to check her room or the old man's as he had taken care of the locks on those windows when he was in the house repairing the alarm. He had assured her that he would make sure the window sensors in the two front bedrooms were operational and used the opportunity to jam the locks.

He was only moments away from what he been dreaming about for the past week. He calmed his breathing and stayed focused. He listened some more and heard her moving around the kitchen.

This is it. She will be mine. She will love me. I know she is the one.

He opened the door and stepped into the hall. Taking in every moment, he walked slowly. He didn't want to rush in and frighten her. She didn't need to be scared. He was here to rescue her. Step by step, he got closer to her. Step by step, he could hear more clearly where she was.

At the end of the hallway where the three rooms met, he stood. He could see her in the kitchen. She was sat at the table with her back to him. He could see a mug in front of her to her right and an empty plate. She was reading a magazine. Her left elbow was on the table and she had her chin resting in her hand. He hair had been pulled into a loose bun on top of her head. She had on a tank top with thin straps, which exposed her shoulders to him. He stood mesmerised by her image. *She is perfect.*

He slipped his backpack off his right shoulder and let it fall to his left side. Without taking his eyes off her, he reached into the front pouch, which he had left unzipped, and pulled out two long cable ties. He pushed them into his pocket and then pulled the backpack back onto his right shoulder. He stretched his fingers and rolled his shoulders. He was ready. This was his moment.

Over many years, he had learned to walk softly on his feet, and he could easily move around a house without making a single noise, making him almost invisible. His trade as an electrician allowed him to become skilled at climbing in and out of small spaces. He never worked in the commercial industry as it did not provide him with the practical experience he needed like the domestic trade. Every day he entered people's homes and climbed in and out of their roofs. And they always left him alone and never questioned why or what he did up there. He liked to be around people in their homes. He liked to watch them as they went about their day, almost forgetting he was there. He would move from room to room, seeing, touching, and, for a short while, becoming part of their lives. He had worked for his employer for over a decade and was able to pick and choose the jobs he took on, so when they rang him this week to go to the nursing home, he knew they were desperate for someone. And by doing the favour, they left him alone, and that was the way he liked it.

Slowly and silently, he walked up behind her. He stood there and looked down at her. She didn't move. He tilted his head to the side to catch a glimpse of what she was reading. She sat up slightly and adjusted herself in the chair, still oblivious to his presence. He leaned forward and, like a shot, put his left hand around her mouth, his right hand pushing down on her shoulder.

Frightened and startled, Kat tried to scream and get out of his grip, but the pressure he had on her shoulder and the grip around her face made it impossible.

He leaned down further and put his face up against hers and whispered, 'Stop struggling, and I will release my grip on you.'

Kat stopped moving, and he moved his hand away from her mouth and placed it on her left shoulder. Too frightened to move, Kat sat like a statue. He ran his hands down her arms and lowered himself until he was squatting behind her. He took one cable tie from his pocket and secured her right hand to the back of the chair and then her left. When he was satisfied she was secure, he stood back up and used his strength to pull the chair back away from the table and turn it to face the doorway he had entered from.

He stepped around the chair and stood in front of her. She was looking at the ground, and he could hear her breathing and her attempt in trying not to cry. He slipped off his backpack and let it drop to the ground by her feet and then squatted down in front of her, making sure he wasn't too close in case she got a burst of courage and tried to kick him. He would only ever let that happen once, and for a moment, he let his mind slip back to another one of his beauties.

He secured Kat's legs to the chair, and as he stood back up, he let his fingers run up her inner leg from her ankle to her knee and then just an inch up her inner thigh. She froze under his touch but looked up to make eye contact with her captor. She held his gaze for a few seconds before she finally recognised him.

'Why?' she asked softly.

He stepped to the side of the table and dragged a chair towards him and placed it in front of her. He sat down and placed his hands on her legs and leaned in.

'Because you are perfect.'

He leaned in a little further and gently kissed her. His nose was filled with her scent, and the touch of her lips on his was almost too much to take. He felt breathless again and sat back in the chair.

'Did you feel that too?' He looked her in the eye, desperate to see if she felt the same.

'No,' Kat snapped back. 'The only thing I feel is sick when you touch me.' She turned away, looking out the kitchen window.

He was confused. *How could she not feel that?* The more he thought about her answer, the angrier he got. He stood and stomped out of the kitchen and into the hallway and up to her bedroom. He opened the door forcefully and stood in the centre of the room and looked around. He spied her vanity table and snatched up her perfume bottle. He placed it under his nose and let the scent fill his brain. Feeling calmer, he carefully returned the bottle to its place and re-entered the kitchen.

He sat back in front of her and gazed upon her beauty. Although her skin looked pale and she glared at him, he still thought she was perfect in every way.

'I like your hair better down.'

He picked up his backpack, which was still on the floor, and placed it on the table. He unzipped the large pouch and reached in. He fossicked around and removed a small hairbrush. He smiled at her, rose from the chair, and went and stood behind her. He pulled at the elastic holding her hair up. She winced as he pulled, but he ignored it and kept pulling until it was free. Her hair tumbled down and fell around her shoulders. He picked up the brush and gently started running it through her hair.

Every few strokes, he would stop and lean in to smell her and let his fingers touch her hair. His breathing became heavier the more he touched her, and he started moving his fingers from her hair to her neck and then her shoulders. And as he leaned in to smell her again, he softly moved her hair to one side and started kissing her neck, starting behind her ear and moving down to her shoulder.

'I need to taste you,' he whispered in her ear.

He leaned around her to his backpack and removed his knife. The sight of the knife instilled fear into Kat. Her heart beat loud in her ears, and she could feel her body start to shake. He leaned back, and she could no longer see him or the knife, which increased the fear that had taken over her body.

He ran his fingers over her neck to move the few strands of hair that had fallen back and then kissed her shoulder again. He slipped the strap of her top over her shoulder to expose more of her back. Then he placed the point of the knife next to her shoulder blade and put a little pressure on it.

She let out a small cry as the knife pierced her skin. He watched as a thin trickle of blood ran down her back. He removed the knife from her skin and placed it on the table. He dropped to his knees behind her and ran his tongue up her back, licking the trail of blood from her skin. When he got to the wound, he sucked at it hard. Kat let out a louder cry. He stopped what he was doing and sat on the chair in front of her again.

She looked at the man seated in front of her and saw his bloodstained lips. He was smiling at her like he had just eaten the most delicious treat. He frightened her in a way she never knew possible.

'Was it good?' She had no idea why she asked that, but she was hoping if she tried to play along, maybe he wouldn't hurt her too much.

He leaned in again to her and kissed her hard, forcing the taste of her own blood into her mouth. 'I never knew a person could taste so sweet. I knew you were perfect from the first time I saw you.'

Chapter 22

It had felt like several hours, but when she looked at the clock, it had only been ninety minutes. The cable ties were cutting into her ankles and wrists, and the pain was getting unbearable. Her shoulder where he had cut her ached.

Who are you, and why me? she thought to herself over and over.

He had disappeared from sight and moved around the house so quietly, she couldn't tell where he was. Kat saw her phone on the other side of the table. She wasn't sure how, but she needed to get it and try to call for help. Little by little, she lifted her weight onto her feet and pushed the chair back. Every time she moved, the cable ties cut into her ankle a little more. She could feel a trickle running down her left foot, and she could see a red smear on the ground from where she had just moved the chair.

Closer and closer, she moved, and she was almost at her phone. She was exhausted from the pain but kept pushing herself. Finally, she had moved enough that she was next to her phone. She chuckled a little as she had no idea how she was going to dial any number with her hands shackled behind her back. She leaned over with her face and tried to unlock the screen with her nose, her chin, and even her tongue, but nothing was working. Frustrated, she banged her head on the table.

'Now what's going on in here?'

Kat looked up and saw him standing in the doorway, smirking at her. He wandered over and stood next to her and spotted the phone. He picked it up and held it out to her.

'Is this what you were after? Is there someone you would like me to call?'

Laughing at her, he showed her the screen as he powered off the phone and then tucked it into his pocket. He crouched down next to Kat and looked her in the eye.

'You belong to me now.' He placed one hand on her inner thigh and the other on her shoulder, and as he ran his hand up her leg and under her skirt, he pressed his finger on the wound on her back, causing her to yelp. 'And you will behave.'

Kat looked him in the eye and spat in his face. 'I will never belong to you.'

Infuriated, he stood up, leaned over the table, and grabbed his knife. Without hesitation, he forcefully plunged the knife into Kat's leg. She let out a painful howl, and tears flowed freely down her cheek. He stood up and walked away from her.

Kat sat there, tied to the chair with his knife sticking up out of her leg, instantly regretting spitting at him. She knew if she were to have any chance of getting out of here, she needed to play his game and get him to trust her.

'I'm sorry.'

Her voice was shaky and filled with pain. He turned back towards her and just stood there, staring.

'I really am sorry for my behaviour. I promise I won't be rude to you again.'

His rigid body language softened, and he came back around to her. He crouched down next to her and place one hand on the handle of the knife. Slowly, he pulled the knife out of her leg. Blood streamed from her leg, and she felt dizzy. He reached up and cut the straps to her top and then cut through the middle of the fabric. He lifted her leg slightly and used her top as a tourniquet.

His hands were covered in her blood. He lifted them to his face and smelled the blood. He looked over the tops of his fingers at her and smiled. He licked at one of his fingers and then stepped behind her to the sink and turned on the tap. Kat was repulsed by him and didn't understand why he had chosen her or what she had done to deserve this.

He finished washing his hands and came and sat on the chair next to Kat and just stared at her. Kat tried not to make eye contact, but every time she looked up, he was staring at her.

The time ticked by slowly, minutes turning into hours, and he just sat there. The pain slowly increased, and nausea was taking over her body. Her lips felt dry, and her mouth like sandpaper. Kat was exhausted. She looked down at the floor and saw a small pool of blood forming under her chair. The sight of the blood made her dry-retch. Kat started to sob; the tears ran down her cheek and dripped onto her leg.

Her crying seemed to amuse him. He got up from the chair he was in and knelt in front of Kat. He put his hand under her chin and lifted her head so she was again looking at him. He kissed her softly, and she didn't fight him. He ran his hands over her bare shoulders, and she didn't shrug him away. Playing along seemed to be working for her.

He stood up, went to the fridge, and opened the door. 'Are you hungry, my love?' His words were soft and caring. 'Thirsty, perhaps?'

'Yes. I am hungry and very thirsty. Your name is Bradley?'

'It is sometimes. And other times it's Simon. And other times it's Josh. How about I make us something to eat, and how does a nice cup of tea sound?'

'Sounds perfect, thank you. So what name should I call you?'

'Let's stick with Bradley.'

He turned over his shoulder and smiled at her. He seemed pleased with her cooperation. He turned back to the fridge and grabbed at a few items. Satisfied with his selection, he placed them on the table in front of Kat. The thought of food made her stomach grumble, and her stomach pained from hunger. She watched him at the sink filling up the kettle and preparing two mugs with tea bags and sugar.

'I really hate this smell.' Bradley picked up the jar with the sticks and held it in her direction. He pulled open the cupboard with the bin and dropped it in. 'I thought I had thrown that out before. Did you get it out of the bin?'

Katrina lost her breath. Her brain had just caught up with the conversation, and she realised that he had been in the house before the day he came to fix the alarm. 'Yes, I did take it out of the bin.' Kat furrowed her brow at him. 'How many times have you been in my house?'

Bradley stood tall and proud. 'A few. In fact, I've been watching you and your family for a while now, and that's why I know I'm going to fit in just fine.'

'So my father isn't going crazy. You have been watching us? And what about all the other things? Moving his stuff around, banging on the window – was that you too?'

He laughed at her from deep down as if she had told him a funny joke. 'Yeah, that was me.'

'So for the past week, I've been thinking my father is losing his mind, and all the while, you were messing with us? Why?'

'It amused me.'

Kat was getting angry now. 'It amused you? Are you serious?'

'Yes. And look at how it ended. You got rid of him for the night, and now we can be alone.' He came up right to her face again and started kissing her cheek and then her neck. 'Don't you get it? You are meant to be with me.'

Kat's brain went onto overdrive. She had to think of a way to get out. The children would be home in an hour, so she didn't have long. She needed to do something. She forced herself to smile at him. 'I think I get it now. How about I finish making lunch?'

He contemplated her offer for a moment before shaking his head. 'I don't think so.'

'What do you want me to do to make you happy?'

'Bleed for me.'

Those three words froze Kat to the bone. Her heart beat so strongly, she thought it was going to come right through her chest, and she became light-headed. She looked at the floor and tried to control her breathing, and for a moment, she gave up hope of getting out alive.

When she finally looked up again, she saw a sandwich and a cup of tea had been placed in front of her. He stood behind her chair and twisted it so she was facing the table, and he shoved her hard so she was close enough to lean forward and eat.

'Do you have any straws?'

'Huh?'

'Straws. You have kids, right? So I figured you would have straws.'

'Yeah, in the pantry, middle to the left in a container.'

He walked away and returned moments later with a pink straw and placed it in her mug. He slid the mug closer to her and bent the straw towards her. 'Finish your lunch, and I will be back soon.'

Kat looked slightly over her shoulder and watched him walk to the laundry room and climb onto the washing machine. Puzzled by what he was doing, she turned her head as far as she could and saw him disappear into the roof.

Fuck! Fuck! Fuck! Dad was right about everything. There was someone in the roof, and we were being watched. The monster is real. He's not imaginary. How could I have been so stupid and not believed him? What the hell am I meant to do now? Fuck!

Kat was furious with herself. She thought if she had just taken her father seriously, she might not be in this position now. She knew she was going to need her strength if she had any sort of chance, so she finished the meal that had been prepared for her. And now she waited for him to return.

Chapter 23

His perfect day had arrived a little earlier than expected, and for that, he was ecstatic. She was a little rude to him to start with but seemed to be coming around. *She is more perfect than I imagined.*

He was back at the camp he had made himself in the roof and started collecting his things. Piece by piece, he packed up. He was diligent to ensure that nothing got left behind. Like any good camper, he made sure that he left no footprint. Once he was packed up, he made his way out of the roof and back into the laundry room. He replaced the cover and slid off the washing machine and carried his bags into the kitchen.

'Ah, my love, I hope I didn't keep you waiting too long. I figured there was no reason for me to hide anymore now that we are together.'

Kat looked at him and nodded, 'Would you like me to help you put your things away?'

'That is a kind offer, but no, thank you.' He looked up at the clock and was pleased by the time. 'Not long to go, and our children will be home from school.'

Kat's body temperature went through the roof, and she felt sick all over. He was right; there was only fifteen to twenty minutes until her kids would be coming through the front door, and she still had no idea how she was going to get free before then.

'You're right. They will be home soon and need to have a snack ready for them. They will be hungry. Can you please let me up so I can get something ready for them?' She did her best to sound sincere but she could hear the fear in her voice.

'It's OK, my love. You work hard. Let me take care of our family for a while.'

Kat was scared. She had tried everything she could think of to get herself free and nothing had worked. She was overwhelmed with fear for her life and the lives of her children. She couldn't control it and burst into tears.

He rushed to her side and lifted her head so he could see her cry. 'You're so beautiful when you cry.' He felt his pulse quicken and the excitement building. He stepped back a little and looked down on her. *She is perfect.*

He leaned to the kitchen sink and picked up a fork. Bradley stood behind her, and with all his force, he plunged the fork into her left arm.

Kat let out an almighty scream as the pain seared through her arm. In between gasping for breath, she looked at her arm and saw the fork protruding from her arm. She dropped her head and cried. She knew she had no hope of saving her children. They would be here any minute, and she could do nothing.

Bradley stood behind her and watched her body shake. He watched blood seep from the fork, and her cries sounded like music to his ears. When the crying stopped, he stepped right up close behind her so he could feel the heat coming from her body. He tilted his head backwards and closed his eyes. He took several deep breaths and let his excitement dwindle.

Back in control of his emotions, Bradley opened his eyes and looked down upon his beauty. There was a steady trickle of blood running down her arm and dripping on the floor. The light from the kitchen window sparkled on the red liquid, and he was captivated by its magic. He dropped to the floor and watched closer as the glistening ruby stream pooled at his knees. His perfect day was better than he had imagined.

Lost in his daydream, he had almost forgot about the children. He sprung back to his feet and kissed his beauty hard. 'You're more beautiful than you realise.'

He dashed from the kitchen, and Kat could hear the front door open. She watched the second hand on the kitchen clock – *tick, tick,*

tick. The minutes became excruciating as she sat there in her kitchen, restrained to a chair with two stab wounds and a fork still in her arm. She was dizzy again as she lost more blood. All she wanted to do was close her eyes and pray for this to be just a bad dream.

The sound of her children running towards the open front door snapped her back to reality. She wanted to scream at them not to come in, but nothing came out. She tried to make some noise with the chair, but she had little strength to move it. And then the voices were inside the house. The little happy voices were coming towards her.

'*Mum!*' yelled Nathan as he rushed through the front door. 'We're home!'

She could hear the heavy steps of her two babies passing the lounge and entering the kitchen, and then she heard the front door close and the deadbolt lock. They were now part of his game.

Defeated, Kat looked up from the table at her children. They looked confused and frightened. Nathan regained focus quickly and rushed to his mother's side. He saw the fork sticking from her arm and the ties that had her locked to the chair.

'Mum? What's going on?' His voice was soft and filled with fear. The sight of the one person who was supposed to protect them bound and bleeding was too much.

Paige was frozen in the doorway. Her school bag, which was almost as big as she was, was still on her back. Her bottom lip was quivering. Kat could see the terror in her baby girl's eyes.

As silent as a snake coming up on its prey, he appeared out of nowhere behind Paige. He towered over her and locked eyes with Kat.

'Look, my love, the children are home.'

Still shaking with terror, Paige looked up over her head at the monster who hovered above her. Her school bag slipped from her shoulders and landed with a heavy thud on the floor. Nathan stood behind his mother, unsure what to do.

'Nathan, please sit down.' He pointed to the chair at the head of the table.

Nathan looked at his mother, who nodded with permission for him to follow the instruction just given. Nathan sat down and stared at the man standing behind his sister, who was still looking up at him.

Kat watched helplessly as he grabbed Paige under her arms and lifted her off the ground and carried her to the chair that was next to her. He retrieved more cable ties from his backpack and bound the little girl in the same way as her mother. Paige put up no fight.

Bradley came around to Nathan and crouched behind the chair he was seated on and grabbed one of his arms. Nathan yanked his arm free and pushed himself against the table, forcing the chair to smash into the monster's face. The monster yelped and fell backwards. Nathan leapt from the chair and tried to run. His foot slipped on the trail of blood that was on the floor, and he fell hard to the ground. Not panicking, he scrambled back to his feet and threw his weight forward in an attempt to get away as quickly as he could.

But Bradley was quicker; he lurched forward from behind the fallen chair and grabbed Nathan by his ankle. Nathan fell hard to the floor again. Bradley pulled Nathan's leg, and the boy slid backwards. Nathan tried to kick with his free leg, but Bradley turned the small boy onto his back and slapped him hard across the face.

From where Kat was, she could not see the commotion that was happening on the floor, but when she heard the slap, she screamed out. Bradley had hurt her child, and she couldn't protect him. She watched as Bradley got to his feet and righted the fallen chair. He stood over the boy, who was dazed on the floor, and lifted him from the ground and sat him on the chair. This time, the boy did not fight as he was restrained to the chair.

With his new family all sat quietly at the table, Bradley sat down and smiled at them all. 'We have a beautiful family, Katrina. We should be proud.'

Kat looked him right in eye. 'Yes, I am proud of my children.'

Bradley looked first at Nathan and then at Paige. 'So who wants to tell me about their day first?'

Both children looked at the monster, but no one spoke.

'Paige, how about you go first?'

Bradley focused only on the little girl, but she said nothing. Bradley sighed deeply as his frustration was building.

'Don't make me ask again, Paige,' he said, his voice now low and gruff.

'Sweetheart,' Kat interrupted, looking at her frightened daughter. 'Everything is OK. So how about you tell me all about your day?'

Paige looked up at her mother for reassurance. Kat nodded.

Paige turned to Bradley. 'Good. I got a certificate for reading.'

'Well, that is fantastic!' Bradley leaned back in his chair and smiled at the little girl. 'Isn't that great, Kat?'

'Yes, that is great. Well done, sweetheart.'

Pleased with how the conversation was progressing, Bradley turned his focus to Nathan, who was glaring back at him. 'Nathan, your turn. How was your day?'

'I got an A on my history test.' His tone was sharp and angry.

'Look at that, Kat – two great achievements today. They look hungry, don't they? So how about I get them that snack we were talking about earlier?' Bradley rose from the table and went to the pantry in search of a treat for the children.

Kat sat at the table, shifting her attention between the children, trying her best to give them comfort. Nathan sat rigid in the chair, seemingly unafraid, and Kat could see his mind was at work. This gave her both relief and fear at the same time. She knew her son was resourceful and had a strategic mind, but she was afraid he would do something silly and make the situation worse. He had already received punishment for trying to get away once.

Bradley returned to the table with a packet of biscuits and placed them in the middle. Both children stared at the packet, hungry from their day. Bradley slid the tray from the packet and removed two biscuits. He placed one in front of both the children and gave them a nod that they could eat. Nathan was able to lean forward enough to pick up the biscuit between his teeth and draw it into his mouth.

Paige was too small. She looked at Bradley with sadness; Bradley smiled back. Bradley leaned over the table and picked up the biscuit and held it out to Paige. Paige tried to bite into the treat but struggled as she was missing her front teeth. For a brief moment, Kat saw compassion in Bradley's eyes as he broke the biscuit into small pieces and fed them one at a time to Paige. She hadn't seen this before, and she began to have hope that she could rescue her family.

'Who wants to watch TV?' Bradley looked at each member of his new family and smiled and waited for them to respond.

They all looked at one other and nodded, hopeful that he would release them from their bindings.

Bradley stood behind Paige first. He leaned down and grabbed the side of the chair. He tilted it backwards and dragged the girl from the room. Kat listened intently in panic as she lost sight of her small daughter. For a moment, there was only a deafening silence. She felt her heart beat quicker and her skin go cold.

She listened harder, and then she heard it. The TV had been turned on, and she could barely make out Paige talking. The channel was changed several times, and then he appeared in the doorway. His head was lowered, his arms by his side. He lifted his eyes without moving his head, and for the first time, Kat saw the true evil that was the man holding them hostage. The sun had moved from the kitchen window as the afternoon went on, and where he stood now, he was partly in the shadow of the hallway.

He just stood there, staring at the boy. He tilted his head to the side and then almost sprinted over to Nathan. He leaned in close to his face and just stared into his eyes. Kat could see Nathan's breathing quicken, and he sat back as far as he could in the chair. The monster was back. He slowly raised his right hand and placed it around Nathan's throat, gently squeezing. Nathan gasped for air and started to struggle. Bradley released his grip and stood towering over the boy, his body language intimidating and his eyes never leaving the boy's.

Kat freaked and yelled, 'What show did Paige choose?' the pitch of her voice high.

The sudden interruption broke Bradley's stare, and he turned to look at her. He stretched his back and stood behind Nathan. 'Some cartoon with talking animals.' He tilted Nathan's chair back and proceeded to drag him away from his mother's sight.

Alone in the kitchen, Kat's emotions became overwhelming, and she cried hard, doing everything she could not to make any noise. She didn't want her children to hear her cry, but she couldn't hold the tears back, and she let them out.

Bradley returned to the kitchen and gazed upon his beauty. He slowly walked around the table and stood behind her. He placed his hands on her shoulders and gently massaged her neck. He leaned down and kissed the top of her head. Without warning, he pulled the fork from her arm.

Kat let out a deep cry and dropped her head, sobbing. Silently, Bradley tied a tea towel around her arm and then proceeded to kiss her neck several times. She could feel his tongue on her skin, and she felt sick. Every time he touched her, she felt her skin crawl.

Bradley tipped her back on the chair and, without saying anything, dragged her to the lounge to join the children.

Chapter 24

'I think it's time the children went to bed' – Bradley looked at Kat, who was struggling to keep her eyes open – 'and then I think we will retire for the night too.' He got up from the comfy sofa and started to drag Paige out of the room but paused in the doorway. 'Say goodbye to you mother, Paige.'

Paige blinked heavily at her mother with a sadness in her eyes Kat had never seen before. 'Good night, Mumma.'

'Good night, sweetheart. I love you.'

Kat's throat closed, and she struggled to fight back the tears and get the words out and then watched as her daughter disappeared from sight. She could hear the clunking of the chair over the tiles and a door being closed. Kat felt her heart break and a pain in her stomach as she sat there helplessly as a monster stole her child away from her.

'Mum?' Nathan twisted as far as he could in his seat to see his mother. His voice was calm and almost emotionless. 'He's going to kill us, isn't he?'

Fighting the urge to cry, Kat shook her head and bit down on her bottom lip. She took several short sharp breaths and then one long deep breath before she spoke. 'I am going to do everything I can to get us out of here, OK? Now I don't want you to think about it. When he takes you to bed, don't fight or do anything that will set him off, all right?' she said, her voice pleading with her son.

'Yes, Mum.'

He turned back towards the TV and said nothing more. Kat knew her son was a fighter, so she prayed silently that he knew this wasn't the time.

Two commercial breaks passed, and Bradley hadn't returned. Kat's heart sank, and she started to struggle in the chair, trying to free herself. Every twist and jerk caused intense pain to surge through her body, and she could feel the blood starting to seep from the wound in her leg. Out of breath, she paused and tried to muster some more energy to try again.

A door closed in the distance, and Kat froze, trying to listen for footsteps. He was silent; he made no sound when he moved. He was like a shadow passing through the house. Kat stared at the doorway intensely, waiting for him to appear from the darkness.

And there he was, half in the light and half still blackened, a figure not unlike you would see from a horror movie. From this angle, he was faceless, almost not real, and Kat felt that all-too-familiar feeling of fear pumping through her veins.

He stepped out of the shadows and back into the light. She saw his face. He looked calm and almost happy.

'Everything OK? Did she go to sleep easily?' Kat just needed to know her baby girl was all right.

Bradley glided up behind Nathan but looked sideways at Kat. 'Everything is fine. I told her a story before she closed her eyes.'

Kat felt a small amount of relief, but without seeing Paige, she would never be completely at ease.

'Your turn to go to bed, Nathan. Say goodbye to your mother.'

'I love you, Mum.' He locked eyes with her and nodded as if he had already accepted his fate.

'I love you too, sweetheart,' she said, her voice full of tears as she watched he son being taken from her and then heard the clunking sound of the chair being dragged on the tiles up the hallway.

A door closed. She was alone once again.

Ten minutes must have passed before he returned to the lounge with a look of satisfaction on his face. 'He's full of energy, that one.'

'Did he give you any trouble?'

'Nothing I wasn't expecting.'

Kat wasn't sure what to make of that. She hadn't heard anything that sounded like a struggle or a fight, so she prayed that Nathan had done what she had asked and he was safe now in bed.

Bradley came and sat beside Kat on the edge of the sofa. He ran his fingers over her shoulder and down her arm. 'Are you ready for bed now, my love?' His voice was soft and almost sincere.

'Yes.' She didn't have the energy to fight. She wanted to sleep and knew the best way to get some rest would be to say and to do what he wanted. In the morning after some sleep, she would find a way to rescue her children.

Bradley pulled his knife from his pocket and flicked it open. He cut at each cable tie and released Kat from the chair. He pushed the blade closed and tucked it back into his pocket. Bradley scooped Kat up from the chair and carried her up the hallway towards her bedroom. As she passed the children's rooms, she looked at the doors, hoping they would be open so she could see them. Heartbroken, the doors were closed, and she shut her eyes, sending them prayers.

At the end of the hallway her bedroom door was already open, and she was carried through and placed in the middle of the bed. He lay over her and stretched her arms to the side. He leaned over the edge and retrieved a cord that had been tied to the leg of the bed. He bound one arm and then the other. He slid off the foot of the bed and leaned over her. He put his fingers under the band of her skirt and pulled it off. He walked to the hamper and placed the skirt inside.

He came back and proceeded to secure her legs. So there she lay in her underwear, now tied to her bed, not knowing what was going to happen next.

Chapter 25

He lay in bed next to her, resting his head on her chest. Her heart beat was hypnotising. He ran his fingers down her chest to her navel and back. Her skin reacted to his touch, and he snuggled in closer. Her skin was warm on his face. His body started to relax, and he felt sleepy. He let his mind drift away to his last true love.

She looks so perfect, just waiting in line at the supermarket. At a guess, I would say she is twenty-eight. Hair pulled back into a ponytail. Dark jeans and a fitted T-shirt. It was not a revealing outfit, but I could tell she looked after herself. She smiles at the girl behind the counter and makes polite small talk. She hands over her bank card and waits patiently for her receipt.

The bag looks heavy, and as she leaves the store, she bends over and places the bag on the seat by the door so she can get a better grip of the handle. She picks up the bag and continues on her way. I follow her. She is perfect.

She walks to her car and puts the bag on the front passenger seat. She closes the door and walks around to the driver's door and gets in. I walk to my van and get in. I can see her on her phone, sending a message, from where I sit. She puts her phone on the seat and starts the engine.

I follow her back to her house and park two doors down. I see her lean across and pull the shopping bag over to herself. She gets out of her car and walks to the front door. I check my watch, and she is home right on cue. I wait one more minute before I go to her door and ring the bell.

I can hear her coming to the door. She opens the door and smiles brightly at me. She is perfect. I introduce myself to her. I am Bradley, the telecommunications specialist. I am here to fix her Internet connection. She does not know that I disconnected it yesterday so she would call me. She invites me in. I smile politely and accept her invitation.

I ask her to show me where she plugs in her modem and any other telephone plugs she has. She shows me everything. She trusts me. She is perfect.

I thank her and set about fixing the problem. She goes to the kitchen and continues putting her shopping away. I start to cough loudly, and she comes back to me. She is obedient. She offers me a glass of water, and I accept. I follow her to the kitchen and wait for her to pour me the drink. I take the glass and drink it all in one go. I thank her and leave the room.

She follows me back to where I was working and asks if I have found the problem. I say I know what it is and if she could pass me my screwdriver from my toolbox. She turns around and bends over to pick it up. As she stands, I take the cable that I have in my hands and quickly put it over her head and around her throat. She struggles for a moment. I tell her to stop and I won't hurt her anymore. She stops. She trusts me. They all trust me.

I loosen my grip, and before she turns, I slip a cable tie over one of her wrists. As she turns, I grab the other wrist and pull it towards me. She does not fight, and I bind her hands together. A tear rolls down her cheek, and she is shaking.

I assure her everything will be just fine. I walk her to her bedroom and lay her on her bed. I put her arms above her head and take another cable tie from my pocket and secure her hands to the bedhead. She lays there looking at me. She is perfect.

I use my knife to cut her shirt so I can see her body, and as I suspected, she does look after herself. I lay my head on her chest and listen to her heartbeat. It beats fast. The sun is going down, and shadows start forming in her room. The sun catches on a red vase, and the room is suddenly turned to a seductive sea of red shadows dancing on the walls.

I look at her face, and she seems calmer now. Her heartbeat has slowed, and her body has relaxed. I stand at the end of the bed and lean over her. I unbutton her jeans and pull at them until she is free. I climb on her and lie on her, feeling her move under me. This excites me. I must taste her.

I sit on her, and I take my knife and run the blade softly over her skin. Her heartbeat quickens, and her skin starts to shiver. She starts to cry and begs me not to hurt her. I let my blade fall slightly to her side, and I carefully pierce her skin. She cries a little louder but not enough. I take my knife and move it to just above her belly button, and this time, I push it in a little deeper. Now she screams. Now she really begs for me to let her go. Now I am happy.

I tell her that she belongs with me and I have been watching her for days. I have been in and out of her house, getting to know her and how she is perfect. She starts to think back and starts remembering all the little things, like the missing food, the window that just won't open, and the light that started flickering. I smile at her and nod. Yes, my love, that was all me.

I remember lying with her all night. As she starts to sleep, I wake her and open her up a little more. I have learned to control myself since my first true love, my beauty sitting on the park bench. I now take my time and let the experience last for hours. As the morning sun enters the window, I look down on my beauty and see her lying so still, so perfect. She lies there in a sea of red, a picture of perfection.

Now I leave. She needs her rest.

Bradley sighed with pleasure as he remembered. He stretched a little and sat up. Kat lay with her eyes closed, hoping he would leave her alone if he thought she was asleep.

Bradley nudged her. 'My love, are you awake?'

Kat did not respond. Bradley huffed in disappointment. He did not like to be ignored. He picked up his knife from the nightstand and looked over her body. He ran his fingers over her skin and watched it react. He liked this. He chose a spot just on the inside of her hip bone. He pushed the blade in slowly while staring at her face. Her eyes opened suddenly, and her back arched off the bed. She let out a throaty cry and fell heavily onto her back. He got excited watching her. As slowly as he pushed the blade into her, he pulled it back out. Blood rushed from the wound and pooled in her belly. Bradley laughed out loud.

'Hello there, beautiful.'

Kat glared at him. She breathed deeply and slowly, trying to control the pain. She said nothing.

Bradley straddled her and kissed her unwilling lips. 'Don't go anywhere. I'm just going to the toilet. We will have more fun when I get back.'

He climbed off and left the bedroom. He didn't close the door. Kat knew she had only a minute to do something.

She pulled her right arm as far as she could towards her face. She breathed in deeply and twisted her aching body so she could reach the knot with her teeth. The cord was thick, and the knot wasn't too tight. She managed to loosen the knot and pull her hand free. With one hand free, she quickly untied her left hand and then her legs. A flood of relief took over, but she knew she had no time to rest.

Quietly, she slipped off the bed and stood at the doorway. She peeked out towards the toilet. He had closed the door, and she could see light escaping underneath. She tiptoed to Nathan's door and quietly pushed it open just enough for her to slip in. She closed the door again and turned to face the middle of the room.

Nathan's curtains were still open, and she saw the silhouette of his sleeping body on the bed from the faint light of the moon. She hurried over and leaned over him. In a whisper that was barely audible, she tried to wake Nathan.

'Sweetheart, wake up.' She put her hands on his shoulders and shook him gently. 'Honey, please wake up. I'm going to get you out of here.'

Nathan didn't move. Kat shook him a little harder, knowing he had always been a deep sleeper, and this time, her voice was a little louder. 'Nathan, sweetheart, you need to wake up now.'

The boy lay as still as ever. Kat leaned over and tried to open the window so she could get him to climb out when he awoke. She tried with all her might – and nothing. She tried once more, but the window just didn't budge.

She returned her focus to the sleeping boy and pulled back the cover as this always annoyed him on school mornings, when he was hard to wake. She put her arms under his and started to lift him.

Her skin suddenly chilled, and her throat closed up. She fought back the tears, and she felt his wet sticky body against her flesh. Holding everything in, she gently lay him back down. The moonlight illuminated his lifeless body enough for Kat to see the gaping stab wounds in his belly.

She collapsed to her knees and covered her mouth with both hands, gasping at air as quietly as she can, her heart broken. She stayed like this for a minute, and then her brain shouted at her – *Paige!*

Her whole body shook as she got to her feet. She let anger take over as her only objective now was to get to her daughter. She stepped to the door and opened it slightly. She glanced up the hallway towards her bedroom. She saw nothing but a slight glow of light from the toilet. *He must still be in there.*

She stepped out into the hall and ran on her toes to the next door. She opened it enough to slip in and closed it. She turned towards the window and stepped in. A shot of pain ran up her foot. She pulled her foot from the ground and dislodged a small building block from the sole of her foot. The pain increased her anger, and she rushed to the side of the bed. She yanked back the covers, expecting to see a bloody mess – nothing. Kat covered her mouth with her hand, trying to stop the tears in relief. She closed her eyes just for a moment.

'Mumma?'

A soft, sleepy voice filled her ears. Kat let the words flood her body, and she collapsed on the little girl, who started to sit up.

'Mumma, is it over? Has the bad man gone?'

'No, sweetheart, he hasn't, so I need to get you out of here, OK?'

Kat released her vice-like grip on her daughter and climbed on the bed to reach the window. She pulled at the handle, and it moved ever so slightly. She tugged again, but it stayed put. She tried one more time and gave up. She knew he has done this. He was prepared.

Kat turned back and sat on the edge of the bed and let Paige climb onto her lap. She just sat there, holding onto her daughter as tightly as she could.

Chapter 26

He could hear her attempting to open the boy's window from the toilet. He smiled to himself, pleased that she still had spirit. He was in the mood for a game of cat and mouse, so he stayed inside the toilet and let her discover his handiwork. He opened the door slightly so he could hear her as she moved around the house. He had a small chuckle when he heard her very faint cry as she found the troublesome boy. If he had just obeyed his instructions, then he wouldn't have been punished, but no, he had to try and run away. *Stupid boy.*

He stood there listening, waiting for her to move on. He heard a tiny click as she closed the boy's door and then the pitter-patter of her quick footsteps to the next door. And there it was, the disgusting, pungent smell of the girl's room filling the air. This was a smell he would never forget – and now a reward for his love.

The small girl did as she was told, so he did not need to punish her. She was like her mother in so many ways but especially her eyes. When he looked into them as he read her a story, all he saw was his true love looking back. This small girl was special; she would grow to be perfect.

OK, that's enough time together. He flushed the toilet and turned off the light. He didn't need light to know his way around the house; he had made sure of that. He knew exactly how to move around the house in the dark. He walked heavily on purpose back to her bedroom so his beauty would know her absence had been discovered. He was curious as to what she would do next.

He waited a minute. He listened. He could hear shuffling in the little girl's room. He heard the door open. It was time to start the game.

'Eight, nine, ten. Ready or not, here I come.' His voice was loud and light-hearted, and it echoed down the hallway.

He started making his way down the hall slowly. He didn't want to catch her too quick; where was the fun in that? Every step he took, he tapped on the wall so she would know exactly where he was. The house was small, so she didn't have too many places to go. He heard a bang and a scraping noise from a box moving across the floor.

'You really should have put those books away, Katrina. Someone might hurt themselves if they trip over the box.' He laughed at her. He liked this game. He was having fun.

Next, he could hear her tugging and banging on the back door and then running from the kitchen to the front door. He paused in the hallway and let her have a go at that door too. It didn't open, and he heard her helpless cry of 'No!'

'Did you think I would let you go that easy, Katrina? Oh, my love, you do not know me very well, do you? Remember when I said you belong to me? I meant it. You will be mine forever.'

He continued down the hallway, this time making not one single sound, his footsteps silent as he wanted to sneak up on her and catch his prize. He peered around the corner and saw his love attempting to open the lounge window. He moved closer to her and then pounced forward suddenly as she picked up a vase from the side table and went to throw it at the window. He grabbed her arm and wrenched it back, pulling her off her feet.

'Which part of "you belong to me forever" do you not understand? Why are you not listening to me?' His voice grew louder and the words came out angry. He turned and started dragging her by the arm. 'You see, your boy did not listen either, and you know how that ended, don't you?'

Katrina's heart sank as the words echoed in her head, and the blurry image of Nathan's limp, bloody body reappeared in her mind. She stopped struggling and tried to get to her feet while being pulled along the hard floor.

'I'm sorry,' Kat muttered softly. 'I won't do that again.'

Bradley yanked her with all his might up to her feet and grabbed both her arms and pulled her close to his face. She could feel his breath, warm and sharp on her face. The pain of him grabbing her wounded arm was unbearable, and she let out a wince and dropped her head to the side. He pulled her even close and then bit her hard on the neck, which she had exposed to him. Her cries of pain filled the house, and he felt his excitement grow. His mouth filled with her blood, and when he pulled back, she could see the red stream running from his mouth. His eyes were fixed on her, and he had a smile that instilled sheer terror deep into her body.

'Please stop hurting her,' a tiny voice came from behind Bradley.

He loosened his grip on Kat, and with a furrowed brow, he looked down to see the little girl standing by his side. Paige put her hand on Bradley's arm and pulled at it gently.

He was confused. There was something about this small child who had a hold of him, and he let Katrina go. He wiped the blood off his chin with his hand and walked them both back to the kitchen, the whole time studying the girl, trying to work out why his emotions changed when she was near him. It felt surreal.

Katrina was back at the kitchen table where this nightmare had begun. He had bound her back to a chair with cable ties. The pain throbbing through her body was exhausting, and she lowered her head to her chest and closed her eyes. She had no more energy to keep them open. In the background, she could hear him clanking in the kitchen cupboards. Little by little, the background noise faded, and she fell asleep.

The sound of buzzing woke Kat. She lifted her head and was reminded of the nightmare she was living by the burning pain all over her body. Light was streaming in through the kitchen window, and it took some time for her eyes to adjust to the light. When she opened her eyes fully and started to focus, she saw the monster who had killed her son standing before her on the other side of the table.

'Good morning, Katrina. I'm so glad you are awake again. Paige and I have been waiting for you.'

Katrina suddenly sat up, and he had her full attention. She looked down to her left and saw her daughter sitting next to her quietly, colouring in an activity book. She appeared unharmed and was not bound to the chair.

The little girl looked up at her mother and smiled brightly. 'Good morning, Mumma.'

She leaned into her side. Kat winced a little but soaked up her daughter's hug. She could feel some energy returning.

Bradley came to Kat's other side and kissed the top of her head. 'See, I told you, Paige. She would be awake soon. Now, my love, you must be starving. Paige and I have cooked you breakfast.'

Bradley walked back to the bench on the other side of the table, and Kat immediately looked down at Paige. 'Did he hurt you? I thought you were hiding like I told you.'

Paige shook her head. 'I'm OK, Mumma. If I do what I'm told, he won't hurt me. He promised.'

Kat shot a look at Bradley, who had turned to listen to the conversation.

'We had a fun game of hide-and-seek, didn't we, Paige? And you even won. I had to threaten you with further harm for Paige to come out of her very sneaky hiding spot. Since then, she has done everything I have asked. She really is a good girl.'

Bradley turned back to the bench and finished serving up plates of food. He placed one in front of Paige, who pushed her colouring aside and started eating straight away. Bradley placed another plate on the table and then returned to the bench for a third. He sat next to Kat and offered her food on a fork, which he held just in front of her face. She was starving, so she ate. Next, he took a bite from his plate and then alternated between his beauty and himself until breakfast was finished. Paige cleared her plate and asked to be excused to use the toilet. Bradley nodded and stood to walk the little girl up the hallway; he did not fully trust that she would not attempt something silly just as her brother had done the night before.

They walked past Nathan's door, and Paige stopped. 'Shouldn't we wake Nathan for breakfast?' She looked up at Bradley with genuine concern for her brother.

'It's OK. Let's leave him to sleep. He had a big night.'

He put his hand on the little girl's shoulder and pushed her forward. Paige continued walking, not saying another word. Bradley let her almost close the toilet door completely and go in private. He stood back just a step so he was close enough if she tried anything stupid. She finished quickly and flushed the toilet. He stepped back when she opened the door and let her shuffle past to get to the bathroom. She washed her hands and then turned to him when her toothbrush was out of reach.

Bradley was quickly becoming fascinated with the little girl. He walked up behind her and retrieved the toothbrush for her. He watched her intently as she brushed her teeth and washed her face. The little girl said nothing, and when she was finished, she pushed past him again and ran back to the safety of her mother in the kitchen.

In no apparent hurry, Bradley wandered back to the kitchen and watched his two girls talking. Kat was doing her best to keep the mood cheerful and praised Paige for the great colouring she was doing.

The day went on, and Bradley had harmed Kat no further. He just sat and watched them together and marvelled in the likeness of the little girl to her mother. He gazed upon Kat and became proud of himself for finally finding the one.

The time turned to half past three, and he knew his day would soon be over. The old man would return soon, and he was not ready to leave. Bradley took Paige by the hand and made her say goodbye to her mother again. He took her to her room and told her not to come out.

He returned to Kat's side and cut her legs free. And then one by one, he released her hands. Kat was confused as to what was going on. Bradley helped her to her feet and then hugged her tight. Kat barely had any strength left to fight back. Her legs were weak and gave out from under her. Bradley lay her on her back on the kitchen floor. He sat over Kat's limp body and admired her. She blinked heavily at him.

He lay with all his weight on her and kissed her passionately. Kat couldn't fight him. His weight was heavy on her chest, and she struggled to breathe. Finally, he sat up, and she gasped in as much air as she could. Bradley put his finger to his pursed lips and indicated silence and then pointed to the hallway, reminding her that her daughter was not far away.

With his left hand on her chest, feeling her heartbeat, his right pulled his knife from his pocket. She closed her eyes. He flicked the knife open. She started to sob. He plunged the knife into her belly. She bit her lip and held back the scream. He removed the blade and then cut down her side from her rib cage to her hip. Life poured from her body.

Kat struggled to breathe as he life started slipping away. Her vision became blurry, and her body started to chill. Bradley stood up and left her bleeding out on the floor. He walked to the kitchen sink and washed his hands. He walked back and stood at her feet; she was still alive but not for long. He stood there, watching over her, waiting for her final breaths, each breath longer apart than the last. Her eyes dulled, and her head rolled to the side.

'Goodbye, my love. You were the one.'

Chapter 27

It was Friday afternoon at the nursing home where the old man spent his days. He sat in the big comfy chair in front of the window to the aviary, looking out at the birds. He had a peaceful night with no one making him feel crazy. He started feeling bad about the past few days with his daughter, and he knew when he got home later that day, he would try to apologise.

He spoke with one of the senior carers at length the night before over a glass of fortified wine the carer kept in secret for occasions just like this, and whilst he was reliving the events of the past week out loud to someone else, he heard just how crazy it did sound and started to understand why his daughter would be thinking he was losing his mind. After all, who would believe that someone was living in their roof and stalking an old man? He knew if someone else was telling the story, there was no way he would believe it either. He needed proof, and he was determined; once home, he would get it. He would set a trap for the man who was haunting him and catch him out. Then Katrina would believe him, and life would go back to what it was only a week ago. It was almost three, and he was ready to go home with his newfound determination.

His thoughts were interrupted by Carla. She came over, clanking two cups of tea on their saucers. She placed them on the table next to the old man's chair and then put her hand on his shoulder.

'I will just grab a couple of biscuits to go with these. Any preference, Al?'

The old man looked up and smiled at Carla. 'Something chocolatey would be nice, thank you.' He reached up and patted her hand.

Carla chuckled and wandered back towards the kitchen to retrieve the treats. The old man looked back at the window and watched two birds hopping around after each other, almost as if they were children playing a game of chasey in the school yard.

Carla returned quickly and handed the old man a small plate with two chocolate-coated biscuits. He grinned at her, and she sat down next to him and started watching the birds with him.

'You going to be OK when you get home, Al? We are all worried about you.'

'I hope so. It's just the look Kat gives me when she thinks I'm making this all up. I swear I'm not. You have to believe me. And then I get so angry, and I don't mean to. I think we both needed this night apart. Maybe I will suggest that I have one night a week here. She's under a lot of pressure with work and the kids and a husband who always seems to be travelling for work, and maybe I am becoming a burden. She would never say that, but maybe she could use a little less responsibility.'

He sat back in the chair and sighed. Carla leaned over to him and passed him the cup. His fingers were clumsy, and some of the hot tea splashed out of the cup and landed in his lap. The burning heat instantly soaking through his pants caused the old man to jerk and knock the cup completely out of Carla's hand, crashing to the floor. The sound of the cup breaking echoed through the day room and stopped all conversations.

Carla leapt from her chair and stood in front of the old man. 'You OK, Al? Are you burnt? Let me go grab a cloth for you.' She darted away before he could answer any of her questions.

Fury raged inside him. He was angry at his body for getting old and clumsy. He was angry at the universe for suddenly being against him. He fought with his uncooperative body to get out of the chair. Once on his feet, he looked around the room and saw a sea of eyes looking at him. He just stood there looking back at them, staring at their aged faces, at the wrinkles and white hair, and he finally succumbed to the realisation that he had got old.

Carla scurried back with a small towel and a dustpan and brush. He waved away the offer of the towel and started to bend to attempt in helping clean up the mess.

A young man came up behind him and stopped him from getting on the ground. 'Come on, Al. You know we will never get you up again.'

He ushered the old man away from his chair and sat him at a table that was set up with a chess set. The young man left him there and went to check on Carla. The old man watched as Carla looked up and smiled at him and then passed the dustpan containing the shattered cup to the young man. She finished wiping the floor and huffed loudly as she pushed herself from her knees to her feet. As she walked past the old man on her way back to the kitchen, she patted his shoulder in comfort to let him know she knew it was an accident.

The old man felt humiliated. He fat fingers struggled to hold a cup, and he knew the young man was right; if he got to the floor to help clean up, it would have taken several attendants to get him back to his feet. The more he thought about it, the more he felt he was being punished. His mind was still sharp, but physically, he was deteriorating fast, and this scared him.

With the commotion of the spilled tea over, Carla came back and sat opposite the old man. 'Don't worry about it, OK? It's just a cup, and we have plenty of them here. If you're ready, though, we have a driver available to take you home now.'

She looked deeply into the old man's eyes. He liked Carla very much; even when something bad happened, he never felt stupid with her. She had a calming effect on him.

He laughed softly. 'Yeah, I'd better leave before I break anything else.'

Carla laughed back and stood and then offered her hand to the old man to help him from the chair. Once he was on his feet, she linked her elbow with his and walked him to the front door. His bag was waiting for him, and the familiar face of his regular driver greeted him. He paused for a moment but found no words to thank Carla. He kind of just stared at her. She read his thoughts and gave him a soft hug, and she pulled her arm away from his.

'See you next week, Al,' she whispered in his ear.

He nodded at her and shuffled behind his driver out to the car.

The ride home was quiet. He was becoming anxious about seeing his daughter and started fearing that she would still be angry with him. He just couldn't stand the thought of her still being angry, and he would say anything to make it better again.

The car pulled into the driveway, and the old man had his seat belt unfastened before the car came to a stop. He opened the door and found it unusually easy to get out. He had renewed energy and was going to make everything right again. He thanked his driver and insisted that he did not need help getting to the front door. Not interested in an argument and seeing Kat's car in the driveway, the driver farewelled the old man and backed out of the driveway when he saw him safely at the front door.

The old man opened the screen door, surprised that it wasn't locked; his daughter was paranoid about keeping the front door locked so the children didn't wander out when they were smaller, and now it was habit, a good habit to be in.

He stepped into the doorway and heard no noise. Normally, the house was filled with voices and either the radio or TV. He became worried. He placed his bag down near the front door and used the wall to keep himself steady on his feet as he shuffled towards the kitchen.

The old man reached the kitchen doorway and was confronted with his daughter's body lying on the ground. His heart stopped, and he lost all breath from his lungs. His skin went cold, and he felt all the hair on his body prick up. His already weakened legs gave out from under him, and he fell into a heap on the floor. As he regained some of his breath, he pulled himself along the floor the short distance to the lifeless body, his hands slippery when he placed them in the pool of blood that had formed around her, and he struggled to move himself. He continued dragging himself along until he was right by her side, his clothes now bloody, and the smell of death hit him hard.

He scooped her head up from the floor and let out a cry so painful, he was sure the neighbours would hear him and come to his aid. He sat there on the kitchen floor, rocking back and forth, cradling his daughter as much as he could. His whole body ached. He ran his fingers over her neck, praying desperately for any signs of a pulse. He felt nothing. His eyes were blurry from tears as they ran from his eyes, and they stung with every blink.

As he felt the bite on her neck, he started seeing all the wounds in her abdomen and her leg, and he sobbed. His heart ached for his daughter; he could see from the bruising around her wrists that she struggled. She fought with everything she had for her life. She lost her fight, and she must have died in incredible pain. His sobbing increased, and he could not control his body as it convulsed as he gasped for breath.

Who did this to you, sweetheart? He repeated it in his head over and over as he rocked her. *What monster did this to you?*

Several minutes passed when a new thought jolted him back to the now. *The children. Where are the children?*

He ever so gently placed Katrina's head back on the floor and pushed himself back a little. His hands were slippery, and he was covered in her blood all over his legs and feet, and he just could not get up on to his feet. Frustration set in immediately, and he panicked as he needed to find his grandchildren.

He called for them. At first, his voice barely came out. His mouth and throat were dry, and he could not produce enough saliva to lubricate his tongue. He called out again and kept licking at his lips, and eventually, he could swallow, and his cries for the children escaped his mouth and filled the air.

In between his howls for the children, he was quiet, listening hard for any noise at all. He was met with a deafening silence. He feared the worst and started scrambling madly, trying to get up from the floor again. His legs were weak, and the floor was like winter ice; he was defeated. He managed to get to his knees and attempted to crawl like a baby to look for Nathan and Paige. The pain in his knees was too intense, and once again, his body gave out, and he collapsed onto his belly, breathless. He had made it to the doorway, and he looked down the hall into the darkness. He tried again to call out, this time to the neighbours or to anyone passing by, but the sadness had taken over, and all that came out were inaudible sobs.

He lay there, his old body too weak to move. He felt fatigued from the stress and struggled to keep his eyes open. He hadn't felt like this since the war, when he was forced to live with the unthinkable evil he was made to do. He remembered the blood and the limp, lifeless bodies all around him, being made to pick up the carcasses of the women and children who were slaughtered as collateral damage. His brain went into overdrive as the memories that he had locked away in a deep, dark corner of his mind were spilled into his conscious thought and took over.

He felt a tightness building in his chest, and a sudden sharp pain shot down his left arm. He concentrated on trying to inhale as much oxygen as he could. The pain in his chest and arm was incredible; he had felt nothing like this before. He had not an ounce of strength to move or to call out for help. His heart was dying, and he could do nothing about it.

From the corner of his eye, he saw a movement coming from the hallway. His tilted his head back a little in an attempt to see. He blinked heavily, trying to focus his eyes. *Feet.* He was sure he could see feet coming towards him. His body was now too numb to move. He blinked again, getting a little more focus with his vision. He could see two pairs of feet coming towards him. He could make out one to be an adult, and one sparkled as they left the shadow and entered the light.

Paige! He got a surge of energy as he realised his granddaughter was alive. He rolled from his belly to his side and then to his back.

He squinted as his eyes adjusted to the sunlight that was coming in through the front door. At first, the two figures standing over him were faceless and blackened. As his eyes accepted the light, he was able to see perfectly the two people standing there. He focused first on his special little girl, who smiled at him as recognised her. And then he shifted his eyes to the much larger figure standing beside her, holding her hand.

It was him. It was the man who had been terrorising him over the past week. As the realisation of the identity of who had killed his daughter sank in, he felt an overwhelming tightness in his chest, and his brain went fuzzy. He could hear ringing in his ears, and his lungs were failing him. He trembled on the floor, and his vision started to fade. He blinked again, trying to focus on his granddaughter, but all he could see was the monster leaning over him. His face was only a few inches away, and he just smiled at him. His dark eyes were filled with evil.

Bradley hovered over the old man for a few more seconds. He stood back up. He took a hold of Paige's tiny hand and started to lead her away from her grandfather.

The old man let his head fall to the side, and he watched as Paige turned back and waved at him. The front door closed behind Bradley as he ushered Paige through first. He never turned back to look at the old man, who was left on the kitchen floor to die next to his daughter's massacred body. He was alone now.

The ability to breathe had left the old man, and he felt his pulse slowing down. He stared at the ceiling and let the reaper come for him.

Chapter 28

Stephen sat there in his hotel room, staring at his phone, guilt seeping from every pore. It had been two days since Kat had yelled at him on the phone and refused to speak to him since; now she had turned her mobile off and taken the landline off the hook. He understood why she was angry at him, but she just didn't understand the pressure on him from the corporate world he was a part of. It was expected of him to travel as part of his job, and it was expected of him to entertain clients, and if a client asked him to stay on a few days and join him for a fishing charter, then it was bad business to say no.

He loved Kat dearly, but over the past few years, he had fallen out of love with her. The passion and excitement had left their relationship. Stephen had married Katrina eleven years ago. It was a magical day. The moment he saw her walking down the aisle, he knew they were meant to be together forever and he would give her his heart and soul. Stephen was forty-five, only nine months older than Kat.

They met fourteen years ago at an art gallery, where a mutual acquaintance was hosting a show filled with pieces created by final-year art students from the local university. Stephen was standing in front of a sculpture of a man bending over his wife, who was lying down. He remembered the face of the man who had his hands on his head, looking up at the sky. The artist had captured mourning and devastation perfectly. The sculpture really got to him, which was what drew Katrina to his side. She had been watching him from the other side of the room, and when she saw the way the sculpture affected him, she had to come over and meet him. Katrina ended up buying the piece and gifting it to Stephen on their first official date. He knew from that moment she was the only woman he would ever truly love.

They had two young children, whom he adored, and much of his guilt was missing out on them growing up. Then there was her father. He had moved in with them a couple of years ago when his health started deteriorating and he was unable to continue to live independently. He had pleaded with her many times to move him into a facility that could care for him the way he needed so she wouldn't be so stressed with all the additional responsibility that he would add to her life, but she refused to let anyone help her. The best he got was getting her to agree to use the day centre when she needed to work.

Stephen rubbed his brow and dialled his wife's number again – straight to voicemail. He threw his head back in frustration and dropped the phone on the table. 'OK, Kat, I get it. You're pissed at me.' Stephen sighed, staring at the roof.

From behind him, he heard stirring on the bed. He looked back over his shoulder and saw the silhouette of his mistress turning over and sitting up.

Sleeping with her happened by accident. He hadn't planned on cheating, but after a few wines one night while dining with a client, Olivia – who was his senior assistant and, for the first time, travelled with him to meet this particular client – started talking suggestively to him. At first, the conversation was innocent enough. The client laughed and made a few comments, and everything was going great. But when the client left the two of them for night, the conversation became less innocent and ended up with another bottle of wine back in his room and a few hours of drunken, passionate sex. Now Olivia travelled with him every time and had started to become very clingy.

'Come back to bed.' Olivia stretched, and the covers slipped from her body, revealing her naked figure.

Stephen turned in his chair and just looked for a minute. He had feelings for Olivia but did not love her. 'I'm going to leave today. I need to go home.' He turned back to the table and opened his laptop to search for flights home.

Olivia sat up and pulled the sheet back up to cover herself. 'You can't leave,' she snapped 'You promised me a whole weekend away.

No work, no distractions, and definitely not your family getting in the way.' Sulking, she rolled over, waiting for Stephen to come over to her and give in.

Stephen kept his back turned to her. He hated it when she sulked like a child. It was seven in the morning where he was, which made it around ten back home. The next available flight left at ten, and with the time zone change, he would be home for dinner time, and he was certain arriving home on a Friday night instead of the Sunday would earn him brownie points.

Stephen booked the flight and shut down the laptop. He walked towards the bathroom but stopped at the foot of the bed. 'I'm taking a shower and then packing to leave. I need to be at the airport in an hour. If you want to stay for the weekend, feel free. I've already paid for the room.'

He didn't wait for a response and continued on his way to have a shower. He stood leaning against the wall with the hot water running over his head. He took in a few mouthfuls of water.

He knew Kat didn't deserve to be cheated on. She had done nothing wrong. All she wanted was to take care of her family the best she knew how. Guilt washed over him with the water from the shower, and Stephen knew from now on, he needed to support her more and do whatever it took to make their marriage work. He turned off the taps and dried quickly. He was now eager to get to the airport and get home to be with his family, including his father-in-law.

Still sulking, Olivia came into the bathroom and slithered past Stephen. She deliberately brushed her body against his, still trying to regain his attention. She muttered under her breath, muffled by the running water of the shower.

Stephen heard her, and rage filled his head. 'I'm sorry, you what? Did I just hear you correctly? You wish my family was dead?' He glared at Olivia with nothing but anger.

She looked back at him, tears starting to fill her eyes. 'Well, I know you are not going to leave her. You've told me that a thousand times, so if they were dead, then maybe I could have all your attention instead of a day here or there when we travel on business. I'm getting sick of being your substitute when you are away from home. I want all of you.' She turned away and let the water run over her face to hide the tears that started escaping.

Speechless and shaking his head, Stephen walked out of the bathroom. Olivia was right with one thing; he had made it very clear he was not going to leave his family for her and their relationship was a casual thing. Olivia had always said she understood and that was all she was interested in. He had noticed that she had started to change a few months ago when Olivia had started making lunchtime meetings but no clients were showing up. After the third no-show, she finally confessed that she just wanted to spend some time alone with him. He should have ended it right then and there, but he didn't; he let the affair continue. He was angry with himself right now for that. He needed to get home and confess and beg for forgiveness. Kat was the only woman he wanted to grow old with, and he would make sure he gave her more attention and stopped making it all about himself.

Stephen packed his suitcase and placed it by the door. He turned to yell out he was leaving, but Olivia was standing right behind him, wearing only a towel.

'I didn't mean it, Stephen. I don't really wish your family was dead. I was just sulking because I wasn't getting my own way.' She dropped her head, ashamed of what she had said.

Stephen put his hands on her shoulders and kissed the top of her head. 'We will talk about this next week, OK?'

He left the hotel room and took the lift to the lobby. The doorman flagged him a taxi, and he was on his way to the airport. He took his phone from his pocket and dialled Kat again – straight to voicemail. Now he was getting worried. She had been angry with him in the past but never had turned off her phone. He would try her two or three times, and then she would finally soften and answer, he would apologise and promise he would try harder, and she would forgive him. This routine had been theirs and had worked for over a decade.

Stephen sat silently in the back of the taxi, trying to recall the last time they had really fought. Usually, it was only ever small tiffs. He missed a school thing or was late home for dinner, but it was never anything big, not like this time. He had never heard her yell like that before. He didn't know she had it in her, and now she had turned off his phone. Something had to be wrong; he felt it in his bones.

The drive to the airport seemed to take longer than normal. Stephen was becoming anxious and irritable. His gut was telling him something wasn't right. Every time the taxi came to a stop, all he saw were happy couples in love. They were walking, holding hands, or sitting outside of coffee shops, eating breakfast. The guilt he was feeling was consuming him deep to his core, and he started thinking maybe he was still completely and totally in love with Kat. Maybe he had just got distracted when things got hectic at home, and it was easier to take the affections of another than do the hard work that was involved in raising a family and taking care of an aging old man.

He needed to be home right now. He needed to declare his love for her again. He needed to hold her, kiss her, smell the perfume she wore, which drove him crazy. *Hang on, my beautiful wife, I'm coming home.* His thoughts now had urgency to them. He felt invigorated, determined. He was coming home, and he would do anything and everything to make it the happiest family in the world.

At the airport at last, he thanked the driver and tipped him generously. The driver wished him a good day and drove off. Stephen stood out the front of the airport and looked up at a plane that had just taken off and started to disappear from sight. He smiled, pulled out the handle from his suitcase, and wheeled it through the large glass sliding doors, which opened and let him start his journey home.

Stephen loved the organised chaos of the airport – late people rushing around like the world was ending and the organised people who arrived with plenty of time, meandering through the terminal without a care in the world, unconsciously aggravating the late people by always being in the way. Stephen stood there for a moment, just watching it all go on around him. Adequately amused, he made his way to the check-in counter.

'Good morning, sir. Where are you off to this morning?' The bright-eyed attendant smiled sweetly at Stephen as he placed his ID on the counter.

'Home.' He chuckled.

The attendant, still smiling, took his ID and punched it into the system, confirmed his destination, and issued his boarding pass. He watched his suitcase wobble away on the conveyor belt, and he wandered to the security checkpoint. Patiently, he waited in line and then emptied his pockets into a tray and slid them to the scanning machine. As a seasoned traveller, he always found it amusing, watching new travellers pass through security – women being forced to remove shoes, men with belts and keys, and the grumpy old people who had opinions for every occasion and weren't afraid to share them.

Safely through security and sat at a table in the business lounge, Stephen tried Kat one more time. This time, it rang – but no answer. The relief was instant. She wasn't mad anymore. He looked at the time and realised she was at work and so couldn't answer until her lunch break, which would be after take-off. Stephen typed a text, apologising and begging for forgiveness. He didn't tell her he was on his way home. He wanted to surprise her and the kids and would get the biggest bouquet of flowers he could find on the way home and some sweets for the kids. He knew she would raise an eyebrow at the sweets, but listening to the sound of the excitement of the children at the sight of the treats would melt her heart, and she would not be angry anymore. She would come over to him and wrap her arms around his neck, and they would kiss tenderly, the way only a couple in true love could.

Breaking his daydream was the sound of his phone ringing. Excited at the sound, he answered it in hope that it was his wife, finally returning one of his hundreds of missed calls. He did not look at the caller ID, and his bubble was burst when it was the wrong female voice on the other end.

'I'm sorry, Stephen. I didn't mean what I said.' Olivia spoke softly, and he believed her words.

'I know you are, Liv, but I was also very clear up front that this would never be anything more than fun while we are away. I know you want more than that, and I can't give it to you, so for both our sakes, I think we need to end it so you can move on and find someone who can give you everything you need.'

Stephen could hear Olivia's breathing change, and he figured she was trying not to cry.

'I agree with you, Stephen,' Olivia finally responded, fighting back the tears. 'If you won't leave your wife for me, then I don't want to continue this relationship either.' She drew a deep breath in and let it out slowly. 'It's a pity though. I thought we were good together.'

Stephen ended the phone call and stared at his phone, relieved that he had ended his affair. He wanted to focus again on his family and get back what he had been slowly losing.

It wasn't too long after the conversation with Olivia when the crackled voice over the airport's loudspeakers called Stephen's flight. He gulped down the last mouthful of coffee, which had gone cold, collected his things, and left the comfort of the business lounge. He wandered down the terminal to his gate and lined up patiently, ready to board the plane. He was soon seated by the window, and excitement was building in his stomach. He plugged the provided headset into the armrest and jabbed at the buttons until his ears were filled with the sweet sound of jazz.

For a moment, he closed his eyes and pictured his wife and children sitting at the table, getting ready for dinner, when he came through the front door unannounced. He pictured his children yelling in excitement and running at him, hugging him tight. And then he pictured his wife, Katrina, her hair falling around her face, her eyes locking onto his, and her face lighting up, pleased to see him home early. She would walk over to him and throw her arms around his neck and hold him so tight, he would struggle to breathe. She would not loosen her grip, and he would hold her around her waist and let his face fall into her neck. He would smell the fragrance of her perfume, the same perfume she had been wearing since they got married.

She would whisper in his ear, 'Thank you for coming home early. I missed you so much.' Her warm breath would tickle his ear and send goose bumps all over his body.

Even the old man would shuffle past him, slap him on the back, and welcome him home. It would be perfect.

The movement of the plane being pushed backwards and the voice of an older lady over the speaker taking the passengers through the safety instructions brought Stephen back to reality. He watched and listened, even though he had flown a hundred times. The plane sped up and took to the sky, and Stephen was on his way home. Once the plane stopped ascending and the Fasten Seatbelt sign turned off, Stephen removed his iPad from his bag, which he had stashed under the seat in front of him, and set it up on the tiny table that folded down in front of him.

He had downloaded a couple of movies before the trip in an attempt to make the long flights less irritating. Olivia had kept him company on the way over, but she talked the entire time, and he could not escape from her endless conversation. Now he had a couple of hours to sit back and relax in peace and watch a movie that wasn't a chick flick or something for kids.

For ninety minutes, he sat quietly, enjoying his movie and completely distracted from the time. When it was finished, he turned off the screen and rubbed his eyes. He stared out of the window at the ground below and waited for the landscape to start changing from the barren country to the outer suburbs. Stephen noticed the plane starting to descend and felt the pressure starting to build in his ears. He fussed in the outer pocket of his bag and found a stick of chewing gum.

With the voice of the co-pilot filling the plane, giving the passengers the usual update of the local time and weather and confirmation they would be landing on time and thanking everyone for flying with them, Stephen's journey home was almost over. He looked back out the window and smiled as the ground was getting closer and closer, and he could start making out the streets and the buildings of the city.

With barely a bump, the pilot landed the plane and slowly steered it towards the terminal. A rush of excitement hit Stephen, and he started becoming impatient, waiting for that moment when the hostess opened the door and started her monotonous farewells to the hundred and fifty or so passengers. He was sat just three rows behind business class, so his wait wouldn't be long.

Free from the confinement of the aircraft, Stephen stretched as he walked up the tunnel and into the terminal. His pace quickened as he saw the sign for the toilets and quickly made a pit stop. Relieved, he walked with a purpose to the escalators that would take him towards the exit and baggage reclaim, surrounded once again by the passengers from his flight. They huddled around the conveyor belt that, in any minute, would start up, and bags would magically appear from behind the wall. Thinking luck was on his side, he spotted his bag in the first few that appeared, and feeling like the chosen one, he snatched it up and walked away from the crowd, who looked on in hope that they would be next.

Being the first to collect luggage also meant a shorter wait in the taxi line. Joining the back of line, which only had a few people who were smart enough to have only carry-on baggage, Stephen was almost immediately whisked away on his final leg home to his family.

One more quick stop. Stephen asked the driver to pull over at the minimart to get the sweets for his kids and flowers for his wife. He was now all set to arrive home. He checked the time again; it was a little after five, and he was just around the corner. The driver pulled up in front of the house, and for a moment, Stephen just stared.

The house looked perfect. Kat's car was in the drive, just where it should be, and now he was home, just where he should be. He paid the driver and exited the car. He retrieved his bag from the boot and stood there on the grass, flowers and sweets in one hand and his bags in the other. He took a nervous breath in and stepped forward towards the front door.

Stephen placed his two bags down by his feet and searched for his keys in his pocket. He put the key in the lock and turned. The screen door was already unlocked, which Stephen thought odd. His wife was very particular about keeping it locked for the safety of the kids. He pulled the door open and used his foot to hold it while he fumbled with his bags, flowers, and sweets.

The door closed with a bang behind him, and he figured that would get his family's attention. He was met with an eerie silence. A ball of nerves suddenly formed in his stomach, and he put the flowers down on top of his suitcase.

Still carrying the bag of sweets, he took a step towards the kitchen. Looking down, he saw the old man's hand on the floor inside the kitchen doorway. He dropped the sweets and rushed forwards, falling to his knees as he reached the lifeless hand.

Stephen grabbed at his hand and then felt for a pulse on the old man's neck. It was there, ever so faint. Stephen pulled his phone from his pocket and started dialling for help when he noticed the old man's clothes were covered in blood. Puzzled, he ran his eyes down his body and then to his feet, where he saw a blood trail. His heart started beating fast, and he felt weak. He let his eyes follow the red trail.

'*Kat!*' Stephen shrieked.

At the end of the trail, he saw his wife's body lying so still on the floor near the table. The room started spinning, and Stephen struggled to move his body. He could hear a voice in his ear, and with a dizzy head, he tried to focus on his words.

'Sir? What is the problem?'

Gasping for air and willing words to leave his mouth, Stephen stammered, 'Blood. It's everywhere. I think she's dead.'

Stephen couldn't contain his grief at the sight of his wife's mutilated body and started to cry. His whole body shook. The voice in his ear was talking, but he heard nothing but ringing in his ears. He dropped the phone, which landed on the old man's stomach, which caused him to groan faintly. Stephen heard the noise and leaned in close to his face. He could feel a soft breath on his cheek. He hurriedly picked up the phone and heard the voice still trying to talk to him.

'Sir, are you there?'

'Yes, I'm here. I need an ambulance. Please hurry. My father-in-law is still breathing but only just.' Talking to the voice, Stephen felt control coming back.

'OK, sir, I will dispatch an ambulance to you now. Can you tell me your name, please, sir?'

'Stephen.'

'Thank you, Stephen. And you said you thought someone was dead. A woman? Are you able to give me any more details?'

'My wife, Katrina.' Tears starting filling his eyes again, and sadness filled his chest. 'She has been stabbed. There is so much blood on the floor.'

'OK, sir, help will be with you soon. Is there anyone else in the house?'

Stephen sat up, and a cold chill surged through his bones. 'My children!' He scrambled to his feet. His legs were like concrete and didn't want to cooperate. He clung to the door frame and willed his legs to work.

'Sir, are your children OK? Help is only a minute away. You should be hearing sirens any moment, OK?'

Stephen made it to Paige's room, and the door was open. He couldn't see her inside, and nothing looked out of place. With heavy steps, he got to Nathan's door. It was closed, and as Stephen put his hand on the doorknob, he was overcome with fear. He didn't want to open the door. He didn't want to face the horror. Fighting with his emotions, he knew he had to go in. There was a chance that his children were both in there, and he needed to help them.

In the distance, he could hear the faint wail of the sirens. Help was almost here. Stephen opened the door with force and stepped in, praying with everything he had that he would see his children sitting quietly in a corner, waiting for him to rescue them.

The room was dark. The curtains had been closed, and he could barely make anything out. He turned on the light and saw his son lying on the bed.

Stephen rushed over and went to pick him up. 'Nathan, wake up. It's Dad. I'm home now.'

With a sorrowful whimper, Stephen knew his son was gone. He felt a cold, wet sensation coming from his son's body. He pulled him in tight and held onto him. He cried for his son.

The sirens were loud now; they were out the front of the house. Stephen heard a banging on the front door, followed by a deep male voice yelling his name. Stephen gently placed his boy back down on the bed and stood up. He slowly walked out of Nathan's bedroom, tears running down his face, and stared at the ground.

The world around him seemed to be faded into the background. There was a scurry of people standing before him. A police officer came up to him and started talking. Stephen just stared at her face but heard nothing of what she had said. Behind her, he saw two paramedics working on his father-in-law. He had an oxygen mask over his face. One paramedic got up and disappeared towards the front door.

The female police officer took Stephen by the elbow and led him away from Nathan's room and down to the lounge. A male police officer walked past and up the hallway and yelled something back. Everyone stopped talking, and as Stephen looked around, he saw a sea of faces staring at him. The female officer, who was still trying to get his attention, picked up a photo from the side table and showed it to Stephen. A rush of blood went to his head, and without warning, Stephen leapt to his feet.

'Paige! My daughter. Did anyone find her?'

He pushed past the police officer and past the paramedic who was coming back in the door with a gurney and ran up the hallway and into Paige's room. He fell to his knees and started scrambling on the floor, looking for her under her bed and then flicking up everything that was on the floor. He yanked open her wardrobe and started pulling things out, hoping she had buried herself under something.

Two police officers burst into her room and tried to pull Stephen away, telling him not to touch anything. He got back to his feet and starting yelling Paige's name, hoping if she was hiding, she would come out. The two officers restrained Stephen as he thrashed his arms, trying to get away to continue his search for his daughter. They forcefully escorted him out of the house, where another paramedic wrapped him in a foil blanket and sat him down in the back of an ambulance.

The female officer came over to Stephen and stood in front of him and waited for him to calm down. 'Stephen?' She spoke softly. 'We will search the house for your daughter, OK? I am going to need you to stay out here though as the detectives will be here in a minute, and they need to see your house exactly as it was when you arrived home. Can you do that for me? Can you please stay here?'

Stephen was exhausted. He did not have the energy to fight with her. He nodded in agreeance and just sat there, watching the circus that was now his house. As he looked around, he could see all the neighbours forming a huddle over near the police tape that had now surrounded his yard. They were staring at him and whispering. He could feel their beady eyes on him. He pulled the blanket tighter around his shivering body and closed his eyes, hoping this was all just a horrific nightmare.

Chapter 29

Det Alice Forbes was thirty-nine and had joined the police force in her early twenties. Her ambition was to be the best homicide detective in the country. She craved the hunt and quickly got herself the reputation of being the fiercest detective in her precinct. She was unmarried, which didn't bother her, and she never felt as if she needed to explain her spinster life to anyone. Alice never wanted children of her own, but when a case presented itself with a child, whether they be the victim or lose a parent, she took on a whole other personality that didn't know how to stop until she had her monster behind bars.

Standing at only five feet and five inches, she felt she needed to have a strong, outspoken personality so she was never overlooked or underestimated. Although she was unmarried, she did have a boyfriend of three years, Josh. Alice adored him and appreciated how supportive he was of her very demanding career. He never made her feel as if she needed to choose between the two, and when she needed to take time after a case to let it all out and collapse in a heap, he would always be there to wipe away the tears and hold her hand as she got to her feet again.

Alice had no siblings, and her mother had passed away when she was a small child. Her father was her hero and had sacrificed everything to make sure she had a wonderful childhood. Alice always smiled when she thought back that far and how her father had done an amazing job as both mother and father. She could not have written a more perfect profile of a parent who went above and beyond for their child. She felt blessed at her upbringing.

Alice sat there, staring at the photo board, five faces looking back at her. She didn't understand it. *What goes through someone's mind to be able to do this? Such rage. Such hatred for women.*

She had been placed on this case two years ago when the first victim was discovered. It was her big chance to prove herself as a detective. It was all she had ever wanted to be ever since she could remember. She wasn't someone who was following in her father's footsteps, definitely not; he was a financial planner. She shuddered at the thought of sitting at a desk all day, looking at numbers and being responsible for other people's money. This was not Alice; she wanted to save the world from monsters.

But this monster was eluding her, and her frustration was starting to show. Alice rubbed her brow and continued staring at the five women who were brutally murdered by her monster. *Why you?* She was struggling to find the connection among the victims.

Alice picked up her ever-growing folder and started at the beginning.

> Victim 1 – Sophia Williams
> Aged 32
> Occupation – Personal Assistant
> Found on the kitchen floor of the victim's own house. Confirmed death by multiple stab wounds. Ligature marks on her wrists show she had been restrained while being attacked. No signs of sexual assault.
> Boyfriend cleared as CCTV showed him at the time of death at a petrol station and then the gym as per his statement.
> Statement from family indicate she was a quiet person who kept to herself. Not many friends. Not very active on social media. Worked long hours. Liked by all at workplace.

Victim 2 – Emma Taylor

Aged 20

Occupation – Student

Found on the dining room floor of the victim's parents' house. Confirmed death by multiple stab wounds. Ligature marks around wrists and ankles show she was restrained when attacked. No signs of sexual assault.

No boyfriend or love interest. Parents out of town on vacation.

Popular student at local college. Very active on social media but nothing too concerning. Studying journalism.

Victim 3 – Ava Johnson

Aged 20

Occupation – Student

Found on dining room floor of victim 2 parents' house. Confirmed death by multiple stab wounds. Ligature marks around wrists and ankles show she was restrained when attacked. No signs of sexual assault. Noting that the stab wounds were more forceful than victim 2. Wrong place, wrong time, perhaps. Thinking not the intended victim.

Victim 4 – Mia Anderson

Occupation – Vet Nurse

Aged 26

Found in hotel room. Confirmed death by multiple stab wounds. No ligature marks but trauma to head. Appears victim was knocked unconscious and not restrained. Bruising on side of face shows signs of being a fist? Beaten unconscious and then stabbed? Change in pattern?

Statement from family states she was in hotel because of renovations at own residence. Very social with no boyfriend. Mother hesitant to admit victim was gay. Active on social media with nothing of concern.

Victim 5 – Lily Wilson
Aged 37
Occupation – Florist
Found bound to bed in victim's own residence. Confirmed death by multiple stab wounds. Report states that she died slowly. Stab wounds were not deep, and some of the first had started to scab. Report indicated victim was stabbed over a twelve- to fourteen-hour period. No signs of sexual assault.

Statement from family indicates not very social, with small group of close friends. Recent break-up with boyfriend who was cleared as was in another state at time of death.

Alice read her summary at least ten times a day. She could understand what she was missing. There was never any physical evidence left behind of the monster, no DNA on any of the victims, no forced entry. It was like they all just let him in.

Alice had cross-referenced all the victim's phone bills, with no numbers crossing over, either outbound or incoming. They all had different utility companies, different Internet providers, and none of them went to the same supermarkets. The only thing they had in common was they lived in the same city.

Her monster had a type though. All the victims were brunette with medium to long hair. They were all of slim build and had pretty features. Alice caught a glimpse of her reflection in the window and raised an eyebrow. She could easily fit his type. Her chocolate-brown hair was pulled back into a ponytail at the nape of her neck, and she worked out at the gym three to four times a week. She needed to stay in shape for the job. If she could just find the connection, she thought she could bait him.

Alice spun in her chair away from the board and back to the table where all the crime-scene photos were spread out. She picked up photos one at a time, looking at every detail. There had to be something there that would give her a clue. Lost in thought, Alice was startled by her phone. She fished under the photos for her phone and answered it hastily.

'Detective Forbes.'

She listened for a few minutes and jotted down an address and then ended the call. She put the phone in her pocket and then leaned on the table with her head hung. She heard footsteps enter the room and looked up at the man who stood before her.

'You all right, Alice?' It was her mentor and oldest friend at work. Det Leo Mason had been a detective forever and had seen what he thought was everything.

'Another one, Leo, this time two victims. That makes six in two years. Every time he takes longer with them. I just can't imagine what they go through, being cut up the way he does.'

'Deep breath, Alice. They all make mistakes eventually. I know that doesn't help our new vic, but maybe this time, he left you something behind. Want me to come with you?'

'Nah, it's OK, thanks. You go home, and I will call you if I need anything.'

Alice walked out the building with Leo and waved him goodbye. She started her car and pulled up the address on her GPS.

'This time, I will get you.'

Chapter 30

Alice drove alone to the new crime scene. She was tired from another long day of looking over all the photos and witness statements from the previous murders. She pulled into the street and looked around. It was a nice neighbourhood, nothing fancy, but all the houses looked neat with tidy yards. She parked a few houses away from the crime scene and got out of her car. She could see the circus that had formed around the house, and the media was already here. She walked towards the house and caught the eye of a young police officer who was doing her best to keep the crowd and media under control. She forced a smile as she approached the caution tape, and the young officer lifted it to let Alice in.

Alice paused for a moment before walking farther. She saw the look on the girl's face, and Alice knew that she had been inside and seen what the monster had done. Alice placed a hand on her shoulder but said nothing. There was nothing that could be said to make the young officer feel any better. Alice knew every time you saw the scene of a murder, you lost a little bit of yourself, and you had to work hard not to let it turn you bitter.

As Alice approached the front door, two crime-scene investigators walked out, carrying with them sealed bags containing evidence. They exchanged pleasantries, and they told Alice what they had taken. One bag had the knife that was lying next to the female victim, and the other had the cable ties that had been used. Alice was hoping with everything she had that this time, there would be fingerprints on something.

Taking a deep breath, Alice stepped inside. The air felt cold in here, and she could hear soft voices. She continued in and stopped just inside the kitchen. A more senior-looking officer came over to Alice and introduced himself. For a moment, neither of them spoke; they just looked down at the white sheet that was covering the body.

'You ready, Detective Forbes? I will take you through what we found.'

Alice looked up and sighed heavily. 'Yeah, I'm ready. Let's go.'

'Where we are standing now is where an elderly man was found lying on the floor, having suffered a heart attack. A middle-aged man who identified himself as Stephen Elliot was the first on the scene. He called for an ambulance. He said his father-in-law was still alive when he got here.'

They stepped into the kitchen a little, being careful not to step in any of the blood trails. Almost on tiptoe, they moved closer to the sheet, and Alice stood at the far end and crouched down. She lifted back the sheet to reveal the victim's head and shoulders.

'Victim is Katrina Elliot. Aged forty-four. Mother of two. Stabbed multiple times, and at this point, I'm assuming she died from loss of blood from the wounds. Husband found her but did not disturb the body. He said he went to find his children, but as you can see, someone has touched her. There are unusual patterns in the blood.'

Alice raised an eyebrow at the officer. 'There were children in the house? And the father? This is new. If it is the same person who was responsible for the other five murders, he has completely changed his choice of victim. All the others have been on their own in the house. And now a family unit? It doesn't make sense. Where are the children now?'

'Come with me.'

Sgt Michael Avery ushered Alice away from the kitchen and up the hallway. He walked past the first door and stopped at the second. He pushed it all the way open and let Alice step past him and into the room. The curtains were closed, and the room was dark and eerie. The light was switched on, and Alice felt her heart drop into her stomach. A white sheet covered the bed. For the first time at a crime scene, she felt tears building up, and her throat closed up. She took several breaths, and controlling her emotions, she hesitantly went to the bed and pulled back the sheet.

There lying before her was the body of a young boy. She estimated him to be nine or ten at the most. She ran her eyes over the body and saw the red bloodstained middle of the T-shirt. Her heart broke, and she gently laid the sheet back over him.

Alice turned away from the boy, and a heavy sadness filled her chest. She looked up at Michael, and he had the same look on his face. He started to talk, but only a crackled word came out. He cleared his throat and tried again.

'A single stab wound to the belly. There is some bruising around his mouth and nose so it appears that he may have been suffocated at the same time. The coroner will confirm more details for you once he takes the body for examining.'

Alice struggled to find words. 'The other child?'

Michael gave Alice a strange look and then walked away from the boy's room back down the hall and stopped at the first door she had seen. He opened the door and stood back, allowing Alice to go in.

She looked around and didn't see anything. She glanced sideways at Michael. 'What am I looking at? There is no body in here, and the room looks undisturbed.'

'Exactly.'

'What do you mean? Where is the girl?'

'We don't know. We have searched the house and the garden, and she isn't here. We spoke with all the neighbours, hoping she had got away, but none of them have seen her. The neighbour over the road remembers both children coming home after school on Thursday as they both said hello to her on their way back from the bus, and no one has seen her since.' Michael stopped, letting Alice look around the room a little. 'And from what we have found so far, there is no evidence that she has been harmed in any way. She's just not here. Maybe your guy took her.'

Alice considered what Michael had just said but shook her head. 'Why would he take a small child? There has been no indication at any other crime scene that he is interested in little girls.' Alice rubbed her eyes, knowing that she was in for a long night. 'Where is the husband?'

'He went with the ambulance to the hospital with his father-in-law. Two officers are at the hospital with him, taking a statement about the girl so we can log her as a missing person.'

'Thanks, Sergeant. I think I will head over to the hospital now and speak with him while the coroner finishes up here. I will come back tomorrow and do what I need to here if that's OK.'

'Sure. I will be here for the next couple of hours helping collect evidence and take statements from the neighbours.'

Alice thanked Michael and headed back to the front door. She looked over her shoulder and watched for a second as the coroner lifted the body from the kitchen floor and placed it into a body bag. Anger started to build in Alice. Her priority now was to find the little girl. *Why did you take her? I don't get it.*

The hospital was a fifteen-minute drive from the murder scene, but it seemed to be taking a lot longer. Alice pulled up close to the front door of the hospital. She got out of the car and checked her reflection in the window. She tucked her shirt into her pants and grabbed her jacket from the back seat. Alice believed that the way she presented herself made a difference to the way people would talk and open up to her.

At the reception counter, Alice flashed her ID to the security guard, who immediately took her back through the emergency area where the father-in-law was being treated. The security guard stopped at the doctor's station and introduced Alice to the doctor who was looking after the old man.

'He's stable and should make a full recovery. We have him resting over here until we can get a bed for him upstairs.'

The doctor led Alice over to a curtained-off cubicle and pulled the curtain back slightly to allow Alice to go in. The husband was sitting on a hard plastic chair next to the bed and took his head from his hands when he heard them enter. Alice introduced herself and shook his hand. The sound of talking stirred the old man, who heavily blinked as he tried to open his eyes.

'Mr Elliot, I would like to speak with you about what happened, but first, I need to ask your father-in-law a few questions.'

'The other police officers already took a statement from me.'

'I know, sir, but my only priority right now is to find your daughter, so I'm going to have to ask you both questions, and I need to ask them tonight. The longer we wait, the more the chances of us getting her back before the man who took her disappears altogether reduce.'

Stephen sat down and nodded at Alice. He knew she was right, and he just wanted his baby girl back in his arms.

Alice sat in the other chair next to the bed and made eye contact with the old man. 'Mr Jenner? I'm Det Alice Forbes, and I need to ask you some questions about your granddaughter, OK?'

The old man nodded, and a tear escaped the corner of his eye, and Alice watched it as it slowly ran down his cheek. Alice's heart stopped beating for a moment as she saw the pain in the old man's eyes. She knew this was going to be painful, but she needed to know what he saw if she had any chance of finding this little girl alive.

'Mr Jenner, can you tell me everything you saw today?'

Alice had her notebook ready and waited for the old man to tell his story. He wiggled in bed, trying to sit up. Stephen stood and helped him and then sat back down. Alice gave him a nod of appreciation and let the old man start to talk.

'I was dropped home by my driver from the nursing home a bit before four o'clock. The front door was unlocked, which I thought was strange as my daughter always kept it locked for the safety of the children.'

Stephen nodded in agreeance, and Alice wrote in her notebook.

'There was no noise coming from the house, which made me worried. My Kat is always singing to herself or talking with the children. There is always noise. But not today, so I got worried. I went into the kitchen and saw her lying on the floor, all covered in blood and not moving. I went over to her and tried to save her, but it was too late.'

The old man stopped talking, and Alice looked up from her notebook. He was struggling to breathe as the grief took over. He started to sob, and Alice could feel his pain. The look on his face told her how much he loved his daughter, and now he had to remember what she looked like after being brutally murdered. She felt for him, but she had to make him retell the story. She hated this part of the job.

'Mr Jenner? I'm so sorry to make you do this, but can you tell me what happened next?'

Stephen pulled a bunch of tissues from the box sitting on the small shelf above the old man's bed and handed them to him. The old man wiped at his face and noisily blew his nose. He sighed and looked at Alice.

'I went to find my grandchildren next, but I couldn't get up from the floor. There was so much blood, and I couldn't get any grip, so I tried to crawl, but I got so much pain in my chest, I just couldn't move anymore.'

The old man stopped again. He was taking big breaths and had turned a greyish colour. The machine next to him started to beep, and a nurse came bursting in and pushed past Alice. The nurse put a mask over the old man's mouth and then put her fingers to his throat and started counting.

'Mr Jenner, what happened to your granddaughter?' Alice pleaded with him for an answer as the nurse started moving her out of the cubicle.

The old man pulled at the mask and stammered, 'He took her. He had her by the hand and walked out with her.'

Alice was pushed backwards as another nurse and the doctor took over the cubicle.

Stephen stepped out from the chaos and stood next to Alice. 'You are going to find Paige, aren't you?'

Alice looked into Stephen's eyes. They were full of hurt and pleading with her. This was the first time she had heard the little girl's name said aloud.

'I'm going to do everything I possibly can.' She spoke with a new determination. 'Mr Elliot, can I buy you a coffee? You can tell me everything you can about Paige.'

Stephen was beyond exhausted and followed Alice away from the emergency area. There was a café in the front lobby, and Alice found a table tucked away in the back so they were away from all the noise. She opened her notebook again and waited for Stephen to drink some of his coffee before she started with her questions.

'Mr Elliot, are you OK to start now?' she spoke softly to Stephen as she didn't want to come across as pushy, but she needed to get started; every minute counted.

'Yes.'

'Please tell me about Paige. What she looks like, the way she talks, how tall she is. Anything you can.'

Stephen rubbed his eyes and huffed. He had just finished a report with the other officers, and now he had to tell it all over again. 'She is seven and about four feet tall. Light brown hair, about shoulder length. Missing a couple of front teeth. Speaks very independently and is always right.' He laughed to himself. 'Just like her mother.'

Tears started building up in his eyes, and he no longer had the coping skills to hide them. He pulled his phone from his pocket and started scrolling through photos. He stopped on one and slid the phone across the table to Alice. 'This was taken a few weeks ago.'

Alice held up the phone and looked at the picture. She was a sweet little girl. Sunshine lit her face, and she looked like she didn't have a care in the world. *Why would she?* Alice thought. *She's seven.* 'Would you mind if I sent this picture to my phone?'

Stephen shook his head. 'Go for it.'

'Thanks. That way, my number will be in your phone if you need me. Do you have somewhere you can go tonight? I'm sorry to ask, but we won't be able to let you into your house for a while while we do our investigation.'

Stephen's mind went straight to Olivia. He knew she would let him in, no issues, except he had left her at the hotel several hours away. His parents had passed, so his only family left was the old man. 'Not that I can think of. There is a hotel near the office my clients stay at when they are in town, so I will just go there.'

Alice stood from the table and collected her notebook and pen. 'At least let me give you a lift there.'

Stephen didn't argue and followed Alice from the hospital lobby to her car. He quietly gave directions to the hotel and thanked her as he got out of the car. He didn't look back, and Alice watched him disappear into the hotel.

She sat back in the seat of her car and rubbed her eyes. She had no idea where she would start looking for his daughter, but she would give it everything she had. It was after midnight, and she knew she had to go home and get some sleep. She would be up in a few hours, and her hunt for little Paige would begin.

Chapter 31

Alice didn't sleep much and was up and ready to leave for work by half past six. She forced down some breakfast, knowing that it would be late into the afternoon before she would probably eat again. While finishing her morning coffee, which was an essential part of her morning routine, Alice heard her phone buzz in her jacket pocket. She pulled it out and couldn't help but smile. Her boyfriend of three years was checking in on her. She opened the text.

'Morning babe, saw the news last night and you were in the background so I know you are busy. Wanted to say I love you and ring me if you need to talk. Hopefully we can still have dinner later tonight.'

Even after all this time, Alice felt blessed to have such an understanding partner. They didn't live together, which she was totally OK with as he told her he would feel like all he would do was sit around, waiting for her to come home. With them not living together and making sure they had lunch or dinner several times a week, he said he would appreciate their time together more. And for them, it worked.

She replied, 'Hey there. Definitely on for dinner, can we make it at 8? This time a kid was taken and today is critical in office. Love you.'

Alice inhaled the last of the coffee and grabbed her keys from the bench. Her phone buzzed again.

'Oh shit! If you want I can bring something to office just to make sure you eat and then leave you to it. Let's say 6.'

'Thank you. I would appreciate that.'

Alice slipped the phone back in her pocket and pulled the door closed behind her. In the car, the new murder was all over the radio, with the added detail of the missing child. At times, she hated that her job was such public knowledge, and the longer a case went, the more her work was scrutinised. But this time, she was hoping her leak to the media of Paige's abduction would work in her favour as now people would be looking for her. She was relying on the public's thirst for becoming the hero that saved the little girl.

Alice arrived at the station at seven, and already, there was plenty of noise. Her office was up one flight of stairs and halfway down the corridor. By the time she entered the room with the photo board and the table covered in files, there was already a new file sitting on top. The crime-scene crew had already created a folder of photos and notes. She was still missing the coroner's report, but you didn't need to be a genius to work out the cause of death on the two new victims.

Alice opened her notes and added three new entries.

> Victim 6 – Katrina Elliot
> Aged 44
> Occupation – Admin Assistant
> Found on kitchen floor of own home. Multiple stab wounds. Ligature marks around wrists and ankles. Bruising and some wounds starting to heal indicate victim was tortured over a couple of days. No signs of sexual assault. Appears he took his time with this one.

> Victim 7 – Nathan Elliot
> Aged 10
> Found in bedroom of own home. One stab wound to belly and bruising around mouth and nose indicate he was held down forcefully. No signs of any other trauma.

> Victim 8 – Paige Elliot
> Aged 7
> Missing.

Alice closed her notebook and leaned back in her chair and stared up at the ceiling. She had never worked missing persons before but knew time was critical if you wanted to find them still in the land of the living. She needed to go to the house and look at it all for herself. Photos didn't always show everything. She made a list of things she needed to be done while she was gone and would have one of the officers help her.

As she walked through the station, she spotted a young officer who was on desk duty after injuring his ankle chasing a shoplifter a few days ago. She felt for the guy as someone caught it on their phone as he slipped down the curb and fell face first on the street. It was all over the Internet.

Alice walked over and sat on the corner of his desk. 'Hey. How's the ankle, Matty?' She tried not to laugh, but she had seen the footage, and it was funny.

The young guy looked up to her and was starting to see the funny side of it. 'It's getting there. I hear you got an interesting twist to your serial-killer case.'

'Yeah. Seven-year-old girl taken. I need your help. I really need to get to the house and start looking around but need some stuff done here. I need phone records of the female vic's mobile and landline. Again, there was no forced entry, so she must have known her killer. Can you also check out the husband? We know that he was away on business, but it could be someone he knows.'

'I'll get right on it for you, Alice. Ring me if you need anything else. I'm not going anywhere.'

He smiled at Alice and took the paper she had the numbers written down on. Alice smiled in appreciation and walked away from his desk as she spotted Leo coming her way.

'Morning, Alice. You get much sleep? You look like shit.'

'Gee, thanks, Leo.' She laughed at his honesty. 'I got some but too many questions bouncing around my head. I'm heading over to the house. Want to come with me? Thinking I need a few sets of eyes on this one.'

'Yeah, I will meet you over there in half an hour. Just need to file a report real quick.'

Leo patted her shoulder as he walked off, and she knew she needed his help.

Back at the house, Alice slipped under the caution tape and flashed her ID at the officer who was standing in the front yard. The hunt for evidence had resumed in the early hours of the morning, and Alice was there to see and hear about everything that had been collected.

There were several rooms in the house she did not go into yesterday. She started at the front door and went systematically through the house. She stopped in the master bedroom for a long time. She stood at the foot of the bed and sighed heavily. What she saw made her skin crawl. At the corner of each bed were long pieces of fabric that Alice knew had been used to restrain the woman. The sheets were stained with blood, and it looked like they had been slept in.

Behind Alice, a woman dressed in protective clothing and gloves was waiting to take the bed linen away. The blood needed to be tested for DNA, and Alice prayed that this time, he had left something behind. Before Alice let her do her job, she crouched at the corner of the bed and looked at the fabric and the way it was tied. It was loose and poorly tied.

This was never going to hold her for long. She could have easily pulled at this. She went to the head of the bed and saw each corner was loose. *Did he want her to get away? Or was she so badly injured, it didn't really matter?* She had so many questions. Every other victim had such bad bruising from where they had been restrained. This just didn't seem right.

Alice put one hand on the ground to push herself up when her fingers touched something under the bed. She leaned right over and saw a mobile phone in the shadows. She sat up and beckoned the woman over. 'Has this phone been documented yet?'

'I don't think so, Detective. Let me go get the camera and a bag.'

Less than a minute later, the woman returned and took several photographs of the phone and then picked it up and placed it into a bag to take to the station to log in the evidence register.

Alice moved to the next room. It was completely untouched. She opened the wardrobe and guessed it belonged to the father. Nothing was out of place. She left and went to Paige's room.

On the edge of the girl's bed was a blood smear. She looked at the linen and noticed that it appeared clean and unstained except for the edge. *Did Mum come in here looking for her?*

From where she stood, something caught her eye. She went around the bed and stood near the window. There were plastic beads in the track, and as the sun hit the window, it made them shimmer. She got her pen from her jacket pocket and tried to prise one out. They were in there tight. *If they had been dropped by a child, they would be sitting on top, but it's like they have been pushed in.*

Lost in her thoughts about the beads, Alice didn't hear Leo enter the room.

'You find something?'

Alice looked up with a puzzled expression. 'Not sure. There are beads wedged in the window track, which I find unlikely done by a child. Not sure if I'm grasping at something here, but that would make it almost impossible for a child to open the window and escape.'

Leo came up beside her and looked. He nodded. They both left Paige's room and walked to the boy's. There was a ruler stuck in the window track.

'He was prepared for the children. There is no way they could have easily got the windows open. Maybe he had no intention of killing them.'

Alice was thinking out loud, and Leo went along with the story.

'So why pick a family then? If the children weren't part of his fantasy?'

'And don't forget, her father lived here too, and he was not attacked.'

The two detectives wandered around the house, trying to work out what was so special about this woman that he would suddenly take on a whole family. They spent several hours going over every inch of the house, but nothing seemed out of place.

Frustrated, Alice went back to the master bedroom. Leo followed, curious as to what she was doing. He stood in the doorway and watched her go into the walk-in robe. She pulled clothes from the hangers and placed them carefully in a bag she had found on the top shelf. She walked back to Leo, who was leaning on the door frame.

'I'm sure Mr Elliot would like a change of clothes.'

'Sounds like a reason for us to go and talk to him again.'

Alice smiled at Leo. He always got her, and she rarely had to explain herself. 'You coming with me?'

'Yeah, I think I will. I will let you do the talking, and I will observe and see if he is telling us the truth.'

Chapter 32

The hotel door was answered by a woman. Alice raised an eye and introduced herself and Leo. The woman stepped aside and let the two detectives in. They found Stephen sitting on the small couch at the end of the hotel room. Alice placed the bag on the bed and waited for Stephen to gesture for her to sit on the chair at the desk.

'I got you some clothes from your house. Thought you might like a change.'

'Thank you.'

'Dumb question, but how are you feeling, and did you get any sleep?'

'I feel numb. I don't want to accept that my wife and son are gone and my little girl has been taken.'

Alice paused and let Stephen breathe before she asked him another question.

'Excuse me, miss,' Leo started at the woman who was standing near him. 'Can you please tell me who you are?'

Taken aback by the bluntness of the tone in Leo's voice, Olivia became defensive. She crossed her arms tight across her chest and glared at him. 'Olivia, and I am Stephen's second at work.'

'Well, then I'm going to have to ask you to leave as we need to talk to Mr Elliot alone.'

'What? You can't make me leave. Stephen, tell them that I can stay.' Olivia stared right at Leo. 'He needs me now.'

'Sorry, but you need to wait outside.' Leo used his size to make Olivia step backwards towards the door. 'We won't be long.' And he shut the door on her.

With Olivia out of the room, Alice resumed her conversation with Stephen. 'Mr Elliot, please tell me about your wife. Where she worked. Was she part of any clubs or went to the gym?'

Stephen stared at the floor and then closed his eyes. A smile crept onto his lips, and a tear rolled down his cheek. Sitting so close to him, Alice could feel his pain, and her chest felt heavy.

'She was amazing. She worked part time and was so good, every few months they tried to get her to go full time. She refused while the kids were still young, and she also was caring for her father. She was so dedicated to her family, she didn't do anything that didn't involve them. The kids played sports, so she was always at the school, attending games or plays or whatever they were up to.'

'When she was at work, who looked after her father?'

Stephen looked up, curious as to the question. 'He went to the nursing home not far from home. They do respite care and helped out whenever Kat needed them, but she refused to let him live there.'

Alice looked at Leo, who took down the details of the nursing home. They would go there and ask about the father.

'Is there anything else we should know, Mr Elliot?'

'No, I don't think so.' Stephen moved over and grabbed Alice by the hand. 'Please find my daughter, Detective. Please.' His breathing was heavy, and his voice shook as he pleaded with Alice. 'I need my baby girl to come home alive to me.'

His voice broke, and tears rolled down his face, and Alice couldn't be near him anymore without crying with him. She stood and stepped away, pulling her hand back.

'We are going to do everything we can. Please know that.'

In silence, the detectives left the hotel room and the hotel. They stood beside their cars, and Leo let Alice compose herself. He could see this missing child was getting to her.

'We will get her back, Alice. I know we will.'

'Thanks, Leo. I needed you here for that today. Meet you back at the station?'

'Yeah. I will grab some lunch and bring it to you, OK? You want to go speak to the coroner on your way back?'

Alice hadn't thought about that; she was too distracted by the heartbreak of Stephen. She took a deep breath and nodded. 'Yep, I will go see what he has to say. See you back in a while then.'

Alice held her hand up and waved as Leo drove off. It was time to go and meet Katrina and her son Nathan.

It was quiet in the coroner's office. Alice stood waiting to be buzzed through to the cold white room at the back of the building. It smelled of disinfectant, and the air was chilled. A shiver ran through Alice as she followed the medical examiner over to the first of the two tables.

'Detective Forbes, this is Katrina.' He flipped open a folder and started reading. 'Forty-four-year-old female. Confirmed time of death, approximately 4:00 p.m. yesterday.'

He stopped reading and placed the folder on the bench behind Alice. He stood next to the body and pulled the white sheet back, revealing the body of Katrina Elliot. She had been washed and was now lying on her back on a stainless steel table naked for Alice to look at.

Alice started at her head. There was a clear bite mark on her neck. 'Doctor, I assume this was swabbed for DNA.'

'Yes, and I sent the sample off to check to see if there are any matches in the system for you. They will send the results direct to you.'

'Thank you. Tell me what you found.'

'Besides the bite mark, she had four small puncture wounds here in the top of her arm.' He pointed to Katrina's right arm. 'I would say it was from a fork if you have a look at the perfect spacing between the holes.'

Alice leaned in and looked. She stood back up and watched as the examiner rolled Katrina slightly to one side.

'See there on the back of her shoulder? She suffered a stab wound. I have taken a casting, and it matches the knife that was taken from next to the body.' He gently laid her back. 'So does this deep wound in her thigh.'

Alice stepped sideways down the table to see the wound in Katrina's thigh.

The ME picked up one of Katrina's hands and ran his gloved finger over the bruising and cuts on her wrist. 'Consistent with the wounds found on the previous victims. Cable ties were taken from this scene too. Mrs Elliot struggled. The wounds are deep on both her wrists and ankles. She was a fighter. There are three other puncture wounds. One on her side here, not very deep and so wouldn't have done too much damage, and then two in her belly. There were the fatal ones. They are deep. She lost a fair bit of blood from her thigh and all the other wounds put together, but then the two in her belly finished her off.'

Alice sighed and crossed her arms. She had no idea what this woman went through while she was being sliced up and trying to get away, presumably to rescue her children. Her stomach cramped for a moment while she tried to imagine the terror she must have felt. Shaking her head, she turned to face the second table.

The ME paused and let Alice deal with her thoughts before he continued. 'If it is of any comfort, she wasn't raped. There were no injuries to her genitals.'

Alice pursed her lips and nodded. She was grateful for that. None of the women were sexually assaulted.

'This is Nathan. He was ten years old. I found some light bruising on his face, so I'm guessing at some point, he put up a fight. He didn't suffer like the others. The bruising around the nose and mouth show the perpetrator held his hand over his face, holding him down while he inflicted a single stab wound to his belly. It is deep and jagged, so maybe the knife was twisted. He would have died within a minute or so.'

Alice hovered over the boy's body and felt a numbness in her throat. *So you tried to help your mother and sister? Brave boy.*

Alice turned away and picked up the folder from the table. She walked solemnly to the door and looked back at the two bodies lying there, still and cold, and prayed that Paige wouldn't be joining her mother and brother.

Chapter 33

Alice sat at her desk in a room that was getting crowded. There were three more faces on her board, and now eight innocent people stared back her, demanding she get justice for them.

She stood up and walked to the board with a crisp new file in her hand from her recent visit to the coroner's office. She opened the cover and looked down at the drawn outline of a body covered in little crosses showing where Katrina had been mutilated. She flipped the page over and started reading the notes. For a moment, she closed her eyes and let the image of Katrina's lifeless body, lying on the stainless steel bench, come back to her vividly.

She let her mind start at her head and work her way down. There was bruising on her face where she had been hit. There was a bite mark on her neck and four small puncture wounds on top of one of her arms. The coroner was convinced it was from a fork based on the size of the marks and the way they were spaced. There were multiple cuts over her abdomen and a deep puncture wound in one of her thighs. Both her wrists and ankles were badly bruised and cut where she had been restrained by the cable ties found at the scene. None of the other victims had so many different wounds. They were all stabbed with one knife. *So why did he do so much damage to you? Why were you so different?*

Alice looked back up at the photo of Katrina that she had taken from her husband's phone and just stared at her. She fit the type the killer had in looks, but the family thing was still odd. Her eyes shifted to the boy. He was killed swiftly and without much fuss. Alice was convinced that killing the boy was not part of his plan. *So why take the girl? Why not leave her in her bedroom?*

Fatigue was setting in, and it had been about twenty-four hours now since the girl was taken, and she needed to find clues soon. Statistically, she was running out of time to find her alive.

Alice heard laughing coming from the corridor. She went to the doorway and looked in the direction of the noise. A second later, a familiar face appeared, and Alice felt a flood of emotion run through her. Carrying a bag from her favourite Thai restaurant was her boyfriend. She smiled brightly at him and waited for him to get to her before she said anything.

'Hey.' She put her arms around his neck and squeezed. 'Just the person I need.'

He squeezed back and kissed her neck gently. 'You hungry?'

Alice was starving. Leo had brought her a sandwich earlier in the day, but it just didn't fill her up. 'Starving.'

She took his hand and led him to the other end of the corridor to the break room. There was a door that opened onto a small balcony, and Alice was relieved to get some fresh air. She gestured at the table and then went back into the break room and returned with two glasses of water.

'Josh, can I ask you something?' Alice stopped eating and looked at her boyfriend.

'Sure, Alice, you can ask me anything.' Josh took Alice's hand and kissed it gently.

'Do you ever think about having kids?'

Josh sat back, a little surprised at the question. He and Alice had never really discussed starting a family, which he put down to her choice of career. He never saw Alice as the housewife staying at home with the kids or even taking a safe job and doing school runs. 'I haven't, to be honest. I'm too selfish, and you have a very demanding job.'

Alice sat back and took his comments in. 'I'm glad we are on the same page. I just don't think I am cut out to be a parent.'

Josh laughed and stared lovingly at Alice. 'So what made you ask? We've been dating for a few years now, and you have never brought up the subject.'

'I don't know. I think this case is getting to me. I had to interview the father today, and to see the pain that took over his body when he begged me to find his daughter was very confronting.' Alice took another bite of her food. 'And it made me wonder if I had it in me.'

Josh smiled. 'I'm sure you do. If it happened one day, I'm sure you would protect a child with your life.'

Alice shuffled her chair closer to Josh and put her head on his shoulder. 'Thank you.'

Josh let Alice sit like that for a few minutes. She needed a break, and he was in no hurry to leave her. At one point, he thought she had gone to sleep, but when voices came from the break room, she sat up and stretched. They both cleared the containers, and Alice walked Josh back to his car.

She leaned on the back door and let him lean up against her. He was only an inch or so taller than her, but he still had a way of being able to lean over her. She put her arms around his neck and let him kiss her. His kiss was firm, and he slid one hand under her shirt and around to the small of her back. He pulled her close, and she could feel the passion building in her stomach.

When he released her, he looked deep into her eyes. 'I love you, Alice.' He kissed her once more quickly. 'You will find the girl. I know you will.'

Alice watched Josh drive away and then went back upstairs to find Matty waiting for her.

'I didn't want to interrupt your dinner, but you need to see this.'

Alice sat at the table, and Matty did the same. He passed her a folder containing the phone records she had requested earlier in the day. There were several numbers highlighted for her.

'So tell me what I am looking at.'

Matty sat up tall and proud. This was the first investigation he had been brought in on. For the most part of his police career to date, he had worked walking the street through the city, making sure kids were behaving and, at night, drunks weren't causing trouble. So he was excited when Alice had asked for his help.

'The first set is the female vic's mobile. I have struck through the husband's number, which eliminates most of the incoming and outgoing calls. The others were to work colleagues or the nursing home her father attended. So nothing of interest here. But the second sheet is the landline into the house. Not much activity here as she mainly used her mobile. But see the two numbers I have highlighted. The first is from a payphone approximately five minutes from the house, and the other is a mobile I haven't been able to trace. Notice they were both on the same day and they were on Wednesday this week.'

Alice looked impressed; this was the first time something unusual had shown up on any of the phone records.

Matty continued, 'So I have taken the liberty of requesting the CCTV footage from the shops where the payphone is located and see if we can get a picture of this guy.'

Alice fidgeted in her chair. She might finally have a lead. Suddenly, all the tiredness that had started to set in was gone, and she had a second wind. 'Matty, this is great work. Thank you so much.' Alice hurriedly stood up and patted him on the shoulder and went over to the map she had pinned to the wall behind the photo board. She marked the location of the shops and put a big question mark on it.

Matty watched her and wanted to do more to help. 'What else can I do for you, Alice? I'm on desk duty for another week and have cleared it so I can assist you with anything.'

Alice turned and smiled at the willing young man. 'Go home and get some rest. Be back here at eight in the morning.'

'Yes, ma'am.' He laughed as he left the room.

Alice wrote the address of the shops on a sticky note and grabbed her stuff. She wanted to drive past now and see what was there.

Chapter 34

Bradley sat on his couch and stared at the small girl he now had in his possession. He had locked her in a large animal cage he had found in a pile of rubbish on the side of the road. The girl couldn't stand, but it was big enough that she could sit up or lie down. He put in some blankets to make it a little comfortable as he had no idea what to do with her. He couldn't risk her trying to get away, and he didn't want to tie her up, so the cage was his best solution for now.

She rolled over and opened her eyes and blinked sleepily at him. 'Can I come out?' she asked timidly.

'No.'

'I'm busting for the toilet.'

Bradley rolled his eyes and huffed. He got up from the couch and walked over and unlocked the door. 'You know what will happen if you do anything stupid, right?'

Paige nodded and tiptoed behind her capture to the toilet. She pushed the door closed and quickly went about her business. When Paige came out of the toilet, Bradley took her by the hand and led her back to the living room. As he neared the cage, she pulled back, and he stopped and glared at her.

Her face crumpled, and she started to cry. 'I don't want to go back in there.'

Bradley was not equipped to deal with a crying child. 'You have to.'

'But I don't want to.'

'So tell me then – where do you want to go?'

'Can't I sit on the couch with you?'

'Fine!' He pulled at her arm and went and sat on the couch.

Paige sat next to him and, without warning, lay down and curled up with her head on his lap. Bradley stared down at the little girl, not knowing what to do next. He put one hand on her shoulder, and with the other, he gently moved the hair off her face. Paige snuggled in closer, and Bradley's tense body softened. She quickly fell asleep, and he watched TV for the next few hours, not daring to move and wake her up.

Bradley woke up early that Saturday morning. His neck ached from sitting at an angle on the couch all night with his little prisoner still curled up on his lap. He watched her sleep for a few minutes. She was just like her mother, and he felt strange inside. He lifted her head slightly and slid out from under her and ever so gently placed a cushion under her head.

He walked to the kitchen and opened the fridge, only to be disappointed at the lack of food. He found an egg carton with four eggs left and half a loaf of bread. It was going to have to do. Bradley sat at the table with a fresh pot of coffee and the paper, which was on his porch every morning. Every few minutes, he would look over at the couch and watch her.

At about seven thirty, she stirred and woke up. Paige looked over at Bradley and rubbed her eyes with the back of her hand. Her hair fell messily across her face, and she shuffled towards him with legs that were still waking up. Bradley stood from the table and pulled out the chair next to him and pushed Paige in. There was a place set already for her, and he came up behind her and filled her glass with milk.

'I'm making eggs and toast for breakfast, OK?' He felt calm talking to her, and wanting to look after her was coming easy.

'OK,' Paige yawned back.

She pushed herself back on the chair and starting to walk away from the table. Bradley immediately stepped in front of her, ready to stop her running away.

She looked up at him and grabbed between her legs. 'I'm busting.'

'Oh, OK.'

Bradley stepped back and let her past and watched her take herself to the toilet. He listened for the flush and then the taps in the bathroom and relaxed when she came back through the door and sat back at the table. For a reason he could not explain, he helped push her back into the table and then tenderly kissed the top of her head.

Bradley didn't understand why, after all the beauties he had over the past few years, he felt different about this one. He wanted to look after and protect Paige. She was going to be his forever.

'Now that you live with me, we should get you some new clothes and toys. How does that sound?'

Paige's face lit up. 'How many toys?'

Bradley laughed. 'Well, that will depend how expensive the ones you pick out are. When you have finished your breakfast, we will put on my computer and see what we can get.'

Bradley placed a plate in front of Paige, and she hungrily ate her breakfast, eager to pick out some new toys.

'Where will I sleep? I don't want to go in the cage.'

Until that moment, Bradley hadn't thought about where she would sleep as he hadn't actually planned to take her. He had a spare room that was almost empty. He would have to fix it up a little, but it would work. 'Come with me and see.'

He led Paige past the bathroom to a part of the house she hadn't seen before. They walked up a long dark hallway, and Paige became scared. She grabbed Bradley's hand and squeezed; he squeezed back. At the door at the end of the hall, he encouraged Paige to open the door. Tentatively, she turned the handle and pushed the door open.

Daylight flooded the darkened hall, and Paige had to cover her eyes from the sudden brightness. She stepped in and let her eyes adjust to the light. Paige looked around. The walls were painted a soft pink, and there were pictures of fairies and furry animals on the wall. A four-post bed was in the corner and had a princess blanket. On the floor was a fluffy rug. There were no toys anywhere to be seen.

Paige looked back at Bradley with concern. 'Whose room is this?'

'It can be yours if you want it to be.'

'Yes. But who did it belong to before?'

Bradley sat on the edge of the bed and leaned forward on his knees, clasping his hands. 'It belonged to Holly.'

Paige sat on the rug, crossed her legs, and twisted her body back and forth, running her outstretched hands through the shaggy pile of the rug. 'Was Holly your daughter?'

'Yes.'

'Where is she now?'

'She died.'

'How?'

Bradley was getting agitated from all the questions and got up from the bed. He stepped past Paige and headed to the door. 'This is your room now.' His voice was stern, almost angry. 'You can play in here for a while, OK? To get used to it. I will be in the kitchen. In a little while, we will order you that stuff I promised.'

He shut the door, and Paige heard a click from the outside. She leapt up from the floor and ran to the door. She wiggled the handle, but it was locked. She banged on the door and cried out to Bradley.

Bradley was still on the other side of the door and placed one hand on the door and then leaned forward, resting his head on the door. In a soft voice, he spoke again. 'Ten minutes, Paige. Please just give me ten minutes.'

Chapter 35

Even though it was a Saturday, Alice was at the station at 7:00 a.m. sharp. She couldn't stop the investigation just because it was the weekend, but she did feel a slight amount of guilt for asking Matty to come in and help her. She sat at the big table, looking at the phone records he had given her yesterday and recalled her drive past the group of shops where the payphone was located. There was a casual restaurant at one end, a newsagent in the middle, and a doctor's surgery and pharmacy at the other end. It was dark when she had driven past and couldn't really see where the CCTV cameras were located. She guessed they were outside the pharmacy.

Today she would go back in the daylight and look around again. She would take Matty with her; two set of eyes right now were better than one, and he had already proved himself useful. Then she would go to the hospital and visit the father and see if he could give her any further information. So far, he had been the only one who had seen him, and she really needed a description of the man who took the girl.

Alice looked over at the photo board and stared at the little girl. She was so innocent and didn't deserve to be taken like this. Her thoughts were interrupted by her phone ringing. She looked at the number and didn't recognise it. She answered formally. It was the nurse from the hospital. The old man was in and out of consciousness, and his words were becoming incoherent.

Alice put the phone on speaker and started taking notes. 'Can you please repeat what you just said? I want to write this down.'

'Yeah, he keeps repeating it was the electrician. At least that is what we think he is saying.'

'Thank you. I will come by later and check in on him. Hopefully, he might be awake enough to give me a description.'

'Sure, I will let the other nurses know. I finish from night shift in an hour.'

Alice ended the call and sat back, staring at her notes. There were no numbers highlighted on the phone records for any tradespeople. *Who is the electrician?* This thought consumed her, and she checked the records going back further than the last week – and still nothing.

She dialled the husband. It was still early, but she doubted he was sleeping anyway. He answered after two rings.

'Detective.'

'Good morning, Mr Elliot. I hope I didn't wake you.'

'No, I was up.'

'I just had a call from the hospital, and the night nurse told me that your father-in-law kept muttering something about an electrician. It might be nothing as I cannot see anywhere on your wife's phone records that she ever called for an electrician, so I need to ask if you had arranged one recently.'

Stephen was silent for a moment. 'No, I didn't, but Kat mentioned in passing earlier this week the alarm was playing up and a technician came out that day to fix it.'

'Do you know the details of your alarm company?'

'Not off the top of my head, but I have them in my email. Give me ten minutes, and I will find them and text them over to you.'

'Thank you, Mr Elliot.'

Alice put the phone down and made more notes. She felt a fire burn inside her. Leo was right; one day the killer would slip up, and she would get him.

Alice got up from the desk and started towards the door when she saw Matty limping up the corridor. 'Let's go, Matty. Looks like we have a couple of leads.'

'OK, and good morning.' He smiled brightly at Alice and painfully turned around and followed her out of the building and got in the passenger seat of her car. 'So what's the plan?'

Alice started the engine and leaned over her shoulder as she reversed from the parking space. 'First to the pharmacy to get that footage and then to the hospital to speak with the old man to see if he can give us a description. Nurse rang me this morning and said he was muttering about an electrician. Spoke to the husband, and he confirmed a technician came to look at their alarm earlier this week. He is going to text me the details.'

'Sounds promising.'

Alice smiled. 'I'm going to get this son of a bitch, Matty. He's not getting away from me this time, and I'm going to bring that little girl home.'

Alice pulled up into the car park of the shops and got out. She took her jacket from the back seat and slipped it on. She walked around for a few minutes, looking at the payphone from a few different angles, and then stood by the pharmacy door, where she spotted the camera. From this angle, the payphone was obscured by the street sign near the footpath. Slightly disheartened, she still wanted to see the footage as he may have parked in the car park where the camera would have a good shot, perhaps.

The sliding doors opened, and the ding of a bell let the pharmacist know they had arrived. He came from behind the tall counter at the back of the store. He waved them over and led them to a small room behind the dispensary. He had his computer ready, and Alice sat in front of the screen and clicked some buttons until she got the footage back to the time of the call as indicated on the phone records.

There he was, standing in the phone booth with his back to the camera. It wasn't a great view as the sign blocked some of the phone booth. She clicked on the bar at the bottom and rewound the footage back slowly and watched where he had come from. The man on the screen walked backwards away from the phone booth and into the restaurant.

'Got ya,' Alice said under her breath.

She asked the pharmacist if she could make a copy of the footage and left Matty there to get it for her. Alice almost ran out the door and to the restaurant. She yanked the door open and stood there, looking around. It wasn't a big place, so she was hoping they would remember the man from the payphone.

A friendly older man came over and welcomed Alice, who instantly flashed her ID and asserted her authority. They took a seat at the counter, and Alice asked if he remembered the man from a few mornings ago.

Harry smiled at her and nodded. 'Sure do. Don't get a lot of customers at six in the morning, and the ones I do are regulars, if you know what I mean.'

'Can you describe him for me?'

'Yeah, of course. Five ten or so. Late thirties, early forties, hard to tell as he had kept a cap on. White guy, not bad looking.'

'That's great, thank you. Is there anything else you can tell me about him?'

'Not really. Quiet and polite. What did he do anyway?'

'He's a suspect in a missing-child case.'

'Oh.' Harry's mood became sombre. 'I have a small camera set up over the register. Not sure if it would have got him or not. You're welcome to take a look.'

Alice straightened up and became interested in the conversation again. 'Yes, please.'

Harry led Alice to the office at the side of the restaurant and turned on the computer. He clumsily clicked through some programs, huffing every few seconds until he found the footage of the morning in question. He was right; the camera only just caught the lower side of the man coming in the door, and when he had left, it captured his back. Alice made a copy of the footage anyway and thanked Harry for his time, and he promised to call her if he came back in.

Matty met Alice out the front of the restaurant and waited for Alice to tell him where they were going next. Alice opened the car and checked her messages; as promised, Stephen had sent details of the alarm company, and she would ring them when they got back to the station. For now, it was time to head to the hospital to see the old man.

'Alice.' Matty was uncomfortable with the silence in the car. 'What did you find out from the people at the restaurant?'

Alice turned for a second to Matty and smiled. 'The owner served him and gave a decent description, and I got a bit of footage from a camera above the register that caught the side of him. It doesn't sound like much but could help.'

'What's it like? Going to a murder scene? Do you ever get used to seeing all the bad things that people do to one another?'

Alice breathed in and held her breath for a moment. 'No, Matty, you don't get used to it.'

Matty looked out his window and was quiet for the rest of the way to the hospital. Alice pulled up out front but didn't get out the car straight away. She turned in her seat to face Matty, who was looking very serious.

'Getting a murderer off the street and bringing closure to a family has its own rewards. Knowing that you found the answers for someone makes it worthwhile. And for this case, it's all about bringing a little girl home to her father.'

Matty got out of the car and leaned on the roof as Alice stood up. 'I want to do more to help you.'

Alice smiled at her new partner. 'You are helping, and I need you to keep watching and observing, and if you see something that I miss or have a gut feeling about something, you tell me, OK? No dumb ideas at this point.'

They walked at a brisk pace through the hospital to the ward the old man had been admitted to. He was sitting up in bed with an oxygen tube under his nose. A nurse was with him, checking his vitals. They waited in the doorway until the nurse had finished, and then they quietly walked over to the side of the bed. The old man looked at them with a blank look. Alice introduced herself to him again, and he still didn't appear to recognise her.

'Mr Jenner, I know this is hard, but I really need you to try and remember for me, OK? Had you met the man who took your granddaughter before yesterday?'

The old man thought for a moment and nodded.

'Where, Mr Jenner? Where had you seen him before?' There was an urgency to Alice's words, and she leaned in closer to the old man's face.

His words were muttered, and she had trouble making them out. An irritation was building in her stomach as she asked him to repeat himself three times before she finally understood.

'He was at your house? Was he the man who fixed the alarm? Mr Jenner, was that the man who took your granddaughter?' Alice was right in his face now, almost yelling.

Matty came up behind her and put his hand on her shoulder to calm her down a little. 'Let him speak, Detective.'

Alice shot him a look and then took a breath and realised she had become aggressive. She sat back down and looked at the old man. 'I'm sorry, Mr Jenner. I just want to find Paige.'

The old man nodded and tried to smile. He understood where she was coming from. He slurred that it was the alarm technician and then stopped and said, 'And he was at . . .' His voice trailed off again.

Trying to contain her urgency for his words, she leaned in and shook her head. 'Mr Jenner, I'm sorry. I didn't get that last bit. Can you please tell me again, slowly and a bit louder if you can?'

The old man leaned towards Alice and mustered up the strength he had and stammered, 'Day care.'

He started breathing heavily again and slumped back against the pillow. The nurse came back in to check on him and politely asked them both to leave. Alice looked back at the old man as she was walking out and nodded in appreciation for what he had told her. This was the biggest lead she had in all the cases, and she had a path to focus.

'Where to now, Detective?'

'Back to the station. We need to speak with the alarm company and find out who this guy is.'

'What do you think he meant by day care?'

'That, I don't know. He has two young grandkids. Maybe they went into school care or something – they are too old for childcare – but maybe he did recognise him from a while ago. We will need to speak with the husband some more later today. But let's start with the alarm company.'

Chapter 36

Bradley and Paige sat at the kitchen table, leaning over his laptop.

'Why can't we go to the shops to get toys?' Paige had been difficult since Bradley had locked her in her new room.

'Because I like to shop online and have the things delivered. It's like a big present that the postman brings in a couple of days' time.'

'But I want stuff now. I'm bored and have nothing to do.'

'Paige, you need to be patient. Your stuff will arrive in a few days, and then you will have lots and lots of stuff to play with and new clothes to wear.'

'I want to go home.' Paige pushed the chair back from the table, and it fell backwards onto the floor. She stormed off and flopped onto her belly on the couch and buried her head into the cushion.

Bradley felt himself getting frustrated and angry with the little girl. He finished paying for the online order and then went and sat on the couch next to Paige. 'You can't go home yet. Your daddy wants you to stay here for a bit longer.'

'Why?' Paige still had her face in the cushion and kicked at Bradley, who tickled her feet, trying to get her to sit up and laugh.

'Because he is still away for work. You know how much he travels.'

'Then I want to go home to Mumma and Grandad.'

Bradley pushed himself up off the couch and knelt down beside Paige's head. 'They don't want you anymore. Remember we had this conversation yesterday. She told me to take you away, and you are to live with me now.'

Paige burst into tears again. Her body rocked with each sob, and he could hear her pain as she thought about the words he had just told her. He didn't feel guilty about causing his new daughter pain as he needed her to forget about them as quickly as he could make her.

He stroked her hair and hummed gently to her. She responded to his kindness and rolled onto her side and looked up at Bradley's face. Paige's eyes were red and puffy, and her nose was runny. Bradly reached into his pocket and pulled out some tissues and cleaned her face. He ran his fingertips down her cheek, and she nuzzled her face into his hand.

'Paige, I know it's hard right now, but just remember that I love you very much, and I want you here with me, OK?'

Paige nodded and sat up, and Bradley turned and sat next to her. He picked up the remote and turned on the TV and found the children's station. Soon, Paige cheered up and started laughing at the silliness that she watched. Bradley could only handle a small amount of the high-pitched squealing and noise that came from the TV and soon disappeared out the back door and into the garage.

He was unpacking his tools from his van, which was safely tucked away from the world behind the garage door, when he received a text. It simply said, 'drinks 8pm usual place?'

He raised an eyebrow and responded, 'yes.'

From out the front, Bradley heard a van pull up. He flicked on a monitor he had set up on his workbench and saw it was the supermarket delivery service. After discovering an empty fridge earlier that morning, he had put through an urgent order at his local supermarket for same-day delivery. He couldn't risk leaving the house with Paige just yet, not until she had submitted to his authority and would not be a risk to running away. He put down the toolbox and walked back through the back door into the house just as the delivery man rang the doorbell.

Paige leapt from the couch and started running to the door excitedly. 'Is my stuff here already?' Her voice was full of glee, and her feet couldn't keep up with her head.

Bradley stepped forward quickly and scooped her up around the waist and spun her around. She giggled and wriggled, trying to get to the door.

'Sweetie, slow down. It's only to food I ordered this morning. Your stuff will be here in a day or two.'

Deflated, Paige stood still and pouted and crossed her arms over her chest. 'That's not fair.'

'I think you will like what I ordered, and I'm going to need help cooking dinner tonight. Can you cook?'

Bradley opened the door and took the first box from the man and put it on the table. He then held the door open with his foot while he was given two large bags full of groceries. He thanked the driver and signed his docket and then closed the front door again.

Paige skipped over to the kitchen to see what was inside the bags. Bradley took each item out slowly and passed them to Paige for her inspection. They put the shopping away together and planned out a menu for the next few days. At the bottom of one of the bags, Paige found two small toys that Bradley had ordered and ran off, holding them tight.

Bradley stood back and watched Paige playing on the floor near the cage, making funny voices as she made the two stuffed animals talk to each other. He was fascinated with her, and he knew she was perfect. He looked at the cage but was hesitant to take it away. He had an idea.

He left Paige playing in the lounge and went to his bedroom and dragged a chair to the wardrobe. He opened the door and reached up high and pulled several blankets and pillows from the very top shelf. He bundled them up into his arms and went back to the lounge and dumped them onto the couch. Paige stopped what she was doing and looked at him, puzzled.

'Thought we could make a secret cubby with these blankets and pillows.'

He took one of the blankets and threw it over the cage. Then he took another and laid it over the bottom. Then he passed Paige the pillows, and she crawled inside and started creating a nest to sit in.

Bradley poked his head into the cubby. 'If you ever get scared or need a safe place to hide for a while, this is your special place, OK?'

She nodded and then pulled the blanket down over the opening and continued playing with her toys.

The afternoon crept away, and soon, the two new friends were in the kitchen, cooking dinner. While Paige was setting the table, Bradley took a pill from a container and crushed it under a glass. He sprinkled the powder over Paige's plate and mixed it in. He picked up the two plates and carried them over to the table. He made very animated faces and noises while eating, which made Paige laugh. Every time she laughed, his heart melted a little more, and the more he looked at her, the more he saw her mother, and she was the most perfect creature he had ever seen.

It wasn't long after the meal when Paige started yawning over and over. Sleepily, she climbed up on his lap, and he put his arms around her, holding her tight. When her little body became still, he carried her to her new bedroom and placed her gently on the bed. He lay next to her for a minute, almost lying on top of her. He smelled her hair, and he ran his fingers down the side of her face. His heart quickened. He touched her arm and watched the tiny hairs stand up as his fingers brushed over them. His heart quickened more.

You are more perfect than your mother. You will be mine forever.

He kissed her forehead and climbed off the bed and walked to his bedroom and changed. On the way back, he locked Paige's door and then left the house for the bar. It was about a ten-minute walk, and the whole time, his thoughts were consumed by his new love.

He walked into the bar and sat at his usual table and was joined by three others who were carrying glasses and a bottle of wine. They exchanged pleasantries and soon became deep in discussion about their lives. Bradley didn't say much, but then he never did. He preferred to sit back and let the others talk.

'Sooo, Liv,' started Rachel, 'tell us what's happening with the guy you been seeing. He leave his wife yet?'

Olivia's face dropped, and tears started welling in her eyes. She wiped one eye and looked up at her circle of her closest friends. 'We were away this week for work, and you know how he promised to stay the weekend with me?'

They all nodded.

'Well, he changed his mind, so we had a big argument, and I told him I wished his wife was dead. I didn't mean it – well, maybe just a little.' A tear escaped and rolled down her cheek. 'Well, you know that woman and kid who got murdered yesterday?'

The group gasped, and Olivia's best friend covered her mouth and started shaking her head.

'It was her. It was Stephen's wife!'

Rachel put her arm around Olivia's shoulders.

'It's all my fault,' Olivia sobbed. 'I wished them dead.'

'No, Liv, it's not your fault. You didn't kill them.'

The friends tried to comfort her.

Bradley smiled at Olivia. 'Liv, why are you getting so upset? You got what you wished for, and not many people get that. Let me get you another drink.'

Bradley went to the bar and ordered another bottle of wine, pleased with himself. One day maybe his friend would appreciate what he did for her. And for the good deed he did, he got a new daughter, one to replace Holly. Bradley didn't think he could get any happier. He returned to his friends and poured another drink for everyone. Olivia had stopped crying, and the fun started to return to the group.

Chapter 37

Stephen sat in the funeral director's office. He never thought that he would be, at his age, planning his wife's funeral, let alone his son's. The funeral director was talking, but Stephen wasn't paying much attention. His body was heavy, and he had trouble moving. He ached all over. The thought crossed his mind several times if he would be back to plan his daughter's funeral in the near future.

Stephen was relieved when the meeting was over. The older man held Stephen's hand with both his hands and, for what seemed like the hundredth time, told him how sorry he was for his loss. The funeral was in two days' time, and now he had the heartbreaking task of ringing and telling people. His father-in-law was coming home from the hospital today, and Stephen now had the obligation of caring for him while processing his own grief.

He sat in his car with his hands in his head and took slow deep breaths while trying to fight the urge to vomit. He drove home slowly and parked in the drive. This would be his first night back in house since the police had finished with it and had it cleaned.

As he got out of the car, he looked around at the neighbours' houses, and he could feel them watching him. They didn't come out, but he saw movement from the curtains, and he felt their eyes on him. He opened the front door and hesitantly stepped in. It was an emotional war being fought inside his head. It was his home, and he wanted to hide from the world, but at the same time, he was stepping into the horror story and standing where his wife and son had been brutally tortured and killed.

Stephen collapsed in the doorway to the kitchen. His whole body convulsed with uncontrollable grief. He crawled over to the kitchen table and lay curled up on the floor where he had found his beautiful wife's near-naked body, bloody and mutilated. The image flashed in his brain. He could still smell her blood; the warm metallic smell flooded his nose, causing him to dry-retch. Stephen used the table to pull himself up from the floor, and he dragged his legs over to the sink, where he vomited violently. He had nothing in his stomach, and the burning from the acid from deep within his guts torched his throat.

He turned on the tap and leaned his mouth under the running water, washing the vile taste from his mouth, and let some of the cold liquid run down his throat and cool the fire in his stomach. He leaned over the sink for a few minutes before standing up straight. He felt light-headed and needed to sit down.

A vibration from his pocket distracted him from the nausea, and he answered gingerly. The doctor from the hospital was on the other end and requested that Stephen attend the hospital in an hour to discuss the discharge and care of the old man. Stephen agreed reluctantly and placed his phone on the table. As he lifted his hand, he noticed that he had several unread text messages and missed calls. He checked the call log, and most were from Olivia. He rolled his eyes and huffed; he couldn't deal with her right now. The text messages were from various colleagues and Kat's family, sending their thoughts and love. He knew they meant well, but he couldn't deal with them right now either.

Stephen walked down the hallway, passing the children's rooms. His breathing quickened, and he could feel sadness filling his chest again. He did not stop at either room and walked quickly to his bedroom. He burst through the door and slammed it behind him. He dropped his head and captured his breath. He looked up and opened his eyes. He had not been in here since he got home from his business trip. The police had ushered him from the house. He stood there, leaning back against the closed door. He was not expecting what he saw. He was not ready for this.

Before him was the bed he shared with his wife. All the blankets and sheets had been taken away, and only the bare mattress was left. In the middle of the mattress was a faint red circle. It was about the size of a dinner plate. He slowly walked over to Kat's side of the bed and leaned over. He ran his hand over the stain, and without warning, rage filled his entire body. He grabbed the bottom of the mattress and flipped it with great force off the base. He screamed at the top of his lungs as it crashed into the side table and knocked a few items onto the floor.

Stephen dropped to his knees, exhausted. He hadn't slept more than a couple of hours since returning home, and he felt like everyone was poking at him – the police with their questions, the funeral director asking intimate details, the phone calls and text messages from everyone wanting to know how he was coping. He knew the truth. He wasn't coping. All he was doing was putting on the brave face they all expected from him, and he hid how he really felt. But now, back in his home, he was going to let it all out.

He screamed again, this time with less rage. He dragged the mattress from his bedroom and, in fits and spurts, dragged it through the house to the front door. He kicked open the screen door, and walking backwards, he dragged the mattress to the front lawn and pushed it as hard as he could away from him. It bounced as it hit the ground, and Stephen gasped for air. He stormed back into the house, slamming the front door behind him.

His body was filled with rage, and he didn't want it to go. He wanted to feel anything other than sadness and grief. He wanted revenge. He wanted to hunt down the monster who took his family and to hurt him in the most painful way he could think of. He wanted to tie him down and mutilate his body the way he did to his wife. Stephen smiled at the thought. He smiled at the image he created in his head of the monster tied down, screaming for mercy.

Stephen showered and changed and headed for the hospital. He had an energy running through him that he hadn't felt for days. He had no idea how he was going to care for the old man, but he knew that was what Kat would have wanted, and he would do this for her.

He arrived at the doctor's office a few minutes late, and as he was getting used to, they all stepped on eggshells around him. In the room was the doctor, senior nurse, and administrator from the nursing home where Kat had sent the old man on the days she worked. Stephen shook everyone's hands and sat in the vacant chair that had been set aside for him. For close to a half hour, they all talked about what was best for the old man. Stephen assured them that he could look after him, but his story wasn't convincing. By the end of the conversation, it was agreed by all that the old man should become a resident of the home. This was a relief to Stephen, and deep down, it was what he wanted.

They all stood and walked in a group to the ward where the old man was waiting to be discharged. Stephen was the first to go in and, completely out of character, embraced his father-in-law. Stephen was aware that he too would have been in pain at the loss of his family and had to live with the recurring slide show in his head of the grisly scene. They all spoke in a mature manner, and Al agreed that he should leave the family home. He said that he didn't want to go back to the house anyway. The doctor discharged Al into the care of the administrator and walked them to the front door. Stephen waited with Al while a car was brought around and waved him off as he was driven away.

Standing alone at the front of the hospital, Stephen felt lost. He had no where he had to be and no one to go home to. He pulled out his phone and dialled Olivia; he knew it was wrong, but he didn't want to be alone tonight. She answered and eagerly invited him over. Pushing his guilt to the bottom of his gut, Stephen left the hospital and went to the arms of his waiting mistress.

Chapter 38

Alice worked all weekend and hadn't seen Josh in a few days. She was craving him; she wanted to feel his hands on her body and his kiss on her neck. The one part to her job she hated was when she had to work endless hours, and this case was the highest priority at the station. She had several people helping her, and she thought she was getting good traction with the few leads she had. She dialled his number and felt a tingle in her stomach as she waited for him to answer. The sound of his voice sent Alice's heart racing, and her body temperature increased instantly.

'Hey there, beautiful.' His voice was soft and eager.

'Hey.' Alice breathed in and let the tingle run down her body. 'I miss you.'

Josh laughed softly, and this made Alice even hotter. 'I know you're busy, babe, so I didn't want to bother you the last couple of days, but if you need a break, I can come to you and, well . . . take care of you, if you get my drift.' He tried to put on a seductive voice, which made Alice laugh loudly into the phone.

'That is exactly what I need.' Alice looked around to make sure no one was in earshot. 'How about lunch at my place in an hour?'

'That sounds perfect to me. Alice?'

'Yeah?'

'You doing OK? I worry about you when you have to work such long hours.'

Alice smiled and let the warm feeling rush through her. 'I'm OK. Had a few leads that needed to be looked into this weekend. I just want to find this little girl.'

'I know you do. Hey, see you in an hour, OK?'

'Yeah, see you then.'

Alice held the phone close to her chest and closed her eyes for a moment. She was so in love with this man, and their relationship was as close to perfect as she could imagine.

Her thoughts were interrupted by Matty, who was like a shadow. 'Alice?'

Alice opened her eyes and smiled at Matty. 'Yeah?'

'OK, so I have finally finished going through the employment records of the alarm company, and nothing seems strange. No one has come up with a record of any kind. Also checked into the family, and the kids never went to childcare. Katrina stayed home with them until they went to school, so I checked the records of authorised tradesmen at the school for the past three years, and none of them cross over with the alarm company employees, so now I don't know where to look next.'

Alice studied Matty's face as he was recalling these facts to her. He had put a lot of effort into this over the past few days, and she could really hear his enthusiasm in his voice when he spoke.

'Did the alarm people tell you who went out to the house?'

Startled by the question, Matty suddenly realised he had missed out the most important information. 'Oh shit, yes – well, I mean no'

Alice cocked her head and screwed up her face. 'Is it yes or no, Matty?'

'What I mean is they have no record of anyone talking to the vic recently. In fact, they said that the alarm had been disconnected at their end at the request of the husband a couple of weeks ago.'

Alice pushed herself back off the table she was leaning on and grabbed at the folder containing the witness statements from the neighbours and noted that two had seen a van parked out the front of the house late on the Wednesday afternoon, the same day the two phone calls were made from the payphone and the mystery mobile phone.

'Did you get any more information on who belongs to the mobile number yet?'

'No, all the carrier can tell me is that it is a prepaid number that has changed ownership several times, and all the addresses that have been provided are for commercial buildings, but I am still working through the names and will see if any appear on the new lists we are making.'

'Thanks, Matty. I need to talk to the husband and the father again. I'm going to go get lunch and then go and speak with them. Can you please keep looking into that mobile number and also check out dads of the children's friends? See if any are electricians. Maybe that is where the connection is.'

Matty nodded and walked off, ready to action his new task.

Alice picked up her jacket and bag and headed for home. She pulled into her driveway and saw Josh already waiting for her, and she got that tingle back in her stomach.

She got out of the car and locked eyes with him. 'You're early.'

'I missed you.'

Alice almost ran the few steps to Josh, who stepped towards her and pulled her close with one hand around her waist and the other hand grabbing the back of her head, and he kissed her hard and passionately. Alice fumbled with her keys and eventually opened the door. They almost fell in, and Josh kicked the door closed.

Alice dropped her bag on the floor as Josh guided her backwards through the house while never breaking the kiss. He stopped at the kitchen table, and Alice pulled herself up on to the edge and wrapped her legs around Josh's waist. Josh stared into Alice's eyes and scooped her hair away from her face. He kissed her again and fumbled with the buttons on her blouse. Impatient, Alice finished unbuttoning her blouse and yanked it off her arms.

Josh kissed her on her neck and put his hands behind her back, undoing her bra. Giggling, Alice bit her bottom lip and lay back on the table, allowing Josh to kiss her chest and belly. Feeling the tension building, he pulled off his T-shirt and unbuckled his belt. Alice giggled as she heard his pants hit the ground and felt Josh pulling at her pants. She lay there submissively and let her boyfriend take her. She loved the way he felt, the heat from his body causing her to sweat. His hands firmly held her waist, and she lifted her back off the table as he moved. She could hear herself moan as he reached his climax, and he lifted her up so she was sitting again. Her naked body was right up against his, and he held her tight. She wasn't in a hurry for him to let her go, and she held him back.

They remained in their loving embrace for several minutes before Josh stepped back and Alice felt the sting of her skin being unstuck from his. She made a funny face, and Josh laughed at her and kissed her softly. He pulled up his pants and then jogged to the toilet. Alice pointed her toes and slowly slid off the table. She picked up her clothes from the crumpled mess on the floor and redressed. By the time she had walked to the fridge to get a drink, Josh was back and had his shirt back on. Alice offered him a drink of water, and he gulped it down.

'Are you hungry, baby?' She stood with the fridge door open, looking for something quick to eat.

'Starving! Happy just to have a quick sandwich or something, beautiful. I have a job on this afternoon.'

Alice smiled at Josh and started taking a few things from the fridge to make lunch. Together, they made sandwiches and went and sat out on the back porch in the sunshine to eat. Alice and Josh sat and talked for about fifteen minutes before they left each other's company again. Alice cherished the time she had with Josh and wished she could give him more, but it just wasn't meant to be. He kissed her tenderly as he left, and for several minutes after, she could still feel him.

With her game face back on, Alice left her home and headed for the Elliot house to speak with the husband again and hoping the father was going to be out of the hospital and save her another trip there. She was disappointed when she arrived at the house to find no one home and was intrigued at the sight of the mattress on the front lawn. She dialled Stephen's number and was oddly unsurprised when a female voice answered. She guessed it was Olivia based on the way she had spoken to her when she met her in Stephen's hotel room on Saturday morning. Olivia put Stephen on the phone, and Alice insisted on meeting him somewhere to ask him a few more questions. Reluctantly, Olivia agreed to Alice coming to her apartment, and Stephen gave the address.

Before Alice started driving, she gave Matty a call.

'Hi, Alice. What's up?'

'Hey. Do me a favour, will you? Check out if you can find anything going on between the husband and his assistant. I have a feeling there is more to their relationship than just business. I'm on my way to speak to him now.'

'Sure thing. I will give you a call with what I find.'

'Thanks.'

Alice pondered on the thought and then started the car. She wasn't sure, even if they were having an affair, whether it had anything to do with the serial killer she had been looking for, but she thought it worth checking out anyway.

Olivia lived in the city not far from the motel Stephen stayed at in a two-bedroom apartment on the twelfth floor of a fairly new building. It was nicely furnished with no signs of kids or pets ever setting foot inside. She welcomed Alice in begrudgingly and offered her the mandatory cup of coffee. Alice accepted so she could get her out of the living room for a few minutes.

She sat across from Stephen and took out her notebook. 'Stephen, we have been looking into the alarm company, and they have no record of sending a technician to your house last week.'

She paused to let him take in what she was telling him. He frowned at her.

'And they told me that you cancelled the back-to-base monitoring two weeks ago.'

The look on Stephen's face told Alice that he knew nothing about this, and then she watched him turn from polite to angry within seconds.

'So you are telling me this . . . this . . . monster who slaughtered my family has been watching us for some time?' Stephen started pacing around the living room with his hands on his hips and his face bright red.

'I think so.' Alice watched him for anything that might give her another clue. 'Your father-in-law said he had met the guy before.'

Stephen stopped and glared at Alice. She waited for him to react.

'Where? Where did he meet him before, and why are you here talking to me and not out looking for him?'

'Because he was vague with the details in the hospital, and I hope you can clarify some details.'

Stephen stood as still as a statue with his arms now folded across his chest. 'What details?'

As Alice went to speak, Olivia entered the room with three mugs of coffee and placed them on the glass coffee table that sat between the two sofas.

Alice flipped the pages in her notebook until she found what she was looking for. 'He said he had met him before at day care?' Alice raised an eyebrow, questioning the statement.

Stephen frowned again. 'The kids never went to day care. Katrina stayed at home with them until they went to school.'

That was what she had already found out in the weekend's enquiries.

Olivia stirred sugar into her mug and looked up at Stephen. 'Didn't her father go to some day care for the elderly during the week?'

Alice and Stephen stared directly at each other and held the eye contact; they both had exactly the same thought. Alice picked up the coffee and skulled down the hot contents in one gulp and got up from the sofa and rushed for the door, with Stephen hot on her heels. Without saying a single word, they both left leaving Olivia sitting on the sofa alone.

'OK, bye!' she called after them.

Chapter 39

Bradley sat on the couch with Paige, watching morning cartoons. She had been with him for several days now, and most of the time, she was quiet and well behaved. Occasionally, she would cry out for her mother or father, and each time, Bradley would tell her how they didn't want her and how they had asked him to take her away and that they only loved her brother. He would then listen to her cry, and then he would tell her that he loved her, and he would comfort her. He would make a fuss over her for the hour or so following a meltdown, and then she was compliant with whatever he asked her to do. He crushed sleeping tablets in her food at night, and when she woke in the morning, he was already up and making her breakfast. He had full control over his new daughter, and he knew over time she would forget about her life before him.

This morning, before she woke, he had called his boss and extended his holidays for another week. His boss laughed and encouraged him to finally cash in on the many weeks he had accrued. So now he had another week alone with Paige, another week to get her to love him and only want to be with him.

It was shortly after ten when there was a knock at the door. Paige looked at Bradley excitedly, and he smiled at her. The only thing he was expecting was a large box full of toys and clothes they had ordered online over the weekend. He asked Paige to wait on the couch as he answered the door. Paige climbed onto the end of the couch and watched as Bradley carried in two large boxes and placed them on the table. He went to the kitchen drawer and took out a knife and gently ran it over the packing tape on both boxes. He opened the flaps and peered in.

Paige sat on the couch and was almost busting at the seams, waiting to see if the boxes contained the treats she had picked out. Bradley picked up the first box and carried it to the rug in front of the TV. He placed it down and smiled sweetly at Paige.

'I think this stuff belongs to you.'

He reached out his hand, and she held onto it tightly while she wiggled of the end of the couch. He pulled her close, and she hugged him tight around his neck.

'Thank you,' she whispered in his ear, and he held onto her just a moment longer.

He released his grip and let his little girl go nuts, pulling the contents of the box out and spreading it all over the floor. While she was distracted with the first box, Bradley went and retrieved the second box and brought that over and placed it next to the first. He sat back on the couch and watched Paige show him everything one by one, and he adored the excitement on her face. She even giggled when she opened a pack of brightly coloured socks.

Interrupting his entertainment was his phone. He looked at the screen and knew he had to take the call. He slipped out of the lounge and into his bedroom. He returned after a couple of minutes and crouched down next to Paige. 'I have to go out for a little while soon.' He kissed the top of her head. 'But I know you're a big girl and can look after yourself, just for an hour or so.'

Her toothy grin stared back at him. 'Yeah, I have all these toys to play with now, so I will be fine.'

He knew in his heart, making Paige his was the right thing to do. She had brought something back to him that he had lost many years ago. He silently watched her for a few more minutes before getting ready to go out. Before leaving Paige, he dead-bolted the back door and all the windows. He made sure no one was getting in and Paige couldn't get out. He made her some mac and cheese from a packet and left it on the table to cool, along with a glass of juice and a small packet of chips.

'Promise me you won't do anything silly while I'm gone.'

Paige put down the doll she was playing with and raised an eyebrow at Bradley. 'I'm not a baby. I can look after myself.'

Bradley scoffed at her and picked up his keys and wallet before looking back at her as he shut the front door. He locked the deadlock and left his house.

He drove for about ten minutes and parked his van under a shady tree. From here, he could see her up in her office. He liked to watch her work. She was dedicated and fierce and stopped at nothing to get results. He had been watching her for years and, in the beginning, slowly found ways to interact with her life. The first time they had met officially was his doing. He had messed with the electrics in her house while she was at work and then left a leaflet in her letterbox, so when she came home and had no power, she would have his details right in front of her. His plan had worked. She collected her mail on the way in from her car after returning home, and his leaflet was on top. She entered her house and flicked at the front switch a few times before sighing heavily and walking around the side of the house to the fuse box. She couldn't find anything wrong and, with the leaflet still in hand, pulled out her phone and called him. He turned up at her house quickly and sorted out the problem. They made small talk, and she made him laugh. He rang her the next night to make sure all was OK with her power. Over the next few months, he just happened to bump into her at various places. Alice was perfect, and he was completely infatuated with her. He would do whatever it took to make sure she was happy.

When he found out she had moved into homicide and she desperately wanted to be the lead on a big case, he knew he could help her, and his search for the perfect women started. He would find them, watch them, interact with them, and then kill them. He made sure they were all in Alice's district and killed them all the same way to make sure she stayed on his case. He had been helping her for two years now, and he enjoyed it.

At first, it was rushed and messy, and now he found the perfect way to make sure he could get the most satisfaction from the hunt. He was annoyed with himself for not thinking of it earlier. By being in the house for the few days before he had killed Kat, he got to see her close up. He got to smell her and touch her things. He got to absorb her energy so when he was with her and he got to taste her, he really felt like he was at one with her. So far, she had been his ultimate prize, and now Alice got to see and enjoy his work up close, and watching her on the TV felt good.

Bradley wanted to do more for Alice, but he knew if he gave her too many perfect gifts, they would bring in more people, and they would take over. He sat and kept his gaze locked on her; he would need to give her something to make sure she stayed focused and on task, and he had the perfect thing. Pleased with his new idea, Bradley started the motor and slowly drove away, lost in his own thoughts.

He returned home after almost an hour and a half and panicked as he backed his van into the garage. His brain raced as he remembered he had left Paige unsupervised for longer than he had expected. He hurried through the side door and into the backyard. He peered through the kitchen window and couldn't see her. He fumbled with the keys and burst through the back door in a complete frenzy, yelling for the little girl.

He stood in the lounge and spun his head, searching. She could not be seen. He rushed up the passage to the bedrooms, and she was not there. With his hand on his head and his heart beating fast, he walked back to the lounge, at a loss at what to do next. He sat on the couch and started at the collection of toys in the middle of the floor and the trail that led to the cage that they had turned into a secret hiding place.

Bradley slipped off the couch and, on all fours, crept over to the cage. His lifted the blanket that was covering the door and peeked in. It was very dark inside the cubby, so he pulled the blanket off the side, and there she was, curled up in the nest of pillows she had made, hugging her new teddy, sound asleep. Relief flooded over Bradley like he had never experienced, and a tear escaped one of his eyes. He backed out of the cage and quietly replaced the blanket, covering his sleeping beauty.

Mentally drained from his panic attack, Bradley put on the kettle and sat at the kitchen table. It had been a long time since he worried about a child, and the memories came flooding out like someone had opened Pandora's box. He didn't want to remember. It hurt too much.

Five years ago, Bradley's life was very different. He had a wife and a daughter. He adored that little girl. She was two years old and a real daddy's girl. She would climb into his lap and snuggle in the evenings before she was put to bed. She loved books. He would read to her every day and watch as her face would light up when he made funny voices for all the characters. But his wife had to ruin everything.

Bradley would leave early in the mornings for work and wouldn't return until late afternoon. Being an electrician meant he worked all over the city and outer suburbs, and one day his job after lunch was just a few streets away from home and didn't take him long to complete. He thought he would surprise his wife and come home early. He stopped at the convenience store and picked up some flowers and chocolates. He pulled up into the driveway but did not put his van away in the garage. The roller door was noisy, and he didn't want to give it away he was home early.

He quietly opened the front door to surprise them, but the house was quiet. He placed the flowers and chocolate on the table and listened. He could hear a noise come from the hallway. He walked silently up the passage and stopped outside his bedroom door. He knew what that noise was, and rage filled his body. He placed his hand on the doorknob and turned it slowly, pushing the door inwards.

As the door opened, Bradley could see what he had dreaded the most. His wife was in his bed, having sex with another man. The other man had tied her hands above her head to the bedhead. Bradley stood in the doorway for a minute before his wife realised he was there. She screamed when she saw him, and her lover quickly climbed off and grabbed at his shirt on the floor and tried to cover his crotch. Still tied to the bed, his wife started yelling at him, and his rage increased to a point he felt like he was watching the events unfold from outside his body.

The other man went to run past Bradley to the door, but Bradley pulled his pocket knife out and flicked it open. It felt as if it had happened in slow motion, but as his wife's lover got near Bradley, he plunged it into his gut with an almighty thrust. The lover dropped to his knees and held his stomach. Blood flowed steadily in a red stream through his fingers and down his leg to the ground. The sunlight suddenly came through the bedroom window and hit the red liquid, making it shimmer like it was filled with glitter.

Bradley just stood there, watching him bleed onto the floor, not moving a muscle. He had tuned out the shrieking from his wife and stayed there, mesmerised by the glimmering liquid pooling around the dying man.

When he finally dropped to the ground, Bradley turned his attention to his wife and walked over to the bed. He liked the way she looked bound to the bed, but he didn't like that she would never let him try anything different, so now was his chance to have his fantasy with her. He climbed over her and sat on her and stared into her face. He hadn't said a single word the entire time. He ran his fingers over her naked torso and leaned over and kissed her ample breasts. He sat up and looked her again in the eye and strangely didn't feel excited at all at the thought of making love to his wife while she was bound to the bed. He still had his knife in his hand, and when he lifted it to look at the blood that had started to dry on the blade, he felt something stir in his belly.

He smiled at his wife, who started thrashing to try and get free, but her restraints had been done up too tight. With his left hand gently stroking her belly and his eyes locked on hers, he slowly pushed his blade into her side. She cried out and started begging. This aroused him more, and this time, he plunged the knife in quicker and harder into the V under her ribs. He watched as he pulled the knife out and waited for the glimmer of the red liquid to start pooling in her stomach. Her belly button quickly filled with blood, and he laughed, feeling giddy with excitement. He shuffled backwards so he was sitting on her knees and leaned forward, running his tongue from her pubic line up and into her belly button, savouring the sweet taste of her blood.

His wife started sobbing and begging for him to stop when he felt eyes on the back of his head. He turned around and saw his precious baby girl standing in the doorway, hugging her teddy. Panicked, Bradley jumped off the bed and scooped her up in his arms and left the bedroom. He placed the little girl into her high chair next to the table and went back to the bedroom.

The screeching was giving him a headache, so he walked over to the side of the bed and plunged the knife into her chest relentlessly. She finally quietened down, and he breathed in deeply, thankful for the peace. His kissed her firmly on the lips and removed her bindings, letting her arms fall heavily to her side. Still fascinated with the taste for blood, he kissed her chest and licked his blood-soaked lips. She tasted so good, and he felt so alive.

A crashing sound from the kitchen broke his daydream, and he ran down the hall.

Before him, lying lifelessly, was his baby girl. He dropped to his knees and crawled over to the limp child and picked her up. She had a bloody wound on her head and was not breathing. He looked up at the table as he felt his heart break and saw blood and skin on the edge of the table. He figured she must have tried to climb out of her high chair and fallen, hitting her head on the table. Bradley sat on the floor, cradling the body, howling for her. His body ached with grief, and he curled up on the floor with his daughter held tightly to his chest, and he lay there, not letting her go until he saw the sun morph into the moon and the day had gone forever.

Bradley had those three bodies buried in his backyard, reminding him every day of the life he used to have, but now he had Paige, and he would eventually have Alice, and his life would again be perfect.

His thought was broken by the movement from the cubby and the appearance of a sleepy little face. He smiled brightly at Paige and beckoned her over. She came to him and climbed up onto his lap and laid her head on his shoulder and rubbed her eyes.

'I'm hungry,' she whispered in his ear, and he knew his life had meaning again.

Chapter 40

Alice drove a little above the speed limit and weaved in and out of the traffic to get from Olivia's apartment to the nursing home the old man had been taken to. Stephen was in the passenger seat, holding the handle above his head, trying to steady himself as the movement of the car threw him from side to side. They pulled up right by the front door and scrambled out of the car quickly.

Susan was sitting behind the reception counter and smiled at Stephen as he came through the front doors. They had met several times in the past when Kat would drag the whole family here for celebration days with her father. The children loved coming here and getting all the attention they could from the residents who had very few visitors. They would feed the children biscuits and cakes, and there was one old lady who always gave each of the children a dollar and told them to keep it 'their little secret', which, of course, was impossible for Paige, who had to spend every cent the moment she got it.

'Stephen, hello.' Susan came from around the counter and took one of Stephen's hands between hers and held it and gave him the same spiel as he had heard possibly a hundred times from people over the past few days.

He thanked her for her kind words and pulled his hand free. 'Susan, this is Detective Forbes, and she is helping us find Paige.'

Susan stepped back and covered her mouth while shaking her head. 'Oh yes, I did hear that she was taken. Stephen, I'm so sorry. Anything I can do to help, you just ask, OK?'

Stephen nodded again in thanks. 'If you could just tell us which room Al is in, that would be appreciated.'

There was a shaky urgency to his voice that made Susan scurry off behind the counter and start tapping at her computer. 'He is in room 28. Just follow this hallway all the way to the end, and it is in the building across the courtyard. Do you want me to take you?'

Stephen shook his head, and he and Alice walked quickly down the hallway until they reached a large glass door at the end. Through the door and out into the courtyard, Alice could count a row of five identical buildings. Just ahead, there was a white wooden sign with painted numbers and arrows directing people to the correct building. Alice followed Stephen to the second building, and he pulled open another glass door.

There was a small counter just inside the door with a nurse sitting on a chair, reading what Alice assumed to be a patient file. She looked up and greeted them with a smile. While Stephen exchanged pleasantries, Alice stepped farther in and looked around. From what she could tell, at the front of the building was a common area, and the individual rooms must have been down the corridor she could see at the back of the room.

The nurse escorted the pair through the common area towards the corridor and then stopped. 'Room 28 is the second from the end on the right. We wouldn't normally leave a resident in their room all day, but Al was exhausted after coming from the hospital. I will be at my desk if you need anything. Just press the buzzer by his bed, OK? Just be warned that his thoughts are muddled right now. The heart attack really took its toll on him.'

Alice and Stephen nodded and walked side by side down the dimly lit corridor until they reached the old man's room. Alice knocked and waited for a response. They were greeted with a gruff 'come in', and Alice let Stephen enter first.

The room was fairly plain. The old man was sitting in his bed, which was in the centre of the wall on one side. There was a TV mounted on the wall opposite him and a two-seater couch to one side. A big window was on the far wall, and sunshine flooded in. A small bench with a kettle sitting on it was by the door, and a bar fridge was underneath. To the other side of the front door was a bathroom. The room had a cheap hotel feel to it.

Stephen sat in the chair next to the bed and was checking in with the old man on how he was settling in here. Alice walked to the window and looked out onto a small flower bed that was between the building and the fence. She turned back to the men and then sat on the couch and waited for her cue to talk.

'Mr Jenner, when we spoke last time, you said that you had seen the man who took Paige before. You said you saw him at day care. Mr Jenner, did you mean you had seen him here, at this place, and not something to do with the children?'

Anxiously awaiting his response, both Stephen and Alice leaned forward, saying nothing.

The old man's eyes shifted to the side as he was searching his brain for the requested information. The old man started muttering to himself, and Alice could see Stephen's patience fading quickly. He went to say something, but Alice stopped him and gave him a look that caused him to sit back in the chair and cross his arms. Alice stood and walked to the bed and sat on the end corner, which caused the old man to break his search for information and look at her.

'Birds.'

Alice and Stephen looked at each other, confused.

Alice turned back to catch the old man's eye. 'Birds? I don't understand. Mr Jenner, what birds are you talking about?'

The old man strained as he tried to sit up more. He pointed his wobbly old finger towards the window. 'I was watching the birds. He fixed the light near the birds.'

At that point, the nurse came in to check on them. The old man was breathing heavily and looked stressed.

Stephen stood from the chair and leaned over the old man to give him a hug. 'Don't worry, Al, we will find Paige.'

As Stephen went to walk away, the old man grabbed his arm.

'The birds out there.' The old man had a desperate look on his face as he pointed to the window again.

Stephen and Alice walked back down the dimly lit corridor and back into the common room. Alice stopped and walked to the window that overlooked the grassed area. There were tables and chairs scattered around, and over the far side of the lawn, something caught her eye. She ran past Stephen and out the door. Stephen ran after her and followed her to the other side of the compound. Out of breath and regretting not staying in shape, Stephen stood in silence next to Alice, who was standing, staring at the aviary that stood before her.

'Do you think he meant these birds?' Stephen asked softly.

'Yes, I do,' Alice responded.

For a moment they stood quietly and watched the birds flitting around and hopping from one branch to another. A couple of birds danced in the water of the small fountain in the corner, fluttering their wings as the water splashed over them.

Alice stepped back and looked around. The aviary was in front of a window of a large building. Her eyes followed the wall until she spotted doors, and she swiftly took off again, with Stephen in tow. She yanked open the door and stepped inside.

A sea of faces stopped and stared at her. She paused and looked around for someone who worked there. Stephen stepped in behind her and was about to talk when he realised they were the sudden centre of attention to the room full of old folk.

A nurse came over to them, all matter of fact, and Alice lifted her jacket to reveal her badge, and the nurse quietened down. Alice walked to the side of the room away from the eyes and whispers.

'Hi, I'm Det Alice Forbes, and we've been here talking to Al Jenner.'

The nurse extended her hand. 'I'm Carla, and I know Al very well. Is there anything I can help you with, Detective?'

'Actually, Carla, there is. Mr Jenner mentioned something about watching birds.' She pointed to the far window overlooking the aviary.

Carla laughed. 'That's right. Al loved sitting over there in front of the window and just watching the birds. He didn't involve himself too much with the other people here, but he does love the birds. I would often make a cuppa and sit with him for a while, and he would tell me stories of his grandkids while never taking his eyes off the birds.'

As Carla was talking, they all started walking towards the window. Stephen walked in front and then sat in the big chair and looked out. He was amazed at how different the aviary looked from this angle, and there were two birds chattering to each other on the window sill. He could see why he loved sitting here.

'OK. And was there a light that got fixed here recently?'

'Hmmm, let me think. There was an issue with the electrics early last week. Apparently, one of the lights in here kept shorting out a fuse. We had an electrician come and fix it. No one was hurt or anything.'

Alice looked at Stephen and raised an eyebrow. 'Carla, do you know the name of the electrician who came out?'

Carla shifted her gaze back from the birds to Alice. 'Sorry, no. I don't get too involved in any of the maintenance issues. Susan out the front probably would have all the details though. I can take you to her.'

Alice shook Carla's hand and thanked her for the information and let her lead the way out. Stephen was right behind them and almost tripped over himself rushing to find out more. Once they were back at the front counter, Carla spoke with Stephen for a minute and gave her condolences for his loss. He was getting good at thanking people. Carla disappeared back to where they had just come from, and Alice stood alone at the counter. She turned to Stephen as he came to join her.

'Susan is getting me the information, which I will take back to the station. Are you OK to make your own way home from here?'

'What do you mean? I'm coming to the station with you.'

Alice put her hand on Stephen's arm. 'I'm sorry, Stephen, but you can't. The information that I'm waiting for is police business, and I can't have you involved at this point.'

Stephen turned red as his anger returned. 'I am involved!' He raised his voice. 'This is my daughter we talking about!'

'Stephen, I know.' Alice lowered her voice and held his eye contact. 'But I need to make sure we get this right and get your daughter back safe. If you react on information we haven't verified, you might do something that will jeopardise this case and catching your wife's killer.'

He knew she was right, but he couldn't sit around and do nothing. It was killing him inside. The helpless feeling weighed heavily on him, and he just wanted this nightmare to be over.

Alice walked him out the front doors and waited for the taxi to arrive before going back inside to go over the information Susan was gathering for her. Alice paced the reception area restlessly, and finally, Susan reappeared with some paperwork in hand. She handed the stapled papers to Alice, who sneezed without warning.

'Oh my gosh, I'm sorry, Susan. I didn't mean to sneeze on you.'

The bubbly receptionist laughed it off. Alice felt another sneeze coming and looked up at the ceiling in anticipation. The sneeze came from the bottom of her chest, and she winced as it stung her nose. Susan handed over a box of tissues, and Alice pulled two and thanked her. Alice looked back up at the ceiling and walked slowly in a circle. Curious, Susan leaned on the counter and looked up.

'Susan?' Alice walked towards the front door, still looking up.

'Yes, Detective?'

'Do you have security cameras installed?'

'We have some, yes, at most entry doors only. We are conscious of the residents' privacy, so we don't have them in the living areas.'

'So you have one on this door?'

Susan got where she was going with the conversation and picked up the phone. 'Sorry to disturb you, Ann. We have Detective Forbes here investigating the Elliot murder and the terrible abduction of little Paige. She needs some footage from the front door camera.' There was a pause and some nodding from Susan, and then she placed the handset back down. 'Ann Adams will be with you in just a minute.'

Alice thanked Susan and walked back over to the front door, looking for the camera. Less than a minute had passed when Alice was introduced to Ann Adams, the director of the nursing home.

'Detective, please come with me, and we will speak with the security company that looks after the cameras and get that footage for you.'

Alice followed Ann to her office, where she got the security company on the phone, and they went through the day and time the electrician was there and what rooms he had gone into. The technician was very helpful and said he would bring the footage on a USB to the station when he had put it all together for Alice.

Alice, feeling full of energy and hope at the thought of finally seeing what the monster looked like and tracking him down, left the nursing home and drove straight back to the station to wait.

Chapter 41

It was late afternoon when Alice arrived back at the station, and most people had left for the day. Her trusted new sidekick, Matty, was still there, waiting patiently for her.

'What are you smiling about, Alice? Did you catch him and not tell anyone?'

Alice liked Matty. He had a personality that everyone got along with and always kept a level mood. He was reliable and hardworking, and Alice had high hopes for his career.

'Not yet.' Alice smirked. 'But I think we might have him on camera. Just waiting on the security company to send over the footage.'

Matty leaned back in his chair and crossed his arms over his chest and nodded at Alice, impressed with what he had heard. 'Where is the footage from?'

'The nursing home where the father used to go during the day. Apparently, he met the guy there.'

'Who? The father met the killer? No way. This is huge.'

'I know, and see this stuff.'

'Yeah.' He hung on her every word.

'These are the details for the company he works for, and he is an electrician.' Alice handed Matty the folder. 'Can you get them on the phone and see if anyone is still in the office? If not, we will have to try first thing in the morning.'

Matty took the folder and smiled. 'I think you got him, Alice.'

He shook the folder at her and eagerly picked up his phone and dialled the number. They both held their breath, waiting for someone to answer. When the answering machine spoke, they both breathed out and groaned with disappointment.

Matty hung up the phone and grabbed his keys and started for the door. As he passed Alice, he put his hand on her shoulder. 'I will be here early and will try again, OK?'

Alice nodded and walked over to the desk and picked up the papers she had got from the nursing home and just stared at them, hoping she would see something else. The desk phone rang and startled Alice. It was the front counter telling her there was someone here to see her. She put down the file and walked downstairs to the front desk.

A middle-aged man in a black polo shirt with an embroidered logo of a mountain peak stood waiting for her.

Alice came around the counter. 'Hi. I'm Detective Forbes. And you are?'

'Hi, Detective. We spoke earlier. I'm John from Apex Security.'

Alice's face lit up, and she extended her hand. 'John! Thank you so much for getting this to me so quickly.'

He handed her the USB. 'I hope this helps, but just to warn you, he had a cap on the whole time, and the cameras didn't really get a great view of his face. Your tech guys might be able to do more with it than I could though.'

'Again, thank you, John. I really appreciate it.'

Alice waited for the technician to leave, and she raced back to her office and opened up her laptop. She impatiently tapped on the desk while it took its time waking up. When it finally was ready, she plugged in the USB and clicked on the file to open it. There were four files labelled by time, and she started with the first and watched them all.

John was right. There was no clear vision of his face, and Alice felt deflated. She took out the USB and put it in an envelope with a note for the tech guys. She grabbed her jacket and keys and delivered the envelope on her way out.

Out the front of the station, Stephen was waiting by her car.

'Detective,' he greeted Alice.

'Mr Elliot. What can I do for you?'

'I just wanted to know if you got anything from the information the nursing home gave you today.'

Just as Alice was about to say something, Josh came out of the shadows and over to them. He eyed off Stephen and kissed Alice on the cheek.

'Hey, Josh. Can you please give me two minutes?' Her eyes pleaded with him to back away so she could finish talking to Stephen.

Reluctantly, he moved a few paces away.

'Mr Elliot, I have made a few phone calls and have received some more security footage, which I have given to our tech guys to see if they can get a picture of him, but until everyone comes in tomorrow, there is nothing more that can be done tonight. Please go home, and I will call you when I have something, OK?'

Stephen looked exhausted and had no energy to argue with her. He stepped past Alice with slumped shoulders and his hands in his pocket. Alice felt bad for him and was doing everything she could to bring back his daughter, but seeing him just now, she had a pain of sadness in her stomach.

'Mr Elliot!' she called after him.

He stopped near Josh and looked back at her.

'I will find her.'

Stephen tried to smile as he walked away for the second time.

Josh looked at him and then back at Alice and walked back to her side. 'Was that the father of the missing girl?' He put his arms around Alice's waist and held her tight.

Alice leaned back slightly and put her hands on his face and kissed him. 'I just can't imagine what he is going through. Anyway . . .' She paused while looking deep into his eyes. 'What are you doing here? I wasn't expecting to see you again today.'

'I missed you, and I worry you are working too hard, so I thought I would come and check in on you. See if you were hungry.'

Alice put her arms tight around Josh's neck and squeezed for a second and then let go. 'Starving. Want to grab a pizza from down the road?'

'Sounds like a plan.'

He took her hand, and they walked slowly to the next corner and entered the pizza shop. They sat at the bench that ran along the window and waited for their order. When it was ready, they went to the park only a few minutes away and set up their picnic at a table.

'So tell me, baby, you making progress?'

Alice grinned from behind the pizza she was devouring, and when she had finished her mouthful, she placed the slice down onto the lid of the pizza box and grabbed a tissue from her pocket and wiped her mouth. 'I think I might have him.'

Josh raised an eyebrow. 'How do you mean?'

'He left a witness who placed him at another location, which has him on camera, and I have details of who he works for.' Alice leaned forward and looked Josh in the eye and smiled with satisfaction. 'Confidentially, OK? I reckon by this time tomorrow, I will either have him in custody or very close to it.'

Josh looked fascinated. 'Wow. My girlfriend is going to be a hero. Catching a serial killer and rescuing a little girl. I can't wait to see you all over the news, receiving the accolades you deserve.'

Alice felt good. She was going to solve this case and put a monster away for good. They finished their meal, making small talk.

'Well, you have a big day tomorrow, Miss, so I am going to walk you back to your car and let you go home and get some sleep.'

Alice picked up the pizza box and put it in the bin and let Josh walk her back to her car. She clung to his arm and breathed in the fresh night air, enjoying being in his presence. She would never admit it out loud, but she was completely in love with him and some days wanted the whole fairy tale. But for now, she cherished any time they had together.

Chapter 42

Bradley felt bad about drugging Paige every night, but he had things to do and needed to make sure she slept through the night. He returned home again after being out for a couple of hours and checked on her. He liked to watch her sleep.

Tonight he walked all the way into her room rather than standing in the doorway. She was curled up on her side, hugging the teddy he had bought her. He put one foot behind the other and pulled off one shoe and then the other. Silently, he walked to the side of the bed and pulled back the covers and climbed in next to Paige. He lay on his side behind her and put his arm over her. His other arm was under his head under the pillow, and he leaned in close to her head.

He closed his eyes and breathed in deeply through his nose. The smell of her shampoo that she had picked out was divine. She smelled exactly like her mother. He moved in closer to her so his body was right up against hers and pulled her in towards him. She murmured but did not wake. He nuzzled his face in her hair. She stayed asleep. He lay there next to her, listening to her breath. His hand moved as her stomach went in and out with every breath.

You are so perfect, little one. No one will ever take you from me. You are mine forever.

He soon fell asleep curled up with her in his arms.

It was late the next morning when Bradley was woken up. He opened his eyes and felt a heavy pressure on his guts, which wasn't helping the fact he needed the toilet.

'What are you doing, princess?'

Paige bounced again on his stomach, and Bradley let out a long groan.

'Waiting for you to wake up. You've been asleep forever.'

'Can you let me up, please?' he begged, trying not to be harsh but desperate to get her off his bladder.

Paige slid off and watched as Bradley quickly got out of her bed and jogged out of the room. She wandered after him. 'Why did you sleep in my bed?' She waited outside the toilet door. 'You snore, you know.'

Bradley flushed the toilet and opened the door, not expecting her to be right there, and almost knocked her over. He turned to the side and shuffled past and into the bathroom to wash his hands. He looked over his shoulder back at the little girl, who was still only a step behind him.

'I had a bad dream.' He dried his hands on the towel hanging next to the sink and turned to face Paige. 'So I thought I would come and sleep with you. I hope that was OK.' He made a sad face at her.

Paige came closer and hugged his side. 'I don't mind. And you know dreams aren't real. They can't get you. That's what my mum used to tell me.'

'That is true. You are a very wise young lady.'

He took her hand, and they walked back down the hallway to the kitchen. Paige sat at the table and waited while Bradley made her breakfast. When the toast popped out, he picked it up between his fingertips and dropped them onto a plate and put it in front of Paige.

'I was thinking.' He went back and put two more slices of bread in the toaster and pushed the button down. 'We should go on a holiday.' He turned to see her reaction.

She stopped drowning her toast with jam and smiled. 'Where are we going?'

'I thought we could drive over to the coast and make our way north. We can stop at all the zoos and nature parks because I know you like animals, and there might even be some fairs or theme parks along the way.'

Paige's face lit up, and jam dribbled down her chin. Bradley laughed at her.

'We could leave tonight. We would spend today packing and loading the van, and then when we are ready, we will just jump in and go. You can take all the new things you just got.'

Paige scrunched her face and tried to lick her chin. 'What about school?'

Bradley laughed heartily and came and sat at the table with his toast. 'There will be plenty of time for school later. While we are gone, I will teach you some things, and we can buy books so you can keep up with your reading.'

The little girl stared at Bradley and pondered his words. Then she wiggled in her chair and picked up her other slice of toast. 'OK.'

They sat there in silence while finishing breakfast, and as Paige walked past to take her plate to the sink, Bradley stopped her.

'You know what would be fun?'

She squinted at him and moved her mouth to the side, and the face made Bradley chuckle at her.

'What?'

'For our holiday, we could pretend we are other people and pick new names, and we could change the colour of our hair and everything.' He spoke in a silly voice and tried to make his new game sound like fun.

Paige gasped in excitement and jumped up and down. 'Can I have red hair?'

'Yep.'

'And can I pick my own name?'

'Yep.'

Paige hopped up and down, clapping her hands. 'I'm going to be Angelica.'

Bradley carried his plate to the sink and slyly looked at Paige. 'And how about you call me Dad? Just like my Holly used to.'

'OK, Dad, but only if you make my hair red.'

'To do that, I'm going to need to go to the shops and buy the colour. So how about you go wash your sticky face and then start packing your things back into the big boxes they were delivered in so we can start our holiday?'

Paige ran off up the hallway and soon disappeared from sight.

Bradley picked up his keys and wallet and walked out the back door, making sure it was locked behind him. He walked along the path to the garage and hesitated before opening the door. He looked out into the garden and, for a moment, thought of his baby Holly, who was resting for eternity under the apple tree at the back of the yard. He often wondered what she would be like now. She would be the same age as Paige, and he hoped she would have the same bright personality and independence.

He broke his daydream and got into his van. His picked up the roller door remote and pointed it at the door and clicked. He could hear the murmur of the motor starting, and slowly, the outside world was coming into view. He would quickly go to the local supermarket and pick up some red hair dye so he could turn Paige into Angelica, and he would get black for himself and wash away the sandy blonde. As the roller door finished opening, the sun came into Bradley's face, causing him to shield his eyes with his hands. He fussed with his free hand in the centre console and found his sunglasses. He put them on and drove out of the garage. He clicked the remote as he reached the road and looked in the mirror, watching the door close again.

The supermarket was about a five-minute drive away, and he parked right by the door. He walked in on a mission and went straight to the beauty aisle. He spent little time looking among the brands and just picked out the ones on special. He had no intention of buying any supplies here; he just wanted to get out as quickly as he could.

Bradley liked the self-serve checkouts as he didn't need to make small talk with anyone. He was in and out in five minutes, and as he got to his car, he heard someone call his name.

'Simon!'

It was Olivia, and she knew him as Simon the electrician. He had befriended her about a year ago after he had started following her, thinking she might be perfect for him to gift to Alice for her career, but the more he watched her, the less he liked her as a gift, and somehow they had actually become friends.

'Hey, Liv.' He tried not to come across as annoyed at the hold-up in the time frame he had put together in his head. 'What's up?'

Olivia leaned up against the van, spying the hair dye he had in his hands. 'New look?'

'Yeah, thinking about it. You know what they say. A change is as good as a holiday.'

Olivia laughed. 'Ain't that the truth. Anyway, I was talking to Rachel, and we were going to have dinner tomorrow night. You in?'

'Maybe. I've been asked to go to the coast for a job, and I need to find out when I need to leave. Usual place?'

Olivia smiled at her friend. 'Yeah, babe. Just turn up at seven if you can get there. If not, have a great trip, and let me know when you get back.'

Bradley opened the door to the van and climbed in. 'Will do, Liv. Say hi for me if I don't get there.'

Olivia smiled and waved as she walked away.

Bradley sighed and started the van and drove home via the backstreets to avoid getting stuck at the traffic lights. He backed into the garage and sat there while the door came down, shutting everyone out once again.

Back inside, he was impressed to see Paige had packed all her things back into the boxes and was sitting on the couch, watching cartoons. She barely noticed him come back until he shook the box to get her attention. She jumped off the couch and ran over to the table, grabbing at the box to have a look. She smiled when she saw the picture of the beautiful model with long lush red hair flowing over her shoulders.

'Are we doing this now?'

Bradley looked down at the excited face looking up at him and tapped his chin with his finger, pretending to think about it.

'Pleeeeeease?' squealed Paige.

'Well, all right then since you asked so nicely.'

Paige skipped away, and Bradley followed. He wrapped an old towel around her shoulders and used clothes pegs to hold it on, and carefully, he mixed the colour in the small plastic bottle and started putting it through her hair. He put the timer on his phone and set it down on the edge of the sink and got Paige to sit on the side of the bathtub. Next, Bradley took his shirt off and took the black dye from the box and mixed it as per the instructions and rubbed it through his hair. He sat next to Paige and picked up his phone from the sink.

He opened YouTube and let Paige pick what she wanted to watch while they waited. Bradley put his arm around her and moved in close so he could see the screen better. For fifteen minutes, Paige giggled at puppies and kittens doing funny things. She paused the video when the timer went off and handed the phone back to Bradley.

Bradley folded another towel and placed it on the floor and had Paige kneel down and stick her head over the tub. Bradley turned on the water and gently washed the excess dye from Paige's hair. He handed her the sachet of conditioner and had her rub it into her hair while he rinsed his own hair. They swapped positions again, and he rinsed the conditioner from her hair. Paige tried to brush her hair but got upset at the knots. Bradley sat on the tub, and Paige stood in front of him, and he ever so gently spent ten minutes brushing.

'How about we cut off the dead ends? That way, it will be much easier to brush.'

Paige nodded, and Bradley went to get scissors from the kitchen. He called for her to follow him. He lifted her onto the kitchen bench and went to stand behind her. Paige picked up the scissors to hand them to him when she fumbled and ran her finger over one of the blades, causing blood to instantly pour from her finger. She let out an almighty scream, followed by crying.

Bradley took her hand and put her finger in his mouth, letting the blood run over his tongue. The sweet red liquid was like sherbet, and he felt a warm sensation run through his veins. He held her hand tighter and sucked at the wound. Paige pulled at her arm, trying to get free, and cried louder when he tightened his grip.

'Daddy, you're hurting me!' Paige yelled at him.

Startled by her voice, he opened his eyes and let her go. His pulse was racing, and he was breathing heavily. He picked up her hand again and showed Paige her finger. 'See? I stopped the bleeding for you.'

Paige looked at her finger and saw that the bleeding had stopped. She sniffed loudly and wiped her nose on the back of her hand. Bradley wet some paper towels and passed them to her so she could wipe her face. Paige sat there quietly while Bradley cut her hair. It was now just above her shoulders, and Paige swished her head from side to side.

'Now, Angelica' – Bradley smiled at her and started his game of pretending to be someone new – 'you can go watch some more TV while I pack up the van. We should be ready to leave in a couple of hours.'

Bradley looked at his watch. It was already two in the afternoon. He was hoping to be gone by five, which didn't leave him much time to pack all his stuff. He lifted Paige from the counter and let her go to the lounge.

He looked around the house. He had been renting here for eight years and would be sad to leave, and most of all, he would miss having his baby Holly near him.

Chapter 43

It was a dark day. Today Stephen would say goodbye to his wife and son. The sky was covered in thick black clouds, and there was the scent of rain in the air. Stephen didn't sleep much and lay there on the floor in his bedroom on a fold-out bed used by the children's friends when they had sleepovers. It was small, and the middle bar stuck in his back, and he had tossed and turned all night. He sat up and looked at the clock. It was only five in the morning, and he hated that he was awake already. Today was going to be hard enough, and now he had several extra hours to sit and think about how the day was going to progress.

Stephen couldn't stand the little bed any longer and got up. He opened the curtains, and darkness greeted him. There was a faint glimmer in the skyline from the streetlight that was two houses up. As he walked away from the window, he caught his little toe on the leg of the fold-out bed. Pain rushed up his leg, and he let out a yelp and hobbled the rest of the way to the bathroom.

The rush of warm water over his body was soothing, and Stephen stood leaning up against the shower wall for ten minutes, just letting the water rush over him. Right at this moment, he felt so alone in the world. His soul mate had been taken from him, and he didn't know how he was going to survive. Kat did everything for him. She cooked and cleaned, cared for the children, and always made sure the fridge and pantry were stocked. She was his sounding board and gave wise advice when he was having a bad day at work. Now it was just him, and somewhere out there was his little girl.

Stephen tried not to think about what the monster was doing to Paige. *Was she even still alive?* He prayed in his mind to a god his wife believed in to watch over her and protect her and to bring her home to him. Looking at his wrinkled fingertips, Stephen turned off the taps and stepped out of the shower. He wrapped himself in a towel and stood on the mat, staring at his hazy reflection in the foggy mirror. Sighing heavily, he dried and went back to his bedroom and dressed.

Hours passed slowly, and with every tick of the minute hand going around the clock, anxiety was building in the pit of his stomach. He tried to force some food down, but nausea had control of his appetite. On his second cup of black coffee, Stephen stood in the front door, looking out at his neighbours getting on with their lives. They were scurrying around, leaving for work and getting their children off to the bus.

He took another sip and closed his eyes and let his brain trick his ears into hearing his family in the kitchen, laughing and carrying on. He could hear Kat reminding the children to brush their teeth and the groans of complaint. He could hear Nathan and Paige chattering away and the heavy footsteps of the old man coming down the hallway to the kitchen, grumbling with every step.

Stephen opened his eyes, and the noise faded away and was now only a distant memory. His eyes stung as tears started forming, and his throat tightened. He could feel the sadness trying to escape, and he fought with it to keep it contained deep within his body. He wanted to get through the day as numb as he could make himself. He did not want to show how great his grief was to the outside world; it was none of their business.

At half past ten, a black car pulled up out the front of the house, and a man smartly dressed in a dark suit exited the driver's door. Stephen watched him walk up the driveway and was at the front door as the driver went to knock. Stephen was in a black suit with a fine pinstriped black shirt. He wore a tie that Kat had bought him randomly a few months ago. It was a dark purple with a gold thread running diagonally across. He didn't particularly like it, but Kat said it was the nicest tie she had seen, so today, in memory of her, he would wear it with pride. He had attached a gold tie pin and wore the matching cuff links. With his chest puffed out and his head held high, he followed the driver to the car and sat alone in the back.

At the chapel where the funeral was being held, the car drove up to the front door. The driver came around and opened the car door, and Stephen stepped out like a celebrity. All the people standing around stopped and stared at him. All conversations stopped momentarily, and Stephen could feel everyone's eyes locked on him. He swallowed, trying to wet his throat, which was as dry and scratchy as sandpaper.

An older lady appeared from behind the glass door and introduced herself to Stephen and then ushered him away from prying eyes. Grateful, he thanked the lady, who seemed to know exactly what he needed before he did. She sat him down in a big leather chair in a room off to the side. She brought him a glass of icy cold water and sat on a chair next to him and held his hand and said nothing. A minute or so passed, and a young lad poked his head through the door, and she nodded.

'Mr Elliot,' she said, her voice soft and unthreatening. 'It's time. I'm going to take you through first and get you settled before we let everyone else in, OK? Your father-in-law has just arrived and is being taken in. We will give the two of you a minute together, and then your guests will get seated. The service will start in fifteen minutes.'

She let his hand go and stood up and waited for Stephen to get out of the chair, and she led him to the main room, where she ushered him to the front row. The old man was already seated, and Carla, his nurse from the home, sat on one side of him. Stephen sat on the other side and held his hand, and in a deafening silence, they stared at the two caskets that sat before them.

He has picked out a glossy white casket with gold trim and handles for Katrina. Upon it lay a floral arrangement of white lilies and white and red roses. For Nathan, he chose a black casket with gold handles and red and white roses for the floral arrangement. To the side of each casket was a large poster of his wife and son. Stephen looked away and stared at his feet. He was struggling to keep his emotions under control and just wanted the next hour to be over with so he could run from this place as fast as he could.

The room started filling with noise. The soft whispers of a hundred people hummed in his ears and made Stephen agitated. He started picking at his nails as he tried to block them all out. Just as he was starting to lose it, the older lady crouched down in front of him and held both his hands. He looked up, and a single tear escaped and ran down his cheek. She passed him a tissue box and went and stood beside the lectern, where the minister was already waiting.

The minister started proceedings, and a silence fell over the room. Stephen watched the minister and listened but spent more time alone in his head, trying to keep calm before he had to deliver the eulogy. Then it was time.

The crowd hushed, and Stephen forced his legs to carry him to the front of the room. With shaking hands, he reached into his pocket and pulled out folded paper. He unfolded his notes and willed sound to leave his mouth. His voice was croaky, and the words wobbled from his lips. It was an excruciating ten minutes. He finished with a letter he had written to his wife and son.

'To my beautiful wife, Katrina, and son, Nathan, I'm sorry I was not there to protect you from the monster that came into our house and stole you away from me. I'm sorry for not being there enough and putting my career first. I'm sorry for all the football games I missed and not being there to celebrate the wins and to work through the losses. I'm sorry for taking my family for granted and not telling you every day how much I appreciate everything that you did for me. I'm sorry I missed so much of the past couple of years travelling and missed out on our beautiful children growing up into the most amazing people I have ever met. I'm sorry that I was not the support you needed and I let you carry so much on your shoulders, which you always seemed to handle with ease, even though I know deep down, you just wanted me to be there more. I'm sorry that I was not the man you deserved.

'But I'm not sorry I met you, fell in love with you, got down on bended knee, and asked you to marry me. I'm not sorry we had children and they had your fire, determination, empathy, and hearts big enough to love everyone who came into our lives. I will love you until the day God takes me from this earth, and I will never let a day go by that I don't thank him for giving me the privilege of loving you and have been loved by you. You are my love, my life, my everything.'

Stephen looked up at the room and thanked everyone for coming and then took his place back next to the old man. The minister continued for another five minutes and then asked people to come up and place flowers on the caskets. Stephen stood first and took two flowers from the basket the minister was holding. He placed a flower on Nathan's casket and then Katrina's. As he went to walk away, his legs gave out, and he fell to his knees and let out a painful cry for his wife. He became so overwhelmed with grief, he could no longer hold it in, and it flowed from his body like a torrent.

The old man stood beside Stephen and placed his withered old hand on his shoulder and squeezed. Stephen looked up at his face and, for the first time, saw something in his eyes that he had never seen before. The old man had given Katrina his eyes, who, in turn, gave them to Paige. Stephen stood and embraced the old man. He finally acknowledged that he too was in pain from the loss of Katrina and Nathan.

They walked together out of the chapel and into the large room out the back, which had been set up with tea and coffee, and slowly, behind them, one by one, the people started filling up the room and paying their respects to the two men. Stephen left after a half hour and let the driver who had picked him up take him away from the chapel and deliver him home.

The car stopped out the front, and the driver came to the passenger door and opened it for Stephen. He shook the driver's hand and walked solemnly to his front door. He put the key in the lock and opened the door but then stepped back. He looked at his front lawn and saw the mattress had been taken away.

Stephen hadn't even got all the way in the door when he heard chattering behind him. He turned to see five of his neighbours coming across his lawn. The two women walked in front, holding bags, and three men walked behind, carrying a new mattress, still wrapped in plastic.

'Stephen, hi,' started whom he believed to be the ring leader. 'We wanted to do something for you and figured filling your fridge with bowls of casserole wasn't right, so we wanted to replace your mattress and bedding.'

Stephen was genuinely touched by their thoughtfulness. He was in no mood for visitors, but how could he turn these people away after they had gone through so much trouble? He held open the screen door and let them all in. He went to the kitchen and put on the kettle and let them fuss with the bed.

One of the women came into the kitchen when they were finished and handed him a container. 'It's not much, just some leftover meat and veg, but I didn't think you would be in the mood for cooking tonight.'

Stephen thanked all the helpers and walked them to the front door and gently closed it behind them. He put the container in the fridge and went to the bedroom to see what they had done.

Before him was a beautifully made bed with a plain blue cover and pillow cases. It was nothing fancy, but it was new and was not stained with the blood from his wife. He climbed onto the bed and laid his head on the pillow. Tears silently cascaded down his face, making a wet patch on the pillow, and he let his body give in to the exhaustion and soon fell asleep.

He awoke a few hours later and knew he couldn't be here for a while. He jammed some clothes into a bag and left the house full of memories behind. Stephen threw the bag on the back seat of his car and reversed hastily from his driveway. He forcefully pulled the gear lever into drive, and the wheels squealed as he sped away.

A minute or so into his unplanned trip, Olivia called for the tenth time that afternoon.

'Yes, Olivia,' he grumbled on speaker phone. 'What is it you want now?'

'I'm worried about you, Stephen. You know that. Are you in the car?'

'Yes.'

'Where are you going?'

'Anywhere that is not here.'

'Come pick me up. I will come with you.'

'Why?'

'So you don't do anything stupid.'

'Fine. Be out the front in ten minutes.'

He really didn't want her anywhere close to him, but she wouldn't stop calling him if he had said no. Even now, after the death of his wife, Olivia was still willing to go to bed with him, and her lack of tact infuriated him. He was mad at himself for going back there again, but right now, in the mood he was in, if she was willing to give it up, he would take it. He would fuck her all night long and not regret his lack of affection in the morning as this was all she was to him now, just a slutty booty call.

Stephen braked harshly out the front of Olivia's apartment building, where she was waiting as instructed. She placed her bag on the back seat and got into the front. She went to lean in for a kiss, but he dismissed her and put his foot down heavily on the accelerator, again squealing the tyres and speeding away.

Olivia sat in silence, not daring to speak. She saw the look on his face, and she suddenly felt unsafe near him. She looked out the front window and prayed that he calmed down soon before he did something stupid.

Chapter 44

Alice sat at her desk, feeling empty. She had just returned from the funeral of the latest two victims, and this one was hard, watching the husband say sorry for all the things he never did when she was alive and then collapsing in front of the caskets in unimaginable pain. For a while after the service, Alice started thinking about all the things she wanted to do and hadn't, but she was grateful that she had no regrets so far.

She had Matty and Leo come with her to scan the crowd and look for anyone who seemed out of place. She was hoping the killer turned up, looking like the odd one out, and she could grab him then and there and put this case to bed. But the three of them couldn't spot anyone who fit their profile and so came away empty handed.

Catching her staring off into space, Matty coughed to get Alice's attention. She looked up at him standing there, and he could sense she felt down from the morning.

'Got some news for you,' he said, standing there proudly, 'but first, you need to tell me how awesome I am.'

Alice laughed and appreciated his efforts to cheer her up. 'All right then, O Awesome One, what do you have for me?'

'A name.'

Alice stopped, leaned back in her chair, and sat upright. 'Go on.'

'The electrical company that sent the technician over to the nursing home sent details, and they are working on a photo for me from their files. They said if we want to head over, we can go through all their employee records if it helps.'

Alice made a hurrying motion at Matty. 'The name, Matty?'

'Simon Clarke.'

Getting up from her chair a little too quick in the excitement of hearing a name, Alice knocked her hip on the desk. 'Oh dear lord.' She grimaced.

Matty tried hard not to laugh. 'That look like it hurt.'

Holding her breath and trying to rub the sharp, stinging sensation that now controlled one side of her, Alice nodded at Matty. 'Yep, just a little.'

Matty took Alice's jacket from the coat stand and handed it to her as she limped by.

'Thank you,' she muttered under her breath and led the way down the corridor. 'Let's go get this son of a bitch.'

The electrical company was thirty minutes away on the other side of the city, and the traffic was heavy. It was mid-afternoon, and Alice was becoming agitated with the stop-start traffic of the afterschool pick-ups as they made their way through suburbs, and she was starving. She had lost her appetite after the funeral, but now, knowing she was about to ID her monster, she was hungry and moved like there was no tomorrow.

Bursting through the front door, Alice stormed up to the counter and flashed her ID. The young receptionist wasn't quite sure what to do. She timidly walked out the back and returned behind an older man whom Alice figured was in his late fifties and who appeared to be in charge. Matty introduced Alice and himself, and they followed him into the back into a small office that was barely big enough for the desk and chair, but he had managed to squeeze in two more chairs for Alice and Matty.

Alice looked at the name on the door and then back at the man staring at them. 'Sam.' She handed him a photocopy of the work order she had got from the nursing home. 'Can you please confirm if this work was completed by one of your staff?'

Sam looked nervous and uncomfortable, and Alice saw his brow start to become shiny, with little beads of sweat building.

'Yes. I can confirm I received the phone call from the nursing home and sent one of my employees over.'

'Thank you, Sam. Can you please confirm whom you sent?'

Trying to maintain his composure, Sam leaned forward in his chair, his hands clasped tight in his lap. 'I sent one of my longest serving employees, Simon Clarke. He has been with me for over a decade, and I trust him.'

Alice jotted down notes in her book and then calmly looked back up at Sam. 'Do you have details and a photo of Simon Clarke?'

Sam's hand was shaky when he handed over his employee file. 'I made a copy of everything I have on Simon. Am I in any trouble? So far, you haven't actually told me what he is accused of.'

Alice took the file and held Sam's eye. 'Let me assure you that you are not in any trouble. Simon is a person of interest, but I am unable to tell you any more because of privacy. I would hate to tarnish someone if they are innocent.'

Sam relaxed and took a deep breath. 'OK, thanks.'

Alice was about to open the file when she paused with a thought. 'Do you know where he is today? You know, just in case we need to speak with him.'

'Sort of.'

Alice frowned at the vague answer.

'He's on annual leave. He was away last week and then called me Monday morning.' He looked up at the ceiling, looking for information. 'Yeah, that was yesterday, and he asked if he could take this week too. I said I didn't have a problem with that because he never takes leaves, and even last week, he did the urgent nursing-home job when I had no one else available, even though he was on leave.'

Alice and Matty looked at each other and nodded. Their prime suspect wasn't working when the murders happened and so had all the time to carry it out.

With her finger under the cover and about to open the file, Alice stopped to ask one more question. 'Does Simon have a wife or partner at home?'

Sam shook his head. 'No, his wife left him and took his kid a couple of years ago. He has a girlfriend from what I can make out, but we've never met her, and from the way he talks about her, I assume she is some sort of lawyer or something. Not 100 percent sure. Can't even be sure it is his girlfriend.'

'Thanks,' Alice responded as she opened the folder.

The first couple of pages were personal details: date of birth, address, and so forth. On the third page was a small photo. It was in black and white and blurry and only around two-by-one inches in size. Alice stared at the photo and felt the image was familiar, but she couldn't make out why.

'When was this taken?'

'Would have been the day he started with us, so ten or eleven years ago.'

'And you don't have anything more recent?'

'No, sorry. He never attends any staff dinners or anything. He has always kept to himself. Look, I have never had any trouble from him. He does his work, and clients say nice things about him when I do random check-ups, which I do on all my staff just to make sure all my guys are doing the right thing.'

'I see,' Alice said aloud while thinking to herself. She closed the file and carefully stood up, her hip still aching from hitting it on her desk. 'Thank you, Sam. If we have any further questions, we will be in touch.'

She extended her hand and shook Sam's with a firm 'I'm in control' handshake. Matty followed suit and then trotted off behind her as she exited the building.

Alice reached for her keys but couldn't find them in her pocket. She patted down her other pockets and realised she must have dropped them inside. She handed Matty the file and jogged back to the front door. She acknowledged the young girl behind the counter but let herself into the back towards Sam's office. She slowed just before getting to the door and overheard Sam on the phone.

'Simon, it's Sam. The police were here asking all sorts of questions about you. Look, if you are in trouble, tell me, and I will help you if I can. Call me back when you get this.'

Alice waited until he hung up the phone, silently stepped back a few paces, and then called out to Sam as she walked, heavily making loud footsteps.

'Sorry, Sam.' She poked her head around the corner. 'Did I drop my keys?' She looked around and saw them on the floor near the desk. 'Ah, there they are.'

She swooped down and picked them up, locking eyes on Sam as she stood up again. She intensely held his gaze for a second and then turned to leave. 'Thanks again for your help, Sam. I will be in touch.'

She walked away from his office for a second time, not too quick to arouse suspicion that she had overheard his call but quick enough that she needed to act on this information quickly before Simon got that message and did a runner.

Back at the car, Matty was leaning against the bonnet, reading the file, when Alice walked out the front door with a look he hadn't seen before. She pointed the key at the car and unlocked the doors and got in without taking her jacket off. She did not wait for Matty to do his seat belt before she was already reversing out of the park a little too quickly for Matty's comfort.

'Hey, whoa there. What happened when you went back in?'

'I overheard Sam leaving a message for Simon that we were asking questions about him.'

'Fuck.'

'Yep, that's what I thought. Hey, can you get Leo on the phone and start giving him the details so he can run through the system? We need a photo that is clear and not ten years old, and I don't want to let another thirty minutes slip by until we get back to the station. If Simon gets that message, it's enough time for us to lose him.'

Matty didn't need to question her instruction and got straight onto the phone with Leo and explained what had just happened. He spent a good five minutes reading the file out loud with Leo on speaker so both he and Alice could hear.

Leo piped in when Matty had finished. 'Sounds like our guy. Away from work at the time and now extended leave, maybe because he has a hostage. Just my thinking, but if he had killed the girl, he would have gone back to work already.'

'Exactly what I thought too,' Alice responded. 'And from what he said about customers always having nice things to say, he is charming and could talk his way into anywhere. They would just open the door and let him in.'

Matty hesitantly spoke. 'Sam said that Simon had a wife and child, but she left him and took the child with her. Do you think he took Paige as a substitute?'

235

Alice turned her head slightly and raised an eyebrow. 'That's a damn fine question. Hey, Leo, can you find information on the wife too?'

'Yeah, sure, I'm on it. See you when you get back here.'

Alice put her foot down and started to weave in and out of traffic. She started straight ahead and gripped the steering wheel so tightly, her knuckles started to go white.

Matty wasn't even sure if she had blinked in a minute and just watched the expression on her face. He could see it in her eyes, and now he understood why she had the reputation that she did. She was determined and uncompromising when it came to hunting down the monsters and bringing them to justice. He felt pride filling his chest as she had chosen him to help her on this case, and he wasn't going to let her down.

Chapter 45

It was nearing five o'clock, and Bradley wasn't close to having all his stuff packed. He hadn't realised how much stuff he had accumulated over the years. He was at the point now he just needed to take what was important and leave the rest behind.

The first things he loaded into the van were Paige's stuff; he wanted to make sure no matter where they went, she had her things and felt at ease. Looking at the mess he had created in the lounge, Bradley only took to the boxes with memories of Holly and a few clothes. After spending hours rummaging through his cupboards, he accepted the fact it was all just stuff that he could replace. He had planned to drive through the night and get as far from here as he could over the next day or two.

There was a town north on the coast that he estimated, with stops, would take around seventeen hours to drive. He had seen it advertised as a perfect spot to take the family to, so he thought this would be a good place to start. If he could keep Paige amused in the car that long, he could get there in two days.

Hot from packing, Bradley went into the kitchen to get a glass of water and make sure all his electronics were charging. He picked up his phone and saw he had missed a call from his boss, who had left a message. He couldn't deal with work right now, so he ignored it.

Anxiety was creeping in, and Bradley just wanted to get out of there, so he abandoned the packing and loaded the last few things he needed to take. He had created a space in the rear of the van behind the cargo barrier for Paige. He couldn't risk her sitting in the front seat with him and being spotted by someone, so he set up the cage that he had turned into her cubby and would let her play in there while he drove. He had a way of turning things into fun, and Paige bought it and eagerly climbed in. When she was safely inside, he closed the door to the cage and locked it. He pulled the blanket down over the side and then placed other boxes in the van next to the cage so from the open sliding door, it didn't look out of place.

Bradley had packed a bag filled with snacks and drinks for Paige and had slipped in a low dose of sleeping tablets dissolved in her water bottle. It wasn't enough to knock her out but would keep her feeling sleepy and hopefully quiet.

Bradley started the van and clicked the remote, opening the roller door, and slowly slipped away from the house. He looked in his rear-view mirror as the house disappeared from sight. Breathing a sigh of relief, he was on his way to a new life with his new daughter.

Less than a minute into his getaway, a light flashed on the dashboard. Bradley looked down and groaned. The petrol light came on. *Shit! How did I forget to get petrol?*

Angry at his carelessness, Bradley looked around to work out the best place to stop. He figured he would get through the city and stop on the outskirts before getting to the freeway. He continued driving through the city, holding his breath at every red light and not making eye contact with anyone. His heart beat loudly, and he had little patience left. He just wanted to be on the open road.

Bradley pulled into the service station on the other side of the city and found a vacant bowser on the very end row as far away from the other cars as was possible. He slid out of the driver's seat and walked to the back of the van. He picked up the pump and started filling his tank. Like everything today, this seemed to be taking forever, and he was starting to lose it. He stormed towards the shop to pay and grab something to eat. In all the madness of leaving his home, he never ate, and now his stomach ached from hunger.

The inside of the shop was buzzing with people. Bradley kept his head down and swiftly moved from aisle to aisle, grabbing a few things for his long drive into the night. With his arms full, he headed towards the counter, only to hear that familiar voice behind him again for the second time that day.

'Oh my god! It is you. I almost didn't recognise you with dark hair. It looks great.'

'Hey, Liv.' Bradley looked around to see if anyone else he knew was with Olivia. 'What are you doing here? It's an odd place for you, seeing you don't own a car.'

Olivia attempted a smile when Stephen stood by her side. The two men looked at each other, and Stephen reacted when he realised they had met.

'You're Alice's boyfriend, right?' he questioned.

'Yeah. And I'm sorry if I was rude last night. I get a bit protective when I see another man talking to her.'

Stephen laughed softly. 'Don't worry about it. I get that.'

'And I'm so sorry for your loss. I've been reading about it in the paper.'

Stephen shook Bradley's hand and nodded in appreciation and continued to the counter.

Olivia tilted her head and squinted a little at her friend. 'So he has met this mystery girlfriend of yours, but your best friends can't?' She was teasing him and smiled. 'So I guess that means she really does exist then. Rach will be pissed. She bet me fifty bucks you made her up.'

Bradley faked a laugh and went along with the conversation. 'Yeah, she's real. Anyway, I got that job I told you about earlier, so I am heading out of town for a few days. I will call you when I get back, OK?'

Olivia leaned in and kissed Bradley on the cheek. 'And you will arrange dinner with us so we can interrogate . . .' She coughed cheekily. 'I mean get to know Alice.'

'Sure, Liv. Let's do that.'

They walked side by side to the counter, and Bradley paid for his dinner and fuel and quickened his pace as he walked towards the van. He got to the passenger door and fumbled with his keys when he felt a hand on his shoulder. Startled, he dropped a couple of things and caught in the reflection of the window Stephen.

Bradley's knees weakened, and he felt his heart jump into his throat as he turned to talk to the man whose daughter was just on the other side of the door he was standing next to. His mind instantly jumped to if Paige heard her father's voice, she might start yelling out to get his attention.

'Sorry, didn't mean to startle you.'

Bradley bent over and picked up the can of drink that was starting to roll away. 'It's all good. Was in a world of my own and didn't hear you.'

Stephen stepped back and bent down and picked up the packet of lollies that Bradley had dropped. He held them for a moment before passing them back to Bradley, sniggering at the same time. 'These were . . . I mean are . . . my daughter's favourite.'

Bradley carefully took them from Stephen, trying not to look into the van. He said nothing and waited for Stephen to make the next move. After a few seconds of uncomfortable silence, Stephen finally spoke again.

'I just wanted to ask you something, and I don't expect that she would have said anything to you, but does Alice know who took my daughter?' His breathing was heavy as he fought off the tears.

'Sorry. man, she doesn't discuss her work with me. She's always been very strict about that which I get.'

Stephen dropped his head and thanked Bradley. Disheartened, he walked away from Bradley back towards Olivia, who was watching them intently from Stephen's car. She waved as she got in, and Bradley turned and opened the passenger door. He placed the items on the seat and let himself breathe again. He looked back and saw Stephen's car leave the driveway and speed off.

Bradley closed the door and leaned against it for a moment longer to allow his pulse to return to normal, and then he opened the sliding door. He moved one of the boxes and lifted the blanket. A bright toothy grin looked back at him, and he saw she had put in the earbuds he had given her and was watching a cartoon on the iPad, so she had heard nothing. She pulled one out so she could hear him.

'You OK back here, Princess Angelica?'

She nodded. 'Yep. This is fun riding back here. Do I have to get out now?' Her grin turned to a frown.

'No, sweetheart, we've only just begun our adventure. I will stop again in a couple of hours, so go easy on your drinks as there are no toilets for a while.'

Paige nodded and put the earbud back in and resumed watching the cartoon, and Bradley closed and locked the cage and put the blanket back over. He put the box back and closed the sliding door. He looked around as he walked around the van to the driver's door and saw no one watching him. He started the engine and slowly drove out into the night.

Chapter 46

Alice and Matty raced through the station when they had arrived back and straight up to her office. Leo was in there, waiting for them, sitting on the corner of the desk with a folder in his hand.

'What did you find?' Alice barked as she came charging through the door. Leo held out the file for her, and she snatched it from him.

'Hey, settle down there, Alice,' he snapped back at her.

Alice looked up and sighed. 'Sorry.'

Leo rose from the desk and put his hand on the file, stopping Alice from opening it. She frowned, and she looked up from the folder. Leo gave her a look, and she knew not to question him. She stood still and watched as Leo walked over to Matty and put his arm around his shoulder and whispered something to him as he escorted him from the room and closed the door. Alice started to feel hot and uneasy, and her fingertips tingled as she knew she was about to be on the receiving end of bad news.

Leo stood near the door and turned slowly to face Alice. 'Sit down before you open that file.'

Alice pulled a chair away from the table and sat gingerly. She placed the file on the table and looked back up at Leo, who had come over to her side, dragging another chair with him. He put his hand on her arm and squeezed gently. Panic had started settling in, and with each short sharp breath she took, she felt a numbness creep up her legs. Alice slid her finger under the cover of the folder and flipped it open. Alice stared at the photo in disbelief.

'This has to be a mistake.'

Alice swallowed with a dry throat. Her eyes started to sting, and her fingers shook. She flipped through the next couple of pages, trying to read the words, but nothing stuck in her brain. She turned the pages back to the front and stared at the photo again.

'Tell me, Leo, how did you come to this conclusion?' Her voice was full of accusation, and anger was creeping to the surface.

Leo put his hand on her arm again in comfort, and she jerked it away.

'Don't.' She swallowed again hard, pushing the contents of her stomach back down.

'Alice. I'm sorry, but it is true. He's been right under our noses the whole time. Your boyfriend, Josh, is the one we've been looking for.'

Alice felt her entire body cramp up as Leo's words echoed in her ears. Her chest tightened, and her stomach was twisting itself into a pretzel. As pain seeped from her eyes, Alice started rocking in the chair, trying to comprehend the information. Alice tried to talk, but nothing came out, her eyes pleading with Leo to tell her it was all a mistake, but he bit his bottom lip and slid his hand under hers. He moved the file away from Alice and turned the photo over so she could no longer see him and started explaining the information on the first page.

'I started with the employment records given to you. When I searched the name matched with the date of birth, the name Simon Clarke came up. I searched the name in the system, which is where I got this photo. It came from an investigation into his missing wife and child. It seems they disappeared without a trace several years ago.'

Leo paused and let Alice digest the information. He waited until she nodded for him to continue.

'They were never found, and Simon had a perfectly clean record. Not even a speeding fine was recorded against him, so after a year with no leads or evidence of Simon doing something to them, the investigation was closed.' Leo turned to the next page. 'I have requested his phone bills and bank statements, but as you know, they take a little time to come in, and you only gave me this info a half hour ago.' He placed his hand back on hers and held it for a moment. 'Alice?'

Her eyes had darkened, and her skin looked white, like someone had just freshly painted her face. She drew in a breath slowly, but her eyes were glued to the page in the file, and Leo watched her as her brain absorbed the DNA results from the evidence collected off the latest victim, Katrina Elliot.

'There was a bite mark on her, Alice. The coroner was able to extract foreign DNA from the wound, which was a match to Simon. His DNA was taken as part of the investigation into his wife. It's him, Alice. There is no doubting that.'

Alice pulled her hand away from Leo and put her hands on her head and leaned back in the chair and stared at the ceiling. She felt like a complete idiot at this moment. She cleared her throat and looked sideways down to Leo.

'How did I not see it?' She moved again in her chair and dropped her arms to her side like they were lead weights. 'I'm like one of those wives you see on the news who had no idea her husband was a rapist who then go on to defend him, telling everyone it couldn't be true.' Alice leaned forwards in the chair and put her elbows on the table and rested her head on her clasped hands. 'OK, Leo, how do you want to proceed from here?'

Leo stood from the table and gently patted her shoulder. 'We need to get the father to confirm the ID as he had seen him at the house taking the girl. Also, the staff at the nursing home interacted with him, so they could ID him too.'

Alice turned in her chair and got up to follow Leo, who stopped her.

'Alice, I should take you off this case right now. You have a personal connection to our suspect.'

Alice pushed past him and opened the door. She looked back at Leo and scoffed. 'Don't you dare. I am a professional and have been on this case for two years. You are not going to take this away from me.'

'Alice.' He spoke like a stern father to her. 'If I feel at any stage you are hindering the case, I will take you off it and put you on leave. You understand?'

Alice rolled her eyes at Leo. She was emotionally exhausted. 'Yes, sir!'

He followed her out with the file in hand and walked past Matty, who was waiting at the end of the corridor, eager to find out what was going on.

'Matty, your day is over. Go home, and we will fill you in tomorrow.'

Stunned and speechless, Matty caught up to Alice and stepped in front of her. 'What's going on, Alice? Are you OK?' He tried to make eye contact, but Alice looked away.

'You heard Detective Mason. Go home, Matty.' Alice pushed past Matty but stopped after a few steps and turned back. 'You will be fully briefed in the morning, OK? So don't be late.'

Alice continued walking away and felt numb. Her feet were heavy and aching, and her stomach still twisted. She was good at pushing her feelings way down deep inside, and she knew this was what needed to happen now. Josh no longer existed. She was alone again and needed to only focus on the case and finding the missing girl. The numbness soon turned to solid concrete, and she felt hard, and she let her heartbreak turn to determination. She now walked with resolve and would let nothing get in her way. Her eyes focused straight ahead, and the world that surrounded her faded into a blur. She was coming for him, and nothing or no one was going to get in her way.

Alice let Leo drive so she could read the information in the file. The first time she looked at the words, they slipped away before she could retain them. This time, every word stuck like glue, and as she stared at the face in the file, a fire burned hot in her. She had been played by him, and he had made a fool of her, and she was not going to let him get away with it.

Leo parked close to the front door of the nursing home. Silently, they both walked into the reception area and waited for someone to come and help them.

Susan poked her head around the doorway to the side, and then her body emerged. 'Hello, Detective,' she greeted Alice with a friendly smile and then turned to Leo, whom she hadn't yet been introduced.

'Susan, this is Detective Mason.'

Leo extended his hand and nodded at Susan. She shook his hand and nodded back.

'Susan.' Leo took over the conversation from Alice, who was about to speak. 'Do you recognise this man?'

Leo indicated to Alice to show Susan the photo from the file. Alice slipped the photo from the folder and held it out for Susan.

She carefully took the photo and started nodding almost instantly. 'Yes, I recognise him. He is the electrician who came out here last week to fix the fuse that kept shorting out.' Susan looked up at Alice and handed the photo back to her. 'That is definitely him.'

Feeling her heart twinge a little, Alice took back the photo and slipped it back into the folder. She had a small part of her heart that was desperately wishing that the monster she was hunting wasn't the man she was head over heels in love with, but the more evidence and positive IDs she was getting, the more that part of her heart started to die.

Leo watched Alice carefully. He was ready to send her home the minute he felt she could no longer be a benefit to the case. He was impressed when she quickly snapped herself out of the disappointment of hearing her boyfriend was the electrician who was here a week ago.

'Thank you, Susan,' Alice said professionally. 'Where could we find Mr Jenner?'

Susan stepped away from the two detectives and went behind the counter to her computer and clicked away. She picked up the handset of her phone and pressed four numbers. She didn't look up while she waited for someone to answer, and when they did, she whispered into the phone. Susan placed the handset back down and regained eye contact with Alice. 'He is in his room. The on-duty nurse will go and see if he is awake. Do you remember where to go?'

'Yes. Thank you, Susan.'

Alice led the way down the hall to the back door. As they crossed the courtyard to the residential building, Leo stopped Alice and stood in front of her and moved his head until he had her eye contact.

'Just checking in before we speak to the father. Now would be the time to tell me if you want to wait here.'

'No, Leo,' Alice huffed at him. 'I don't want to wait here, and I don't want to be treated like a child.' She walked on and put her hand on the door handle. 'I am fine.'

Leo didn't push it as now Alice had become the best witness to the case and had built trust with the family, and he needed to use that to get to Simon.

Once they were inside the building, the nurse was waiting for them, and Leo introduced himself. She escorted them down the hall and stopped outside his door.

'He's not doing so great, so please be gentle with your questions. The stress of everything has started to take its toll on him. I will be back in five minutes, all right?'

Leo nodded and opened the door to let Alice in first. She smiled at the old man, who was sitting up in the large recliner chair that was next to the bed. He looked tired, and for the first time, Alice thought he looked very old and frail. He attempted a smile back at Alice and, using all the effort he could muster, lifted his weak old arm and beckoned her over to his side. Alice sat on the bed as close to him as she could and placed the folder next to her. She held out her hand to Leo and introduced him. The old man looked at the couch and gave permission for him to sit. Alice held the old man's hand with both of hers and let him get comfortable again.

'Mr Jenner,' she spoke softly, 'I need to show you a photo of a man we believe took your granddaughter.'

The old man nodded and held out his hand.

Alice took the photo from the file and handed it to him. The old man reacted in a way both Alice and Leo knew he had recognised the person in the photo. The old man passed the photo back, and his breathing became laboured, and Alice could hear him starting to wheeze. She reached for the buzzer and summoned the nurse to his aid.

'Mr Jenner' – Alice took his hand again – 'I need you to confirm or deny out loud. Is the man in the photo the same man you saw at your house and the same man who took your granddaughter?'

With a raspy voice, the old man spoke. 'Yes. That was the man I saw take Paige.'

Leo stood from the couch and extended his hand to the old man. 'Thank you, Mr Jenner. You have been very helpful.'

The old man shook Leo's hand and then grabbed Alice as she went to move aside for the nurse who had entered his room. 'You will bring my Paige home, won't you, Detective?'

Even as the life was slowly leaving the old man, Alice could see straight into his soul when she looked into his eyes at that moment, and she could see the pain ran deep into his core. She was not going to let him leave this world until he had one more hug from the little girl he craved to see one last time.

She crouched in front of him and took both his hands. 'Mr Jenner, I will never stop until I have your granddaughter safely here with you.'

The old man smiled at her, and she left his room. She followed Leo out of the building, and they stopped in the courtyard again. Alice pulled her phone from her pocket, and Leo raised an eyebrow at her, curious as to who she was calling. The sun had disappeared, and Leo checked his watch. It was almost seven, and his wife would have been wondering where he was. He would wait until he had found out what Alice was up to, and then he would ring her and put her mind at ease. Even after several decades together, he was still touched that she worried about him at work. He smiled to himself as he let his mind wander for a minute to his wife.

'Hey.' Alice's voice filled the silence. 'Not really, I've had a shit day.' Alice was looking at the ground as she spoke and then raised her head slightly and looked at Leo.

He had never seen this look before. Her head was facing down, but her eyes were rolled up, staring at him, and she had a grin on her lips that almost frightened him.

She continued her conversation. 'I thought I had a lead in this case, but it seems I was wrong, and it turned out to be a dead end.' She sighed heavily, and she started sob. 'Josh, I really need you. Can you come and pick me up?'

She paced around and winked at Leo, who was impressed at her act. He watched her intently and secretly hoped he would buy the story.

'Oh.' She sobbed a little more. 'I can come to you.' There was silence while she listened to the voice in her ear. 'You're driving to a job site? At this time of night?'

For a minute, she made the mandatory 'uh huh' and 'oh' sounds before she smiled at Leo with a plan.

'Josh, please.' She burst into full tears and between sniffs. 'They've suspended me and given the case to someone else. They told me because I have made no progress, they don't have a choice.' Alice fussed in her pocket for a tissue and blew her nose gently into the phone, adding dramatic effect. She raised an eyebrow and rolled her neck. 'OK, I will see you there.'

Alice ended the phone call and wiped her eyes and looked very matter of fact to Leo. 'He is driving north on the freeway and said he will stop at the next town and check into a hotel and ring me with the details.' Alice started walking towards the main building, and Leo was right behind her. 'I'm going to go home and get changed and have something to eat, and then I will head off.'

'Alice, you need to send me the details as soon as he rings you. I will follow you there. We need to be in two cars so he doesn't panic when he sees you arrive.' Leo grabbed Alice's arm hard and pulled her to a stop. 'Alice, don't be a hero and go on your own. He is dangerous.'

Alice glared at Leo and pulled her arm free. 'My only concern is getting to that little girl, Leo. I'm not going to put her at jeopardy, all right? I'm not stupid.'

'I know you are not stupid, Alice, but I also know how stubborn you are. We are a team, and we will take him down together.'

'I got it, Leo. Jesus, I heard you.'

They were interrupted by Susan, who came through the door to the main building, looking for them.

'I was about to lock the doors and just wanted to make sure you didn't get locked in anywhere.'

'Thanks, Susan.' Alice walked away from Leo and back into the main building, making idle chit-chat with Susan.

Leo sighed and followed them. He knew Alice was going to go after Simon alone, so he had to do something to protect her from herself. He took out his phone and sent a text to one of the senior tech officers at the station. It was a simple instruction.

'Keep track of Detective Forbes's phone. I want to know where she is at all times.'

Alice looked back at Leo, who put the phone to his ear after quickly dialling his wife's number and nodded at Alice to let her know everything was all right. Leo dropped Alice off at her car and told her again to let him know where Simon was so he could back her up with an army of officers. She agreed and waved him goodbye.

Alice texted Josh before driving home. 'Baby I need you so bad right now. Where are you?'

She received a heart symbol back almost instantly, followed by 'I will call you real soon'.

Alice had him right where she wanted him, and it felt good. She turned the key in the ignition and looked over at the file sitting on the passenger seat and flipped open the cover to see Josh looking back at her.

'I'm coming to get you, you evil piece of shit. You're not getting away from me again.'

Chapter 47

Bradley put his phone back in the cradle on the dashboard and wondered what to make of the phone call with Alice. She seemed very distraught, and he knew how passionate she was about her work. He could feel anger starting to emerge at the thought of all his hard work going to waste. He did this for Alice and not someone else. No one else would appreciate the work he put into finding just the right gifts for her. Bradley thought he had done enough to keep the investigation going with her in charge, but maybe he had underestimated her skills. He would see her tonight and reassure her of how perfect she was. He would renew her confidence and make sure she left in the morning determined to resume her chase.

Bradley felt good inside, and he loved watching Alice work. He patted the box of trophies that was keeping him company on the passenger seat. He would still go away for a while with Paige and work out what to do next to get Alice reappointed to the case. He needed a few days for it to settle, and then he would get her another gift, and he would present it to her in a much more spectacular way. Warmth filled his body at the thought, but for now, he needed to find somewhere to wait for his love.

He saw a large road sign approaching, and as it flashed by, it told Bradley the next turn off was not far away. He had only been driving a couple of hours and was disappointed that he hadn't reached the state border as per his plan, but he knew Alice would have started driving almost straight away, so he would need to find the nearest roadside motel and check in.

Bradley turned off the freeway and headed for the small town only a few minutes away. He heard a rustling coming from the back and glanced up into the rear-view mirror to see the blanket being pulled off the cage that was nestled among the boxes in the rear of the van. Bradley came to a stop at an intersection and saw Paige looking through the cage at the back of his head.

'Hello, princess.' He looked back at the road and continued driving. 'How you doing back there?'

'Good,' came a sleepy voice. 'I need to go to the toilet.'

Bradley glanced in the mirror again and saw Paige yawn. The sleeping pill he put in her water was working. She would be sound asleep by the time Alice arrived and would be no trouble. She was a good girl, and he was surprised at how easy it was to influence her.

'We are going to stop in just a couple of minutes for the night. I will find us a nice place to stay. You think you can hang on for a little bit longer?'

Paige hugged her teddy and lay down. 'Yeah, I can hold it but not for much longer.'

'OK, princess, it won't be long. I promise.'

Ahead in the distance, Bradley could see a blue neon light. He slowed as he neared and could make out the logo of the hotel chain. He pulled into a parking space and got out of the van, making sure he locked all the doors. He approached the office door and saw a light on inside. He knocked on the door and watched as a man came from the back room and unlocked the front door. He welcomed Bradley and held the door open for him and then stood behind the counter.

Bradley completed the guest registry and handed over cash to pay for the room for one night. 'Any chance your kitchen is still open?' Bradley was starving and figured he should feed Paige before she went to sleep for the night.

The man looked at his watch and then back up at Bradley. 'It's going to close any minute now, but if you give me your order straight away, I will get them to stay a bit longer.'

He handed Bradley a menu and stared at him while he read the options. Feeling he was being watched made Bradley uncomfortable.

He put the menu down and slid it back across the counter. 'I will have two burgers with fries and two chocolate milkshakes, please.'

'I will bring it to your room shortly. You want to pay for that now or after breakfast before you leave?'

Bradley opened his wallet again but didn't have enough cash left, so he gave him his credit card. 'I will pay now, thinking we will head off early in the morning.'

'As you wish.' The man took his card and swiped it through his machine and handed it back. 'Food won't be long.'

Bradley thanked him and went back to the van. He backed out of the space and slowly proceeded through the car park until he reached the unit on the very end. He backed the van into the space so the sliding door was away from sight. He slipped out of the van again and walked around to the other side and opened the sliding door.

He smiled at Paige, who sat up and was by the door, waiting to be let out. Bradley slid some boxes out of the way and unlocked the cage door. Paige climbed out, still clinging to her teddy, and Bradley picked her up and carried her to the unit door. He placed her down, conscious to keep her in front of him, and used the key given to him to let them in.

Bradley ran his hand up the inside wall and found a light switch. He flicked it on and let his eyes adjust to the light. He could see the bathroom to the back and let Paige go on her own. She ran through the room and closed the bathroom door behind her. Bradley went back to the van and grabbed a bag with clothes and locked the van. He came back in and closed the front door and placed the bag on the bed. The man who checked him in said the unit had a separate bedroom and a second bed in the living space. Bradley needed a space for Paige where he could shut the door. He wasn't ready for Alice to meet her just yet.

Paige emerged from the bathroom and sat on the bed next to Bradley. He put his arm around her and pulled her closer so she would climb onto his lap. She sat with her back leaning up against his chest, and he put his arm around her waist and held her. He could smell her hair and leaned his head against hers so his nose was right up against her. He breathed in deeply and held it, letting the fragrance fill his head. He squeezed her a little tighter and put his other hand under her chin, holding her firmly by the throat. His pulse quickened, and he felt the heat in his stomach rise to his chest. He inhaled through his nose again on the back of her head and groaned as he let the breath out.

Paige wriggled and got free of his grip and stood in front of him, frowning. 'Stop that. I don't like it when you smell me like that. It's weird.'

Bradley let the warm fuzzy feeling subside and then apologised to Paige. 'It's just I love the smell of that shampoo you picked out. Maybe you could let me use it. Then I wouldn't need to smell your hair.'

Paige thought about what Bradley said and nodded. 'OK, I will share it with you.' She smiled at him slyly. 'You're still weird though.'

'Oh, really?'

Bradley laughed and grabbed Paige and started tickling her. She wiggled and twisted, trying to get away, laughing so hard, it was infectious.

There was a knock at the door, so Bradley let her go. He could see the familiar face of the man from reception and got up from the bed to let him in. He carried a tray and placed it on the table and acknowledged Paige, who ran to the table to see what treats had just been brought to them. He let himself out and shut the door behind him.

Paige pulled out a chair and sat at the table without being asked. Bradley removed the covers off the plates and passed one over. With impeccable manners, Paige thanked Bradley and hungrily stared, devouring her dinner.

Bradley didn't start eating straight away. For a minute, he just watched Paige. When she frowned at him and told him to stop staring, Bradley picked up some fries and shoved them into his mouth. He picked up his phone and realised he had forgotten to tell Alice where they were. He stood from the table and walked out the front door, leaving Paige to be entertained by the TV. She answered after two rings, and he gave her the details. Alice told him she had only been in the car ten minutes, so she would be there in a couple of hours.

Bradley leaned up against the wall and listened to her hang up. He couldn't wait for her to get there. He missed her, and he wanted to tell her everything he had done for her. He wanted to show her his new daughter and tell her to run away with them. He wanted her to be his, but he knew she wasn't quite ready. He was a patient man and knew she was worth the wait. When she was ready, she would see him for the man he really was, and she would appreciate the effort he had gone to for her, and she would give herself freely to him, and they would live happily ever after.

Bradley returned to Paige, and while she was hypnotised by a cartoon, he had crushed a full sleeping pill into her milkshake. He called her name several times before she turned to him. He handed her the drink and told her to finish it off as it was bedtime. She took several big sips and put the glass back on the table. He watched her for the next ten minutes. As each minute passed, he watched as her eyes became heavy, and she started yawning. She fought hard to try and get to the end of the show, but the medication won.

Bradley scooped her up and carried her to the bedroom. He laid her on the bed and covered her with the blanket. He got down onto his knees and hovered over her, letting her warm breath tickle his face. He leaned in and kissed her tenderly on the lips and then whispered into her ear.

'You are perfect in every way, and you will be mine forever.'

Chapter 48

The drive to get to Josh was going to take Alice around two hours. She had gone home and changed and was back in the car in record time. Alice rang him again once she was on the road to find out exactly where he was. It seemed he had bought her story on the phone earlier, and she had got him to stop driving.

Alice played over in her head why, all of a sudden, he had taken off, and then it hit her. She had told him the night before when she thought he was Josh, her boyfriend, and not Simon, the serial killer, that she had a strong lead and would be arresting her suspect the next day. She must have spooked him, and that was why he had left, and now she had to draw him back to her.

Finally on the freeway, Alice put her foot down and sped towards his location. She turned up the radio and focused on her story. With one hand on the wheel, Alice texted Leo with the details. Before sending the message, Alice decided to put more distance between her and Leo. She needed time once she got there to make him believe that everything was OK and they still didn't have the faintest idea whom they were after. She was also going to make him believe that she needed him more than anything.

Alice had plenty of time on the drive to think over the past two years since the bodies started turning up and her relationship with Josh. She was angry at herself that she was so blinded by his love that she has missed every sign possible that he was a killer. She thought back to the first body.

I remember walking into the victim's house and being escorted to the kitchen. The body was covered with a sheet, but I could see the pool of blood on the floor next to the body. The sheet had started absorbing some of it and was turning red.

I remember the medical examiner pulling back the sheet for me so I could see the victim. Her name was Sophia Williams. Her blouse was unbuttoned, and there was a section that had been cut off. I remember thinking that was strange. Her pants had not been touched, so it did not appear to be sexually motivated.

I remember seeing many stab wounds, and from where I was standing, I quickly counted twelve. To me, that indicated rage. What did she do that was so bad for someone to have that much hate in them?

I remember walking around the house, and nothing appeared out of place, and there were no signs of forced entry, so we ruled out theft.

I remember questioning a man who was thought to be her boyfriend, but he assured me that they were only friends and nothing romantic, but I didn't buy his story.

I remember the look on his face when I told him of the brutality of her injuries. The colour drained from his skin, and his eyes filled with tears. He started shaking and put his head in his hands and cried. I had never seen a man cry like that before. You can't fake that kind of deep-down pain. He could not have done this to her.

I remember going home and feeling empty. It was my first week after being detective and being placed in homicide. I remember being told the first few cases are the hardest, but once you learn to distance your emotions and focus on facts, it gets easier. I remember Leo telling me this after I left her house feeling sick.

I remember calling Josh, and he came over and held me and assured me that everything was going to be fine and how I would find the person who did this and I would be a hero to her family. I remember letting him touch me. He touched me with the same hands he used to kill Sophia earlier that day. I let him kiss me and take me to bed, and I let him make me feel better about the world. I let him make me fall in love with him.

I don't remember anything about his behaviour being unusual or suspicious. Nothing he said gave away that he knew anything about what happened. He sat quietly and listened while I talked. He held my hand while I tried to explain how I had felt when I saw her butchered body. I saw his face looking at me. There was nothing in his eyes to give away his secret.

I remember feeling safe in his arms. How could that be? How could I feel safe in the arms of a killer?

Alice felt a heaviness in her heart. She wondered what the families of the victims were going to think of her and say to her when they discovered that she was sleeping with the murderer who took their loved ones from them. So far, Leo had played it cool, but she knew him too well. He was keeping her on this case because she knew intimate details of Simon and she was the best chance they had to catch him and rescue the missing girl.

Alice now had an hour head start on Leo. She sent him the message detailing the location and continued driving, with every minute bringing her closer to the monster she had been hunting. The next hour was exhausting for Alice. Night-driving on the freeway was making her sleepy, and she rubbed her eyes again. Alice turned up the radio and wound down the window. The rush of cold air swept through the car, and Alice felt reinvigorated. The thick warm air that was sending her brain to sleep was quickly sucked out and had been replaced by a steady stream of a sharp coldness that pulled her back to reality. Alice wiggled in her seat so she stopped slouching and was sitting up tall and proud. She was only minutes away now, and it seemed butterflies had come in with the cold wind and nestled in her stomach.

Her turn-off approached, and she slowed down as she floated around the sweeping bend and off into the darkness, away from the other cars. The voice from the GPS started talking to her again, and she obediently followed the instructions as they were given. A little way in the distance, she could see a bright blue neon sign, and it was calling for her. Alice slowed the car almost to a stop as she was told she had arrived at her destination and leaned over the steering wheel, looking up the driveway of the motel. She could see two cars close to the front, and the rest looked abandoned.

Alice reversed a little and then turned into the driveway and crept along, looking at the golden numbers shining in the night, counting upwards from one. She was looking for twenty. One by one, she crept by the rooms. Her car was silent in the night. At the very end, she was greeted with the sight of a white van, which she recognised. She turned off her headlights and reversed her car next to his, parking as close as she could to the driver's side. She figured if he did, for some reason, try to run from her, she would block the driver's door, making it a bit harder for him and to slow him down.

Alice turned off the motor and got out of her car. She slipped her phone into her pocket and reached back in to grab her hand bag from the passenger seat. She quietly closed the car door and stopped. She reached into her bag and took out a small bottle of perfume. Josh had given it to her on her last birthday, and whenever she wore it, he would become almost mesmerised and very affectionate. Alice needed him to be off his guard, and she would pull out all her tricks to seduce him and make him vulnerable. Only when he was at his weakest would Alice take the opportunity to capture him. She had seen the evidence of what he was capable of and would not risk giving away her secret too early.

Chapter 49

He was patient. He sat and waited for her to arrive. He sat across from the door to the unit he was staying and hid in the shadows. His heart beat slowly as he focused, and his breathing was quiet. He saw her car pull into the motel driveway. He watched her slowly drive away from the main road towards him. The lights from the building illuminated behind her, and he saw her as a silhouette. *She is perfect.*

He was motionless as he waited. Her car was silent as it delivered her to him. She parked next to his van, very close to the driver's door. *Why so close, Alice?*

He watched her get out of her car. She put her phone in the front pocket of her jeans. She reached back in the car. He just sat and waited. Curious as to what she was doing, he squinted a little to try and focus for more detail.

She closed the car door but did not lock it. *What do you know, Alice?*

She got something from her bag, a small bottle of perfume, and sprayed herself. He was close enough that he could just make out the faint fragrance as the gentle breeze carried it through the air. It was his favourite and made his temperature rise. *Clever girl, Alice.*

He watched as she walked around his van and looked in the windows. *See anything you like, Alice?*

She disappeared from his sight, and she went around the rear of the van. He did not like this. He must see where she was. She came back into view, and he calmed himself. She finished looking at the van and walked towards the front door.

He had left the door ajar for her so she did not need to knock. She leaned on the door frame and tried to peek in. He moved closer to her. She pushed the door open just enough for her to enter. He moved closer again to her. She did not know he was out here, watching her. He was so close, he could smell her.

She tentatively stepped inside. He watched as her fingers slowly let go of the door frame, and she was consumed by the dark. She did not put on the light. He inched towards the door. He could see her outline faintly lit by the streetlight in the car park. She was halfway in. He watched her. *She is perfect.*

She walked through the unit and waited by the door at the back. It was closed, and she was cautious. She looked back over her shoulder at the front door, but she could not see him. She put her hand on the doorknob and turned it. Her body language changed. He was pleased she had found the surprise he had left for her.

She stepped into the room and pulled her phone from her pocket. He entered the unit and closed the door, not making a sound, and turned the lock. He watched her as she pressed the screen on her phone to unlock it. She looked nervous, and she had trouble. She looked out of the room and saw the front door had been closed. Her face was lit up from the light of her phone, and he saw fear on her face. He was hidden in the shadows, and she could not see him.

She stepped out of the room and held her phone out in front of her for light. She still could not see him. She stepped forward again and moved her arm in front of her, trying to fill the corner of the room with light. He remained unseen. He was patient and waited for her to come to him. She stepped forward one more time, and as she held the phone out, the screen turned off, and she was plunged into the unknown.

He could hear her breath. Each breath was short and filled with distress. She made a small whimper, and she hastily tried to activate the light on her phone, but she fumbled, and he heard the phone hit the floor with a thud. He heard her swear under her breath, and it amused him. The phone woke up again, and she sighed quietly with relief. She held the phone up and screamed.

He was standing before her, no more than a foot away. She looked past him at the door and then back to him. His face was brightly lit from her phone, which she was still holding out in front of her. They locked eyes, and he smiled at her.

'Hello, Alice.'

Chapter 50

Alice was terrified, and her legs seemed to be frozen. She was holding her phone out in front of her, and the light from the screen was showing her the face of the monster she had been hunting. Fear had set in as she saw she had no quick exit. Her phone once again plunged them into darkness. She broke free from the spot she was frozen onto and lunged forward in an effort to get to the front door. She felt her shoulder hit him as she made her desperate attempt to flee.

Pain burned the back of her head as Alice felt her momentum come to a halt. She grabbed the back of her head and located his hand woven into her hair and holding it tight. He pulled upwards, and she had no choice but to push herself to her toes to reduce the tension of his grip. He walked forward, forcing her to move. He released his grip and shoved the back of her head.

Alice blinked several times, and her eyes adjusted to the dark. A small glimmer of light from the window helped her make out the frightening outline of the monster. She turned and stepped towards the door and grabbed at the handle. It was locked, and Alice couldn't get her fingers to work and turn the lock. She looked over her shoulder and could not see him anymore. She continued fighting with the lock when she felt a hand come around her face and pull her backwards. Another hand was pulling at her stomach, and she lost her grip of the handle. She was being dragged back into the room.

Alice clenched her fists and swung them behind her and made contact. She heard a small grunt and tried it again. As she swung, she was pushed and stumbled forward. Before she could get upright fully again, he was on top of her and used his body weight and size to force her to the ground. Alice could not move, and he wrenched her arms above her head. His hands were strong, and he leaned forward and put his weight on her wrists. She fought with all the strength she could find, but it was pointless. He had tied her wrists together and was now in control.

Holding her wrists in one hand, he got up off her and started to drag her on her back away from the door. He lifted her hands up, and the pain seared through her arms as the cable tie cut into her skin. She was forced to scramble to her feet and then sit on the corner of the bed. He climbed on the bed next to her and pulled her backwards until she fell onto her back, lying diagonally across the bed.

For a moment, he stopped pulling at her, and the pain subsided. He was above her head, and she could not see him. Alice tilted her head backwards and watched what he was doing. He was upside down, but she saw he had tied her to the post of the bed, and now she was his. She rolled her head forward and closed her eyes. Her only hope was that Leo got to her before it was too late.

Alice heard the curtains close, and she opened her eyes. She was blinded by the iridescent white light of the fluorescent globe above her head. She scrunched her eyes tight and slowly blinked until she adjusted to being in the light once more. She looked around the room and stopped when she reached him. He was standing by the front door, watching her. When she looked at him, he smiled and wandered over to her. He climbed on the bed next to her and rested his head on her chest.

'When did you know, Alice?'

'Today. You left a witness who identified you.'

Simon laughed heartily. 'Don't tell me that old man survived. Tough old codger, that one. I thought for sure he would have died from shock. You should have seen his face when I walked past him. I'm sure he thought I was the reaper coming for him.' He sighed, pleased with the memory.

'Why did you do it? What did they all do to you?'

Simon sat up and looked at her with a puzzled expression. 'Are you serious? Do you really not know?'

Alice glared at him, her anger building inside at his condescending tone.

He straddled her and brushed the hair from her face. He leaned down and kissed her gently on the mouth. 'Baby, I did this for you.'

Rage exploded from Alice as she thrashed under his body, trying to force him off her. He stayed seated on her and waited for her to settle down again.

'You finally made it to be a homicide detective, and I wanted to give you a gift. And when I saw how the passion for your new career developed and grew inside you as you dedicated yourself to the first gift, I just wanted to keep getting them for you.' Simon smiled at Alice and started unbuttoning her shirt.

'You're a sick bastard.' Alice turned her head so she no longer was looking at him.

Simon growled and grabbed her face hard and turned it back to her. 'Don't be ungrateful, Alice. I was only trying to help give your career a boost.' Simon sat up on his knees and reached into his pocket. He pulled out a pocket knife and flicked it open. 'You said on many occasions that you could never imagine what it felt like. You know, what it felt like to be . . . what was your word . . . "butchered", I believe it was. So let me help you with that too.'

Simon ran the cold metal blade over Alice's stomach, teasing her with the tip. He smiled at her and closed his eyes.

Terror filled Alice to her core, and she couldn't stop the shaking that had commenced uncontrollably. The tip of the blade stopped near her belly button. She could feel the pressure on her skin and started to cry. Alice lifted her head to see the knife being pushed into her belly. The pressure wasn't enough to pierce the skin, but it was enough to scare her. Alice looked at Simon's face, and she could see the pleasure on his face as he thought about pushing the blade harder.

'Josh, baby,' Alice whispered.

Simon opened his eyes and tilted his head to the side. Alice had his attention.

'I get it now. I think I understand why you did it, and the more I think about it, the more I appreciate the effort you have put in to help me.'

Simon lifted the knife away from her skin and listened to her.

'Baby, can you untie me so you can tell me in detail all the things you did? And I will tell you how I felt and what we should do next.'

Simon smiled brightly at Alice. 'You don't know how happy hearing that makes me.'

'Bradley?' From the background came a tiny voice. 'What are you doing to her?'

Alice and Simon looked over at the door and saw Paige sleepily rubbing her eyes, clutching her teddy close to her chest.

'Hey, princess,' Simon spoke gently. 'This is my friend Alice. Can you say hello to Alice?'

'Hello, Alice.' Paige looked at Alice tied to the bed and frowned. 'It's not nice to hurt your friends, you know.'

Bradley climbed off Alice and walked to Paige. He got down on one knee and hugged her. 'We were just playing a game, sweetie, is all. Nothing to worry about. Why don't you go back to bed?'

'Can you bring me a drink?' Paige turned and walked back into the room

'I will be there in a minute.' Simon closed the door and came back to Alice. 'She is my next gift to you. She needs a mother, and you would be perfect.'

Alice tried to smile at Simon. 'Oh my gosh, she's beautiful. Thank you. How about I take her that drink?'

Simon looked at Alice and thought about it. His thoughts were interrupted by a buzzing on the ground. He picked up Alice's phone and pressed the button to answer the call. Simon put it on speaker to hear a gruff male voice already mid-sentence.

'Ten minutes away. Don't do anything, and we will take down this motherfucker together, OK?'

Simon glared at Alice and ended the call. His face turned red, and he snorted as he breathed through his nose. He raised his voice and yelled at Alice. 'After everything I have done for you, I find out you have betrayed me!' He paced around the room, twitching, clearly agitated. 'Alice, I don't understand why.'

Paige re-emerged from the other room and stood in the doorway. Alice looked at her and screamed for her to run. Simon looked away from Paige and focused back on Alice. He stormed over to the bed and plunged his knife into her side and left it there. Still shaking with fury, he leaned over her face until their noses touched. Spit dripped from his lip into her mouth.

'I love you, Alice.'

Simon stood up and walked over to Paige, who hadn't moved. He took her little hand in his and led her towards the front door. He opened the door and turned off the light switch, filling the room with darkness.

Alice could see his silhouette in the doorway and called out to him. 'I will find you again, Simon!'

She pulled at her hands again, and he turned to face her.

'I will never stop hunting you down. That, I promise.'

The dark shadow of the monster laughed back at her, and the evil noise rang in her ears.

'I'm counting on it.'

And he closed the door, leaving her to the eerie black of the night.

Printed in the United States
By Bookmasters